SNOW MOON

Karma Bites.

Piper Duncan

ISBN 978-1-66788-140-9 eBook 978-1-66788-141-6

CONTENTS

Preface ix

1. Devotion 1

2. A Sinner Like Me 3

3. Temptation Calls 5

4. Snowman 13

5. Consequences 21

6. Violence Leads To Silence 24

7. Deliver Me 26

8. My Love For Her Is Tragic 42

9. What You Seek Is Seeking You 46

10. Dead Inside 50

11. Shiny Things 65

12. Synergy 67

13. Only Emptiness Remains 91

14. Love You're Born To Find 92

15. Law Of Attraction 115

16. From Friends To This 119

17. Sipping On Emotion 125

18. Use That Rage 133

19. Numb 137

20. Ugly Scar 147

21. Cruel Winter 149

22. It's Not Me, It's You 160

23. Falling 167

24. We All Fall Down 168

25. Blind But Still Alive...172

26. Ice In My Bones...182

27. Fragile Strength 185

28. Watch Your Back 188

29. We Are Stars Wrapped In Skin 198

30. Under Your Spell 202

31. Progress 209

32. I Crave More 214

33. Like Magic..220

34. I Like The Way It Hurts 226

35. Big Witch Energy 228

36. Crippled Anger..236

37. Gravity 243

38. I Bet My Life...248

39. Inhaling Every Moment 252

40. Desperate Times..270

41. Come Closer 273

42. Dancing In The Star Light......................................282

43. Dancing In The Moonlight 285

44. Every Little Thing She Does Is Magic......................287

45. Your Heart Takes The Fall 297

46. All The Pretty Lights..300

47. Cut..303

Epilogue – Set Me Free 312

When people see things as beautiful, ugliness is created. When people see things as good, evil is created. Being and non-being produce each other. Difficult and easy complement each other. Long and short define each other. High and low oppose each other. Fore and aft follow each other.

Tao Te Ching.

Preface

THROUGHOUT HISTORY, A LARGE NUMBER OF BOOKS HAVE been banned or burned by the Church due to the fact that they contained various uncomfortable truths. Some copies have even been poisoned—giving them a reputation of being cursed—after those who read them ended up dead. Such was the case of books telling tales about the entity known as iL Separatio. According to ancient writings, only two entities had ever seen him before: God and Lucifer— and they'd each only seen him once.

The Bible reads: "God said, 'Let there be light,' and there was light. God saw that the light was good, and he separated the light from the darkness." Legends long kept secret reveal that when the separation occurred between light and darkness, something unexpected happened in the space in between. The separation took form. That form was an entity called iL Separatio, or "The Separation." This entity was neither good nor evil. Instead, it represented perfect and absolute neutrality. Balance.

According to the Church, good people went to Heaven and bad people were destined for Hell. iL Separatio provided a third option, one not recognized by the church. This entity could claim souls who had done as much good as they had sinned.

Only two types of books mentioning iL Separatio have survived: Compendium Augumentum and Codex Lugubrum. Two surviving copies of Codex Lugubrum were both found in private European collections. They tell the story of a fierce warrior named Amantes, a medieval royal paid assassin who one day has an epiphany and decides to make amends with the families of his victims. He dies in this pursuit and when his soul leaves his body, a demon and an angel fight over his soul. That fight is settled when iL Separatio appears and tells them that his good deeds and sins were perfectly balanced and that he therefore belongs in perpetuity to the separation.

He belongs to Karma.

1. DEVOTION

EARLY 5TH CENTURY, EUROPE—I REMEMBER QUITE CLEARLY the first time I saw Amelia. Funny, really, considering how wasted I was that night, and I don't remember much else. Things were a little fuzzy, but I know I'd snuck into the neighbor's cottage looking to drown my sorrows and stole a huge jug of ale from their cupboard. Alone in the woods, consuming to the point of passing out, I saw purple and silver shimmering eyes peering at me through the trees.

At first, I thought I was hallucinating. Before I could muster the energy to run, those eyes were directly upon me, piercing my soul and examining my face like a lion does its prey. She was the most intoxicatingly beautiful thing I had ever seen in my short fourteen year life, and I was instantly hexed by her—paralyzed by both her beauty and my fear. She smelled my face, and then my neck, lingering there before licking the skin below my chin, as if to prime it for devouring.

"Men get this drunk either because they've majorly screwed something up or they are about to," she whispered in my ear. "Which is it for you?"

She used the term 'men.' I was both flattered and terrified. "Both," I replied before passing out.

2. A SINNER LIKE ME

PRESENT DAY, DENVER, CO—DR. ROGAN WAS WORKING LATE, as usual. His nurses and PAs had all left hours ago, and as he finished up the final details on his daily paperwork under the pale glow of a shiny, modern, extraterrestrial looking desk lamp, he took one final drag from his cigarette. A terrible habit he had picked up in college and only revisited after nights like this. Nights that both exhilarated and exhausted him. He looked across the room into the mirror on the wall behind the door and admired his reflection. That's when he noticed the drop of blood on his cheek. He grabbed a tissue from the box on his desk, dipped it into his water bottle, and wiped the last bit of evidence off his face. He put the tissue into his pants pocket, making a mental note to throw it away in the trash can in the parking garage. Being smart like that had kept him out of jail.

He extinguished his cigarette in his antique ashtray—a trophy from last month's trip overseas—and closed his laptop. He grabbed his briefcase and made his way out of the office and to the elevators that led to the parking garage. Fumbling with his car keys and looking down when the elevator doors opened, he never saw what hit him. His skull cracked. Blood rushed down his face. A being gripped his head and licked away every delicious drop of salty blood off his cheek before biting into his neck and sucking hard. Right before Dr. Rogan lost consciousness, he saw a distorted reflection in the glowing blade that would seconds later slit his throat. Shimmering blue and silver eyes bored into his soul as the beast muttered three words to him, "*Nam-tar, Tesh, Kur.*"

3. TEMPTATION CALLS

As a creature of Karma, I had four rules.

Do not directly kill. Do not resurrect. Do not alter emotions. Do not alter time. That's it. It may not seem like a lot, but for the feat I had to pull off to save her and save this world, it was limiting. It meant I did a lot of watching and popping into physical existence to set things in motion or fulfill Karmic energy. Some referred to me as a guardian angel, when a serendipitous positive event took place; others mistook me for the Devil, when I must set chaos in motion.

Now, I as peered inside to watch this particular scene, the lights were dim inside the two-story office, but from the low buzz, I knew the vamps were already hard at work monitoring accounts. When Julian opened the door, he saw Thane's large silhouette lounging, legs kicked up in his usual favorite beat up black leather recliner. Pleather, to be exact. God forbid they have an actual animal product in the house.

He was eating his favorite poison, neon blue Taki chips made from every known chemical on the planet plus some salt and washing it down with a diet caffeine-free cola. Caffeine made Therions, especially wolf forms like Thane, literally rabid. The others were feverously typing away, the glow from their laptops illuminating their pale white skin, making their normally silver-blue eyes take on a greenish tint. The obvious leader of the group—a former colleague and mentor of mine from eons ago—walked over to his stand-up desk and placed his sleek laptop into the triple monitor console. He then surveyed the digital scene in front of him on three huge screens. The monitors encapsulated every last detail and nuance of the measly lives of about twelve hundred students and 450 staff members at the private and overly expensive Valiant High School in Emberglow, Colorado. Thousands of social media pages popped up on the screen with notifications pinging at a feverish pace.

"Give me the rundown," Julian said to no one in particular.

"There are about a thousand photos to scrub from dumbass Therions and Vampires uploading to social media in this sector, but other than that it's a pretty normal night," said Thane. "Mia and her crowd are status quo, umbras leaning dark but not too dark. Don't really need to worry about them. Abbey and Aubrey are bullying Madison, and their umbras are shifting slightly, so may want to start there tonight."

"What about Luke and his new soccer friend?" Julian asked, never really one to care much or remember names of the creatures he manipulated.

"You mean Liam? He's fine. He's trying to fit in with Finn and his group, but he doesn't lean as bright as the rest of them. You could start there instead. Whatever, no skin off my back. He's kind of an ass clown anyway."

I could see Julian homing in on Liam and his social media history. A couple keystrokes later and he'd hacked in to send off a quick DM to Madison.

Pics?

Then he deleted it on his end to erase all proof and waited. Creatures today and their computers. Never in the history of the world has it been easier to manipulate earth dwellers. It was a Vampire's digital playground, and Julian was the playground bully. He glanced to the left of the screen. Like clockwork, Madison, thinking she got a direct message from Liam, had sent a photo of herself from the neck down in a bikini. Stupid teenage girl.

"Hold that delivery so she thinks he's leaving her on opened," Julian instructed his minions out loud. "Then intercept that text from Liam to Finn. We don't want him backing down. Send the dots like he's typing, then hold, then remove."

"Jules, check this text string out between Abbey and Madison," said one of the vamps. The screenshot popped up on the orchestrator's monitor.

OMG OMG

ABBEY

ARE YOU THERE

Liam just asked me for a pic

What? Did you send?

Not full, but the one you of me took at the cliffs last summer before I jumped into the lake

You did not!

What did he send back?

Idk he literally left me on opened

So annoying

ikr

Alex left me delivered for like 24 hours yesterday (eye roll emoji)

And then today when I asked for his number he never answered

Don't send him anything

K

I hate my face in that photo

Omg whatever you look good

No I don't. My neck looks so fat. It's true

Thane slumped even lower in his recliner staring blankly ahead. The Therion always seemed perpetually put out during these late-night computer stalking sessions. He let out a loud yawn, opening his mouth so wide someone could stick an entire fist in there. *Tempting,* I'm sure, to Julian, as he rolled his eyes at his lifelong friend. They'd been friends for years. Like hundreds of thousands of years. More out of necessity than anything else but after all this time, Thane was probably Julian's most trusted advisor. So many books and movies pit Werewolves and Vampires against each other, when in reality, they depended on each other to survive. It fell under the concept of dualism: balanced equals that the universe is so fond of creating.

Without their bond to one another, each would live in hiding with their own kind or in stasis. Underground tunnels or a cryo chamber for Julian and isolated tent camps in the mountain woods for Thane. Alliances among their species have allowed them to remain hidden to humankind for the most part in modern times. And after all, if you go back to the origin of their species, they were in fact half-brothers.

Negativity consumes Vampires so completely that they are incapable of seeing the light in themselves or in others without the aid of a Therion.

Their blackness, their cold heartedness, exists at an altered, lower vibration than other creatures and they must feed off blood, the ultimate elixir of life, from humans who exhibit negative emotions. They are the darkest of souls that have walked the Earth since the dawn of time. They are the ultimate deceivers, like Lily was.

In today's modern era, they have tricked society so that they are celebrated in movies and on TV, and some confused and lost humans even desire or claim to be one. For years they have fed human society silly stories about how they can be kept at bay or killed. Garlic, sunlight, stakes through the heart. All nonsense. Well, mostly.

Therions, like Thane, keep Vampires in check. They are protectors of Humans who possess the light. Thane, however, has little regard for Humans. Especially now during modern times when Humans, in particular teenage Humans, allow themselves to be so easily manipulated.

A Therion bonded with a Vampire, a deep kinship rooted in basic universal energies, allows both to live out in the open, balancing each other's energy with equal light and dark. In my day, you'd see those types of connections often. It was a friendship that could not be broken. But now, and ever since the Alliance was torn apart, it was extremely rare.

The screen lit up like Christmas lights. The addicting notifications are all it takes to suck a teenager in. They could be full on into an in-person conversation, when a little red notice of instant gratification demanded their full attention. I knew Julian rather enjoyed delving into the lives of unsuspecting teens. When you've lived as long as he had, being around young people was a necessity in order to stay relevant in a world that changed faster than ever.

"Send Derek a few ads about guns, and blog posts about that crazy social media group we created last month," Julian said. "We really need to cultivate his friend group into leaning more gray. And then you'll want to have some emo blog posts pop up on his feed over the next few days. How's our friend Erick?"

"Nope—he's off limits," Thane perked up at the mention of Erick's name.

"Just making sure you were awake," Julian responded.

There's that old Native American proverb about two wolves fighting constantly inside every living creature and the one you feed is the one who wins. The proverb got it mostly right. It's actually a Therion and a Vampire fighting over souls. Of course, free will is present so humans can un-invite Vampires with positive thoughts and actions as easily as they invited them in. It doesn't mean they wouldn't try to push their luck though. Like with Erick.

"Erick is right at the midpoint. Too soon to tell if he's ok to mess with," Thane said.

"You're such a rule follower," Julian announced.

Thane inhaled deeply and let out a slow sigh. He responded, "I have high hopes for him. Yeah, he's down on his luck, but I think he's born for greatness."

Thane was an eternal optimist, always trying to protect the humans who hunted his kind for ages. It was utterly annoying to Julian. Once in a while, a human figured out the rules. Thane lived for those moments. While rare, sometimes a bullied kid who was challenged constantly as a youngster chose to face their hardships head on with positive energy and channeled their hardships into light. Sometimes, even an adult who faced enormous adversity, used it as a learning opportunity and came out stronger on the other side. But usually, humans let the bad times push them over the edge and allowed their umbras to shift gray or even black, inviting the demons in to stay. That is what happened to me, at first.

As Julian scrolled through the thousands of social media accounts on the screen in front him, carefully cultivating news feeds for teenagers based on their past preferences and watch histories, I saw him feel it. He grabbed the back of his neck and gently massaged it and his gaze turned cloudy. He felt something…odd. A stirring of sorts, as I did, deep within our souls. He brushed it off, probably thinking he was three days overdue to feed.

"So hey, here's something interesting," Thane said. "That private social media group that popped up over the weekend now has more than five hundred likes."

Julian closed some windows on the screen to better focus in on what Thane was talking about. The private Facebook group named *Students With Light* was definitely gaining momentum, and faster than usual without demonic interference. Its profile picture was a logo that looked like mountains that formed the letter "W" with the triangles inside the letter colored into a turquoise and silver seal. Understandable that so many would be drawn to a group like this since there was a huge outpouring of support and demonstrations after a school across town lost five students in a shooting three weeks ago.

The school had been oozing with negative energy and was a Vampire feeding ground. All of those dark umbras have to manifest and be released. Police were able to enter the school within minutes, but before they found the shooter hiding in a closet, he'd already killed five kids. The event sent shock waves of devastation throughout the community.

Negative actions result in opposing positive reactions. After the event, students throughout the state banded together to speak out against school bullying and violence but also memorialized the students who lost their lives with vigils and moments of silence almost daily since it happened. The sense of unity and light that came from the tragedy was a direct result of the universe enacting balance.

Funny how Demons and Vampires get such a bad rap when humans can be the evilest creatures of all. The devil's messengers don't have a choice. Humans do.

"Make sure you two join the club," Julian said to two others across the room, Breck and Scarlett. "And turn your notifications on. We want to know what they're up to."

He took a screen shot of the monitor and texted the photo to himself as a reminder to check back on it later. Then The Stirring came again. It was stronger, but more familiar this time.

"Dude, you're looking a little, um, pale," Thane said to his friend with a chuckle.

"I'll take that as a compliment," Julian snapped back, looking into the screen in front of him and using it like a mirror. His hair lacked its usual luster and hung limp on his head. He was wearing it longer these days like when I knew him on Earth, with the chestnut fine strands hanging just slightly over his eyes and barely covering his ears. His deep blue eyes showed several strands of silver—a sign that he was hungry. And his skin was paler than usual, but not anything out of the norm. I thought for a moment that he'd ask Scarlett to bloodshare like he had frequently over the past few months, but he hated admitting needing help from anyone. Then it came back again. The Stirring. It called to us both. The family was close.

"You guys have a handle on this for the night?" Julian asked the crew. "I have something to take care of. I'll be back in a few hours."

And with that he grabbed the laptop out of its holder and was gone, exiting the room in a black blur.

4. SNOWMAN

Since the dawn of time, the rules of the universe have been so simple. So basic. So easy to follow. Yet earth dwellers find them too elusive to grasp.

Would you live your life differently if you knew that every single thing that you thought, said and did, reflected directly back upon you or your closest loved ones? Would you spread gossip or speak poorly about someone if you knew everything you said would come back upon you, only ten times worse than what you were projecting upon others? How would you feel if every time you spoke a negative word about someone, it brought positivity and prosperity into their life, and took it away from your life?

That is exactly my calling in this world. A push here, a tug there. My actions enact balance, and they cannot be stopped. Once a human's choice is made, my action is solidified. Only since illusions of time and space prevent the blowback from being immediate, earth dwellers have a hard time recognizing the game of Karma. It has great rewards for those who master it, but deep disappointment for those who don't.

After centuries of such ignorance on Earth, darkness from evil choices fueled The Stirring like a black cloud creeping across the heavens.

The balance had shifted, more and more with each passing generation, threatening the liberation of those who want to destroy this world. I could feel the shift. And yet here we are. With the Old Ones gaining power and infecting souls like poison, this was the last chance for life on this planet. All they had to do was follow the rules, but chaos was intoxicating. So many earth dwellers were enticed by negativity that darkness threatened to reach a tipping point, and that point would empower the evil souls imprisoned below the Earth's surface to rise.

From my vantage point high atop the mountainside I could see so many souls. There was something about watching each car drive by and listening in that made me feel slightly guilty but also alive. It's not that I missed my earthly existence, but I longed for the emotions I felt when I was here. While going through them I was at times tortured, but now after being gone for so long, even the faint memory of pain, heartache and loneliness felt welcome. Mostly because for all of the despair, there was love and light, and there was her.

Each conversation in the cars below was a microcosm of the joy and despair that filled the world. Some families were happily cruising home from a vacation in the mountains with sounds of laughter and happiness filling their vehicles and others were filled with hatred, fighting and fear. Each one like its own movie.

So many creatures are always seeking what is next, what is "deserved," and what they do not have, instead of appreciating the things right in front of them. More concerned with what others have, creating false perfect narratives to inspire envy in others, rather than realizing the unique blessings in their own lives.

Through the connections made with others, the metaphysical veils that have been placed on all earth dwellers to create illusions of separation, will vanish to reveal that we are all truly one. All things interconnected.

In the beginning, before the separation, we were all one. There is a peace in that balance. When there is too great of an imbalance, the world suffers through catastrophe like floods, droughts, earthquakes, or plagues.

In the foreground were the snowcapped mountains looming over the lights of the city below but far beyond that I could sense each light of the Alliance. Separated long, long ago, and hidden to prevent their unification, the Monk's original goal was about to be fulfilled unless they could restore the Alliance. Only the Alliance kept the evil ones at bay and since the Monk destroyed it, the Great Old Ones gained power with every passing generation. Now, in the Age of Aquarius, we had one shot to regroup. One shot to reunite. One shot to find her.

I wasn't supposed to care. My only purpose was to maintain karmic balance. But I had to find her. I had to know her one more time if this world were to end. I had to apologize and let her know I had been tricked. Over the years I had sensed her consciousness but could not get through. She was locked away and hidden well. I watched Julian and Thane more than I should to try and guide their quest to find her location but to no avail. The tourmaline blade deep inside her chest kept her well-hidden. If she'd only known the truth before she plunged it into her body. I tried to push her face out of my mind, concentrating on the task at hand. I knew that Gabriel and Phebe would be passing below any minute and this was the only way.

I had to enlist help to try and find Amelia and reunite the Alliance. That meant taking unusual measures and stretching the bounds of my existence to help the others. I knew what I was doing was right. It had to be done. And with that, I removed the gemstone from around my neck and grasped it tightly in my left hand. I closed my eyes and placed my right hand on the snow. I felt the power pulse into the sparkling ground. And then I focused in specifically to watch the events unfolding in one more car below.

...

"Put a cork in it, bruh," she told him with an elbow to his side.

"Shut up!" he said. "Mom! Sera elbowed me."

"You're so annoying, dumb one," Sera scolded as she stretched her long legs out across the back seat of the car, prodding her brother with one foot and the dog with her other. The dog looked up briefly and fell right back asleep, but her sibling did not let it go as easily.

"Get your feet off me! Dad! Her disgusting feet are on me. You're such an idiot!" Steele yelled at her.

Little did the twins know how interconnected they had been for centuries. Probably a reason they annoyed each other so much. They knew each other as well as they knew themselves. They'd protected each other throughout the ages and would ultimately die for one another, even though in this life, at age sixteen, they'd never admit it.

"It's bad enough I have to sit in a car with you for two hours, but now this traffic is ridiculous. *Why* is there so much traffic?" Sera whined.

"Steele Parker Grayson! Seraphina Paige Grayson! Get your hands off each other. BE-HAVE or I am serious your phones will be gone the entire trip back to Florida!"

Their mom, Phebe, liked to threaten taking electronics away. It always made me chuckle. I may have caused some of those punishments from time to time with just the slightest bit of malevolent interference. This generation's dependence on those things confused me. It separated people from each other and made it so much easier for the darkness to settle in. That was one of so many contributing factors to the predicament this world has now found itself in.

"Oh, that will be a long flight home without electronics," their father, chimed in from the driver's seat.

Their Dad liked to antagonize. It was a personality trait that followed him throughout the ages. It was the main reason that he and I met so many thousands of years ago. His constant prodding about the Alliance needing their own assassin, forced the issue of Amelia presenting me to the group for consideration as their hired killer.

Sera rolled her eyes and gazed out the window at the snow on the ground and the dark green Christmas trees that lined the mountainside on their drive from Beaver Creek Mountain where they'd been on vacation skiing all week to the Denver Airport. I knew she loved the mountains. Her mother had once told me there was something magical about the way the snow sat on the ground like a thick blanket, untouched and sparkling when the sunlight hit it just the right way. Phebe had always been innately connected to nature since her first life in the world. Even while on the Alliance, I remember her uncanny ability to guide my tasks by knowing exactly when the fog would lift, or a storm would be setting in. Even now in human form, those traits must have carried through.

They had been driving for about an hour when the traffic stopped. They were in the right-hand lane next to a guard rail with a huge drop off below. Seraphina shuddered ever so slightly as she looked over the side with a somewhat psychic sense of dread. I knew Steele felt her uneasiness. Even though he was usually the most annoying human on the planet to her, they always shared a close psychic connection. He could feel her thoughts intensely. Sometimes when she was in a bad mood but keeping it to herself, he would act out what she was feeling. It frequently sent him into fits of rage that made him unpopular with friends at school when he was younger. It also made him easy to manipulate when needed.

"Is there a crash or something?" Seraphina groaned, shaking off her premonition.

"Just shut up!" Steele raged back, not understanding completely that his sudden anger was caused by his sister's uneasiness.

Cars were bumper to bumper on their side of the road with zero traffic on the side heading to the mountains.

"Honestly, how much longer until the tunnel? Are we even close?" Steele asked.

"We're about a mile away. After that it looks like smooth sailing to the airport. We should be fine to make our flight," replied Phebe.

The Eisenhower tunnel separated the warmer weather from the colder. East of the tunnel the trees and grass stayed greener longer and the other side looked like a winter wonderland as drivers emerged from the darkness. It also separated the Therions from the Vampires with a mutually agreed upon treaty. Years of magic and a broken Alliance blinded them to the fact that they needed one another to survive but the geographical treaty allowed for a peaceful co-existence in this life.

"I could run faster than this," Steele complained. "I'd be to the airport by now if I was running," he said.

"You'd beat everyone but one person in this car," said their father, Gabriel.

"Yea, whatever, Dad," said Steele.

It was a running joke between them who could run faster. Gabriel was super-fast, but Steele was definitely faster when he tried and when he wasn't complaining about something hurting. Just then the dog let out a huge fart.

"Oh, wow. That was a good one!" Steele cackled as he rolled down his window.

Omega, their rescue husky was known for ripping super smelly ones at the most inopportune times. Well, everyone thought he was a husky. Omega had been sworn to protect the royal family eons ago and had done so valiantly. His reward for that in this life was to be born as a beloved dog who was doted on by his owners and who had up until this point in time lived a life of naps by the pool and playing in the snow.

As the moon disappeared behind the clouds, the sparkles on the pure white snow that glisten in the light went into hiding and faded. When I saw the car hit the precise angle I needed, I mentally vacated from watching the scene inside the car and pressed down further on to the surface of the ground.

Phebe heard the slow rumble for about two seconds before seeing where the noise was coming from. As I set the event in motion, I looked inside one last time. I could swear Phebe locked eyes with me. The snow that looked so peaceful just moments ago awakened and became a raging monster as it began to crumble. It broke away from the mountainside almost in slow motion, at first. Then faster, and faster, and louder and louder, like a freight train on a violent mission to destroy anything and everything in its path, it raged down the mountainside. Steele felt his mother's fear before he saw it.

"Honey," their mom said, as she gripped Gabriel's hand and her eyes looked up the mountain.

"Shit," he said.

And that was it. Those were the last words I'd ever hear them say in this life. Before the snow plowed into the roadway with a force like no other, smacking into their car and steamrolling into them at what seemed to be a thousand miles per hour, for a fleeting second, I had a sense of remorse.

The force knocked their car over the guard rail, along with hundreds of other vehicles in front and behind them, sending them tumbling, over and over for what seemed to take forever until everything was completely still.

5. CONSEQUENCES

OMEGA WAS THE FIRST ONE TO GAIN CONSCIOUSNESS. EJECTED from the car but still close enough to see it a few feet away, blood was dripping from his mouth and he had a huge gash on his head. *Open Your Eyes.* I silently commanded him. *Seraphina. Steele. You must protect them. It is your duty. What you are sworn to do. Open your eyes, dog.*

The eerie silence that pervaded briefly after the fall from creatures in shock, had turned into thousands of screaming, dying humans. Cars lay crushed over and under the snow, scattered like toys of an angry giant, many with shattered headlights gleaming like laser beams through the icy surface. The tumble pushed many bodies beyond the tunnel's border. Some were on the surface of the snow and others beneath it, with muffled moans coming from below. Dark red blood stained the perfect white ground, marring it like a battlefield. The screams of those who survived the fall— attracted beasts to feed.

Omega opened his eyes and scanned the surface for his family. Gabriel and Phebe were gone, their heads completely under the snow and their bodies motionless. He saw Seraphina and Steele in the back seat and seemingly still alive, trapped by their seatbelts, hanging inside the car that was almost upside down and half buried in the snow. He tried lunging for the car, but something was wrong. One of his legs was stuck below the surface, trapped by the wheel of another car. He couldn't break free. His eyes darted to the edge of the forest. That's when he saw it. Glowing eyes betrayed them as they emerged from the trees like an army about to wage war against a helpless, injured enemy. One was headed right for Omega. He pulled at his paw to no avail. The monster came closer, floating on the surface of the snow, taking its time. His brothers and sisters were already fast at work draining the injured and dying, ending their suffering quickly and with precision. But this one was coming straight for Omega. Strange because human blood was much more fulfilling than canine.

He could not get that paw free. Behind him Steele was awake and yelling at an unconscious Seraphina. He was definitely alive; that was good.

"Seraphina! Seraphina! Wake up! Answer me! Mom! Dad! Omega!"

Omega squeaked out a weak bark. Steele unbuckled himself and climbed out of the car, running over to his pet.

"Omega—Oh my God. You're alive. You're alive. Let me help you, buddy."

He frantically buried into the snow making a hole around Omega's trapped leg so the dog could break free. But the demon still headed their way. Steele didn't see him.

"Come here, buddy. Oh, thank goodness you're alive. Help me get Sera, Mom, and Dad, okay bud?"

Just then he must have felt what Omega was seeing because his eyes darted beyond in terror.

"What in the hell..."

The creature wasn't coming toward Omega. It was Seraphina he had in his sights. He moved toward her motionless body that was hanging head downward, unconscious and half buried in snow, now with speed and urgency. The monster grabbed her, ripping her right out of the seatbelt and the car, and bit into her neck.

This is not what I had planned. He shouldn't have been attracted to her blood. I could set things in motion, influence thoughts with ideas, whispers, and dreams but I could not interfere directly unless I took human form. I watched as my entire plan was about to dissolve before it had even begun. As the Vampire sucked the lifeforce from Sera's body, Steele jumped on top of him.

"Stop!" His eyes turned bright yellow with rage, a trait I'd never seen in him before, and he ripped the creature from Sera's neck.

The beast turned with ease and knocked Steele down with a blow to the head. Sera's blood dripped from the corners of his mouth as he returned to feed on her. His demonic comrades worked their way through hundreds of humans, draining the blood of those who didn't die in the fall. Steele attacked the Vampire with a fervor I hadn't seen in him for several lifetimes. Watching a Vampire attack his sister must have awakened the ancient oath he'd made. Something primeval inside of Omega raged to emerge as he let out a deafening growl, his body shaking as it blurred and elongated. He returned to his human form, locked eyes with the beast and yelled an ancient command.

"Pacta. Sunt. Servanda."

The Vampire instantly dropped Sera from his grasp. Steele, shocked by the broken connection with his sister, and exhausted by his supernatural exhibition of strength, collapsed beside her in the gore-stained snow.

6. VIOLENCE LEADS
TO SILENCE

SERA'S BLOOD SHOULD HAVE REPELLED JULIAN, BUT AFTER several lifetimes as a human her original soul DNA must be heavily diluted. I didn't think he would attack her, but their connection must have confused him. The nostalgia drove his hunger. He was connected to her ancient soul.

I debated the pros and cons of entering their physical realm and directly intervening. She may have too much venom in her system to fully recover. If she died, the plan died along with her. The next time all elements would be perfectly in place wouldn't be for another 156 years. But if Julian could save her, it could still work. He wouldn't want to, as it was forbidden but this may be exactly the advantage the group would need. Maybe this was the universe intervening. If the Old Ones were awakened fully, there would be no more time and my efforts to find Amelia would be for naught. We would never be together again, separated by vast realms of time in space. Still, I waited before getting further involved.

"What is a Therion doing with humans, pretending to be a dog?" Julian sneered at Omega.

"Think, Julian. Think!" Omega yelled back. "Why would you feed on a Therion? It's forbidden! You may have killed her!"

"A Therion? A Therion?" Julian repeated. "I… what are you talking about? She's Human, or isn't she? Or..." his voice trailed off, slowly realizing his mistake.

"You need to turn her. *Now*," Omega commanded.

"I can't," Julian muttered. "Follow me. We'll have to bring her to the Therion camp nearby. I took too much blood. And you know it's forbidden. She'll either stay dead or be healed by them, but they can help and will have to make the call. I'm sorry. I didn't know."

He had no way of knowing who she was. Julian had never met Seraphina or Steele. He only knew their parents in their original form, not as Humans. Legends passed down through the ages told of Witches who may have hidden the children as Humans right before the Monk's curse. It was folklore, though. Julian wasn't there when it happened and had no way of knowing it was true.

Julian threw the unconscious and barely breathing teenage girl over his shoulder and Omega transformed back into animal form before wrangling Steele up onto his back.

7. DELIVER ME

I FELT MY SOUL LEAVE MY PHYSICAL BODY. AS IT HOVERED nearby, I could sense separate energies battling for its existence as if the universe was weighing some cosmic decision. I wasn't sure what happened, and I didn't quite care. I felt oddly at peace and ready to move on.

"Who is she?" I heard someone ask, pulling me back toward reality.

"They are the Alpha children. The hidden ones," a familiar voice replied. I lost consciousness again, drifting above my physical form once more. I was free.

A decision was made that injected me into my familiar Human form. The suit of skin and bones trapped my soul, locking me in for good.

Cold wind hit my face. I was on someone's back moving at a ridiculous pace. It almost felt like I was flying, and then I fell back to sleep.

When I regained consciousness, my vision was clouded. I had to blink a few times to get a clear view of the room. It was like a photo filter over my eyes made everything seem extra vivid, crisp, and clear. I felt cold but also warm, safe, rested, and strong. My muscles were tight, and my body was heavy, almost pinned down, but also strong and full of excitement. Something small and hard rested on the center of my fore-head, sending a surge of energy through my body. I could sense every-thing around me—the warmth of the fire burning in the fireplace by the door but also the people and animals outside. I knew exactly how many of them there were—fifty-seven shapes in the clearing plus eight more lurk-ing in the woods, I could smell intensely the piney logs popping in the fire, the grass buried under the snow, and the musky scent of insects cocooned among the evergreen's branches. While I marveled at these new heightened sensations something deep within me felt a sense of dread.

As I sat up, a crystal fell from my forehead. I caught it in my hand. The power and clarity I felt seconds before disappeared, and my normal eyesight returned. Beautiful and sparkling, the crystal glistened silvery white and reflected both the light and shadows that filled the room. I tried putting it back on my forehead, but again it fell. I clasped it tight trying to regain the newfound senses I felt before. No luck.

A quick scan of the room revealed that I was in a huge tent, like one of the ones Mom and Dad used to talk about renting in Montana. What did they call it? Oh right—*glamping*. Glamorous camping. Huge cream-col-ored canvas material formed the walls, floor, and roof, complemented by giant plastic windows, wooden beams overhead, a furnace, and a large cloth door. Two oversized cots and a suede maroon sofa filled the room. Steele lay asleep in the next cot. He had a crystal on his forehead as well but his was a pale yellow, emanating a soft glow, like an aura around his entire body. No sign of Mom and Dad.

I whispered my brother's name, but only a whimper came out of my dry mouth. Next, I sent the thought to my brother telepathically, which worked for us when we really tried. He slowly stirred.

Growing up we always tried to play psychic games with each other and amaze our friends when we could guess each other's cards or a word that was hidden on a piece of paper. We never thought much of it and our parents always said it was our twin connection. When we were really young, I guess we even had our own language that no one else could understand but the two of us. This kid always slept like a dead person.

"Steele!"

This time I screamed it inside his brain.

He opened his eyes. They were blood shot and, upon closer inspection, he looked awful. Somehow, I could sense that his blood vessels were constricted, and his energy level was low. His nerves were on fire, his throat was sore, he had a dull headache, and his eyes felt heavy as if he'd been sobbing. Before my brain even registered my decision to move, I was by his side. I'm not sure how. I just wanted to be near him and the next second I was. He sat up and hugged me. Tight. The crystal fell off his forehead and tumbled onto the ground. And then he started to cry.

"I thought you were dead," he said.

"It's okay," I said. "It's okay."

We sat there together for what seemed to be an eternity before we broke our hug. His head jerked uncontrollably as he sobbed, and he let out a chirping noise. Steele had a tic disorder that made him have uncontrollable body movements and sounds when he was stressed, tired, or hungry. It plagued him since age five but with a specific diet, behavioral therapy, and stress and sleep management it was controlled most of the time. I tried to remember how we ended up here. But my mind was blank.

"Steele, it's okay. Can you tell me what happened?"

He pushed me away and looked at my face incredulously.

"I thought you were dead. I didn't think you'd ever wake up. And Mom and Dad," he chirped and started sobbing again.

"What happened to Mom and Dad?" I asked, feeling my palms getting sweaty.

"Sera, they're gone. They're dead. One second, we were on the road, I was yelling at you. And then an avalanche knocked our car over the rail. You were attacked by, by..."

"By what?" I asked.

Chirp. "I...I think a Vampire."

The word struck a chord in my soul. Brief flashes of memory taunted me, and pictures flashed in my brain. Something biting me. Draining me but then filling me up again with magic and venom. I thought of my parents. Of my mom. I saw her face. I called to her mentally and smelled her essence inside my mind. My mom, my best friend. She couldn't be gone, could she? My dad, my strong and fierce protector. I could still feel them. They were ripped away from us so suddenly. Why? How could this have happened?

"I think—I mean—I know they are okay," I said as I pulled Steele against my chest for a hug while rubbing his head. "I feel them. They are with us." I tried to convince myself as well as Steele.

As we held each other, I felt a oneness with Steele's heartache, but I also felt at peace with an ancient knowledge that I would meet them again. That didn't stop it from feeling like a stab to the chest, leaving a hole that would never be filled.

I mentally reached into Steele's soul and calmed his heart. *How did I do that?*

"I don't know. How *did* you do that?" he said aloud.

Before I could ask him about what just happened, the door to the tent edged open and a black nose pushed its way through. Omega rushed inside. He tackled us and we ran our hands through his thick fur, which was both familiar and comforting.

"Omega, come here you little cutie. Omigosh, I am so happy to see you," I said as he climbed into my lap, and I pulled him in close to me.

Omega was the best dog ever. My parents had never allowed us to have any pets until Steele and I turned seven because I had horrible allergies. Our constant nagging convinced Mom and Dad to take us to a nearby rescue to 'test' whether we'd grown out of my allergies. Several trials and hive breakouts later, we were resigned to the fact that our parents were never going to let us have a dog, until one day when we found the cutest little abandoned puppy in a construction dumpster near our home. We had set up a few self-made ramps to jump our bikes over and were just about to test the first one out when we heard a faint crying coming from up the street. Always curious and ready to investigate, we walked toward the dumpster where the crying got louder. Steele hoisted me up over the edge to look inside and I saw the absolute cutest ball of fur with bright-blue eyes staring back at me from under a pile of papers. I scooped him up and it was love at first sight. We hid him on our back porch for a week until Dad found him while cleaning the pool one Saturday morning. Amazingly, I had zero allergic reaction to the little cutie and Dad helped us convince Mom to let us keep him. I think she fell in love with him instantly as well. Her only condition of keeping him was that she didn't have to bear any responsibility for him whatsoever—no walking, no bathing, no picking up his poop. If we swore to care for him, we could keep him. So, we did. Well…we swore to it, sure. But Dad wound up with most of the care responsibilities. He was always the Alpha. There had been a few threats over the years of bringing Omega to the kennel when we refused to take him on an early morning walk or bathe him, but we all knew they were empty threats. Mom and Dad both loved that dog as much as we did. He was a fierce protector.

As we cuddled and snuggled with him, it was as if the emotional toll was easier to bear. I stared into his captivating blue eyes and as I did his image began to blur. It was like when you stare at a picture too long and everything becomes blurry, but it reveals the hidden image inside. He let out a loud yawn and then before our eyes, our best friend's shape blurred into a gray cloud of dust and sparkles spinning like a dust devil in the wind. It got bigger and longer and twisted in every direction until suddenly staring back at us was a full-grown Human. The eyes were the same, but Omega had turned in to a rugged and gangly guy who looked like he was about twelve years old with long lean muscles, a mop of curly black hair, and a giant smile revealing ultra-perfect big white teeth. He grabbed a bed sheet to cover himself.

"Well, hello there," he said meeting our bulging eyes with his wide grin.

"How did you do that?" Steele said. "Are you a werewolf or something?"

Omega chuckled. "Not exactly. Think deeper. You know what we are · deep inside your soul."

"Wait, what? We? Does that mean I can change into a dog? Or a wolf?" asked Steele.

"Not exactly," Omega sighed. "Let's start from the beginning."

Omega then began to tell Steele and I about who we were. Who we really were.

"Adam longed for a mate, so God gave him Lilith. The couple had a passionate love affair and bore children of great strength who commanded the other warm-blooded earthly creatures. One of them was your father, Gabriel. Their offspring, called Therions, were able to take the form of any animal on the planet. At age twelve Therions chose one particular animal, and then used the power of the sun to shapeshift at will. They were immortal and free, roaming the Earth as Humans or as Animals, living in peace. And for a time, life was good."

"Let me guess," I interjected. "Until Eve came along?"

"Well Adam and Lilith fought. A *lot*," Omega continued. "And eventually, Lilith cheated on Adam with, a demon, for comfort. Adam and her Therion children turned against her and banished her. She was heartbroken and vengeful. She mated with the demon and with dark magic powered by moonlight they purposefully created a race with the spiteful intention of being superior to her first-born children, spawning the first Vampires. In nature, and in the universe, everything centers on balance. They balanced the sun driven shapeshifters perfectly."

"So if dad was a Therion, was mom a Vampire?" Steele asked.

"You mom was a Daughter of Eve," said Omega. "Just chill. I am getting there. The Therions and Vampires, blinded by their hate, didn't realize how much they needed each other. The children went to war, vowing to destroy each other. Great chaos ensued on Earth. As the wars raged between the races, they almost wiped each other off the planet. Small pockets of each survived but went into hiding. It was a dark time."

"Wait," I interrupted. "The story about Adam and Eve is not real?" I asked, hanging on Omega's every word.

"Oh, it is real," he replied. "Most stories just have Eve out of order. After the war ended, God made Eve for Adam to mend his broken heart and in an effort to start over. The two bore Human children—two boys and four girls."

"Girls?" Steele said.

"History has a funny way of omitting things to serve a certain purpose," Omega explained. "Most stories have a vein of truth but miss a lot of the details. The girls are never mentioned in the Old Testament but if you study genealogy, you will find all Humans on the planet today can be traced back to the seven Daughters of Eve. Four Humans and three Witches."

"Three *Witches?*" Steele asked.

"From when the demon seduced Eve," Omega said. "As the snake in the garden."

"Well, that must have pissed Adam and Lilith off," Steele replied.

Omega scoffed. "Well, yeah. It sure did."

He continued on about Adam and Eve bearing Cain and Abel, and that each had a twin sister. They had two other daughters after Abel died. Adam eventually forgave Eve for her betrayal, but Eve and Lilith hated each other and so did their children, activating the same vicious cycle of hatred as before with the Therions and Vampires. The Humans and Witches were constantly at war with each other, inviting even more chaos to encompass the Earth and reflect itself back into the universe, just like it does today.

"Did the Therions and Vampires take sides in the Human/Witch wars?" I asked.

"Good question, Sera," Omega replied. "They did take sides randomly, creating even more death and destruction and plunging the Earth into darkness. That all-encompassing darkness attracted The Third Air, a group of unique, malignant beings of great power. Formed out of threads of primordial darkness that had predated the universe, its power grew with the great wars between the half siblings on Earth. The Third Air gained strength from chaos slivers in the deepest, coldest corners of the cosmos, like what exists in black holes. The Third Air thrives on hatred, fighting, and is evil in its purest form. When it gains enough strength, it spreads, slowly poisoning all lifeforms it encounters with its influence."

A shiver ran down my spine and I grabbed the blanket off the bed for warmth.

"God and Lucifer, sensing The Third Air's growing power, created a joint army to find and eradicate it. They knew the only way to preserve the planet and their Earth dwelling children was to work together," he said.

We nodded silently in unison.

"Their armies traveled to the darkest depths of space to eradicate the menace. While they were mostly successful, they were unable to fully prevail. Since it was impossible to completely destroy The Third Air, Earth's soldiers imprisoned them in either different dimensional planes of existence, deep within the planets' cores, or in uninhabited places in space."

"Divide and conquer, I guess," I muttered.

"Yes exactly, Sera. They broke them up, and scattered them in different places, and in essence exterminated them. But there are slivers of The Third Air that remained. They escaped by hiding and remaining dormant, some of them here on Earth. The earth dwellers, learning from God and Lucifer, knew that the only way to prevent The Third Air from awakening and destroying the universe was to continue to work together. That was why they formed Arete 8, a holy alliance. Two members from each earthly faction put aside their differences to protect the planet in perpetuity from The Third Air. The combined power of the magical alliance ensured The Third Air remained imprisoned and in a state of slumber. In this state they could still command and torment the weakest, darkest souls but were no longer necessarily malevolent to all earth dwellers."

"This is all, uh, interesting I guess," said Steele. "But what does it have to do with us, mom and dad and the Vampire who tried to kill Sera?"

"The Third Air are older and more powerful than angels, demons, monsters, and even Gods," replied Omega. "If they are ever released again, they will plunge the universe into darkness and death. Your parents both sat on Arete 8, the Alliance formed to control them. Two Therions, two Vampires, two Witches, and two Humans."

At this point we hung on his every word.

"Only together were they strong enough to control the darkness and protect the planet with their forced allegiance," Omega said. "They were sworn to protect the world, and each other, from The Third Air. The factions still fought, but now their troubles seemed small. The Alliance passed a set of planetary guidelines and enforced them valiantly, together. That Alliance held strong for many thousands of years, until it was destroyed in the 5th century. Your mother, or an earlier incarnation of your mother, was pregnant with the earliest incarnation of the two of you when Arete 8 was destroyed. To protect you and your parents from being found, a powerful Witch put a cloaking spell on you before you were born and altered your Therion DNA—made it dormant—so that you would appear Human and would reincarnate as Human. When you were born and for every generation afterward, for many, many lifetimes you have been born Human with your Therion DNA dormant among your genes. You are called the hidden children of the Royal Therion family. And I've been protecting and watching over you ever since—reincarnated usually as your dog."

I grabbed Steele's hand and closed my eyes. Something about the story resonated deep within my soul and I knew it did for him too. Together, in our minds, we tuned in to ancient images of our parents, my beautiful mother with long blond wavy hair hanging past her shoulders and a bulging belly that looked about to burst, sitting next to my father at a strange octagonal table, surrounded by candlelight. He looked troubled, his green and gold eyes stormy, and his dark eyebrows turned downward. His hand rested on my mother's stomach. I felt their emotions and knew Omega's story was true. I opened my eyes and the room was spinning.

"Are you ok?" Steele asked me.

"Just, a little queasy," I said. "I just can't believe they're gone."

"What happened to Mom and Dad?" Steele asked, his voice cracking slightly and his eyes welling up with tears. His chin began to tremble.

"Do you mean then or now?" Omega asked.

Steele cleared his throat. "Then. Now. Both, I guess. Where are they now?"

"They died in the avalanche. They never knew their true nature in this life. But their souls will renew. It is the natural cycle. I promise," he said as he reached out and squeezed my arm. "After the avalanche I tried to save them, but they were buried too deep in the snow. They died quickly, as Humans tend to do. They loved you two so much and would do anything to protect you. And so would I," Omega said.

"I was attacked," I muttered as my hand flew reflexively to my neck. "Did I, die, too?"

"You did, Sera, but only for a few moments," Omega said. "And then we were able to get you back."

"It was a Vampire and I'm going to kill him," Steele said with a conviction in his voice I'd not heard in long time. He jumped from his cot and ripped the covers off it, throwing them violently against the wall. He picked up the bedframe and threw it across the room.

"Steele, it's okay. I'm okay," I said, trying to calm him down, which has always been an effort in futility when he was unable to manage his emotions like this. Albeit this time, he had a pretty good reason to be angry.

"Do you know him?" Steele screamed at Omega, ignoring my efforts.

"I do," Omega replied. "His name is Jules. Jules Blakewell. He was once a sworn ally of your parents and a member of Arete 8."

Steele's face was flushed with anger. His nostrils flared and his eyes glimmered with golden flecks. I stood up and put my hand on his shoulder.

"Get off of me!" he yelled and pushed my hand away. "Mom and Dad are dead! A Vampire attacked you. He killed you! And you're not even upset. What is your problem?"

His anger sent a chill through my soul.

He tended to have a bit of an anger management issue, and understandably the events of the past few hours set him off. Growing up, Mom had always been the best person to calm him down. They worked on breathing exercises, chakra cleansing, and used essential oils when he got worked up but usually after he'd punched a wall or two. Mom would always tell him that anger is an ugly emotion. That would get him even more worked up.

"How can you say that?" I yelled. "I am upset. I am just trying to process everything," I said. "Yes, he attacked me, but I *am* fine. I have this instinct that mom and dad are okay, too. Just calm down. Please. Take your breaths. And listen to Omega," I pleaded.

That seemed to alleviate his anger momentarily, allowing Omega to continue.

"Jules, the Vampire, should have been repelled by your blood. When Arete 8 formed, the Witches cast spells using balance and natural elements to bind the laws of the day and prevent the factions from killing each other. It bound them together, made them dependent on each other. Vampires, half siblings of Therions, aren't allowed to kill one another, and they can only feed on Humans who invite them in. Even being disguised as a Human, your true nature should have repelled him. Nevertheless, he brought you to the brink of death, and then just beyond it. Most people would have died from that, from losing so much blood."

"Why aren't I dead?" I asked.

"Vampires are forbidden to turn a Therion. Once he realized who you were he stopped feeding on you and we brought you here," said Omega. "We convinced him to try and save your life, and between his venom and the Therion healers, they did. Even Vampire venom, which cures most minor Human ailments and turn Humans into half breed Vampires when drained, wouldn't have been enough to save you. You lost a lot of blood from him, and the crash."

"Speaking of my crash injuries, they're gone?" I asked taking an inventory of my limbs.

"Yes. Therion crystal magic healed you both," Omega said.

I opened my hand to reveal the stone that had earlier fallen off my forehead.

"This?" I asked.

"Yes. It's an activated amethyst, but, Sera, you shouldn't be alive. Jules broke an ancient oath by bringing you back. Even though you are technically Human, you have Therion DNA, and we're not sure what that will mean for you, and him."

"Why would he do that?" I asked.

Just then the tent door opened again and an older man, looking to be in his mid-sixties walked in. He was surprisingly fit for his age and taller than my dad had been. He stood about six foot four, if I had to guess, with a salt and pepper military looking haircut. He wore a dark blue fleece, blue jeans, and flip flops. Not exactly a combination you'd imagine fitting for the 20-degree weather outside.

"Hello, I'm Brock," he said, looking at Steele pacing around the room. "I'm sure you must be bewildered, tired, and hungry. We're about to have dinner outside. Please join us."

I was starving. And my head was reeling from our newfound knowl-edge of the history of the world taught by none other than my dog.

"That sounds great, thank you. We'll be right out," I said.

I stood up and grabbed Steele's hand and pulled him toward me.

"Come on, let's eat. Umm…Omega? Are you staying like that or…" I asked.

"I'm going to change back—it takes a ton of energy to shift and remain Human, especially at night, but I can only talk to you this way. I want to conserve energy just in case."

His voice trailed off. I didn't really want to inquire about what the "in case" remark meant so I just told him we'd give him some privacy and meet him back outside.

Steele and I headed outside the tent and the sounds of chatter, and the smell of a feast drew us across a wide-open field to a bonfire pit. There were a group of about twenty people eating around the fire, and a handful of others lined up outside another tent. Brock motioned us to the food tent and told us to help ourselves to the spread inside.

I could feel every eye on us and sensed hesitation and excitement from the crowd. Inside the food tent we found a buffet table filled with salad greens, grilled fish, rolls, rice, and fruit. I loaded my plate to its limit and Steele did the same. We walked outside and Brock had saved us two seats by the fire, next to him on logs that made for makeshift benches. As we sat, the others did as well, and a hush fell across the group. Everyone joined hands and closed their eyes. We reluctantly played along, wanting to be polite, and as my hand met Steele's on one side and Brock's on the other, I felt a surge of intense energy shoot through my body. It sent a shock wave through the circle that was palpable.

In the energy came a sense of family, of ancient knowledge, of peace and of power. Everyone around the circle opened their eyes and when they did, they were glowing gold. All eyes turned to Brock as he gripped my hand a bit tighter.

"The wisdom of the Gods is upon us tonight, as we thank our ancestors for this plentiful bounty and protection from our enemies. We look to the sun whose reflection glows on the moon and strengthens our souls. We find solace in solitude but are grateful for our pack connection and to one another. Tonight, we ask for answers and blessings and welcome our new friends. So be it."

"So be it," said the group in unison. Everyone's hands separated and the glow left our gazes.

"Steele and Seraphina, please eat. We know you've had a very long day and must be famished. We want you to know that you are most welcome here. We want you to feel like family. You are, in fact, family and we've been waiting to meet you both for a very long time."

I knew he was right. The connection formed from the circle had imparted a historical knowledge into our brains that was clear and succinct. Long, long ago when our parents sat on Arete 8 and we grew inside our mother's womb, the Alliance was strong. Friendships had formed among creatures that began their existences as enemies but were forced to unite against a great evil. Those relationships were the foundation of the Alliance's success.

Brock broke my train of thought.

"The ancestral knowledge ran through you, correct?" Brock asked.

Steele and I nodded our heads in silence.

"You are the hidden Alpha children, and our kind has been searching for you and your parents for more than fifteen hundred years. I'm not sure how, but the universe has sent you back to us, and now we need to find out why."

8. MY LOVE FOR
HER IS TRAGIC

TAKING PHYSICAL FORM IS NOT PARTICULARLY PLEASANT.
Things hurt, the body has a lot of involuntary urges, and there are, *smells*.
Before I knew better, these things didn't bother me as much, but now, having shed my physical form so long ago, it was somewhat uncomfortable and itchy to be in this claimed body. I chose one whose soul moved on after the avalanche, one that looked similar to the body I once inhabited—young and lean, muscular and tall, with shaggy dark hair that covered my ears but wasn't so long that it got in my green eyes.

As Brock led the group ritual, I wondered if Amelia would recognize me this way. Beautiful Amelia, with her long, raven shiny waist length hair and her mesmerizing steel purple eyes. Her perfect milky white skin and full pink lips drew me in from first sight. The creature next to me whispered in my ear and interrupted my lovestruck memory.

"I don't buy it," the creature said.

I tilted my head to the side and repeated back to him, "You don't buy it?"

"Yeah," he said in a hushed tone. "That they are the Alpha children. Do you?"

I wasn't sure what this person next to me what asking. What was he wanting to buy? I thought I might be missing the meaning of his words, so I decided to avoid his question.

"Shh," I replied. "I'm listening."

That seemed to work as the creature opened his mouth as if to respond, but then made a strange huffing noise and leaned away from me. Not being in Human form too often made common phrases confusing for me. I wondered how the children would be accepted into this tribe and guessed that was what the comment was about. If I wanted to find Amelia and help the twins reunite the Alliance, I would have to get them to trust me.

"We also welcome a new friend to the circle tonight," I heard Brock say as he motioned toward me. "Please extend your warmest greetings to Hunter, who is passing through for a few weeks and joins us from his tribe in the Andes."

The group focused their attention on me, and all gave me welcoming nod or smile. Hunter was the name most people knew me by when I lived on Earth, and only the Alliance members knew my real name, Amantes.

"Thank you," I said, knowing Therions were always gracious to visitors from other tribes. The slightly yellow glowing iris modification I made to this body would convince them I was in fact, one of them. If only Amelia knew I was pretending to be a Therion. She would be amused. I had tried to convince her for so long to make me a Vampire but since it was forbidden by the Alliance, she never would. I'd tell her how it would make me such a better assassin, but she refused to break the oath.

She knew I didn't need Vampire speed or powers to succeed. She was, after all, the one who recruited me. I was Arete 8's hired gun, an assassin who never failed and who systematically took out anyone who spoke against them.

It *was* for a noble cause: to keep the peace in a dangerous world and protect it from falling deep into chaos. No one was better than me. When Amelia and I worked as a team, we were unstoppable... until I betrayed her.

Mara convinced me to deceive them all by rescuing and freeing a dark force—an evil monk with ties to the Great Ones. Turned out the Monk was her father and she had seduced me only to trick me into rescuing him. After her need for me was complete and her father was free, Mara murdered me, severing off my head, while Amelia watched.

Unbeknownst to me she had followed me one night as I left for a job and watched the traitorous scene unfold before her eyes. Engulfed in rage, she ripped Mara to shreds and then turned the dagger on herself. When the Monk found out Amelia killed his daughter, he was furious. His powerful anguish unleashed a dark power that cursed the Alliance and drew strength from the Old Ones he worshipped. He cursed the Arete 8 members to walk the Earth forever hidden from each other in that lifetime and any others.

Just before the darkness reached a pregnant Phebe, the Witches on the council cast their own spell of protection. They hid the twins from the Monk and magically submerged their Therion DNA under Human genes. They'd lived many lifetimes as Humans, never knowing their secret identity.

I debated whether to reveal myself to them. I knew it would be a necessity at some point but didn't want to overwhelm the twins with too much too fast. No one on the council knew what happened to me after I died. No one knew I had been claimed by iL Separatio and how sorry I was about betraying the council. And no one knew that in order to defeat the Old Ones, they would have to eventually trust me.

After the ceremony, I retreated to the guest tent Brock so graciously offered to me. Just outside the entrance were pungent wild white flowers, seemingly immune to the cold and snow.

Sights, sounds, and smells brought flashbacks of the life I lived a thousand years ago. Memories of the sweet smell of jasmine permeating the summer air as I chased Amelia through flower fields, knowing I'd never catch her.

As I lay down on my cot alone, and left this body for the astral plane, now, it was the smell of burnt rubber that permeated my nostrils as I hovered near Julian's house and saw him speed into his driveway.

9. WHAT YOU SEEK
IS SEEKING YOU

DRIVING FAST USUALLY ALLEVIATED SOME OF HIS STRESS BUT not tonight, it seemed. Not even the Tesla Model X insanity mode heading eastbound on I-70 on an empty stretch of highway provided him with any relief. His blood engorged body should be sleepy, but he was too amped up to even notice. He'd been drawn to the sight of the avalanche by the smell of dying humans. That much death had a stench that reached about five hundred miles for a Vampire. But there was something else that drew him there.

The Stirring.

And now he suspected why. He entered the house through the garage and yelled for Thane. No answer. He turned on the lights, threw the key fob on the counter and yelled louder.

"Duuuuuude, what's the emergency?" Thane answered groggily from the couch.

"We have an issue," he told him. "I killed a Therion. By draining her. And then I turned her."

Thane shook his head, confusion marring his face. "Are you feeling ok, Jules? I mean, you know that's impossible right?" When Julian didn't respond, Thane sat up straighter on the couch. "Man, just start from the beginning. Like…what happened when you left the office two hours ago?"

"And it gets worse from there," he told him, rubbing the back of his neck and pacing their shared living room.

As Julian recapped the evening's events, Thane's eyes widened and his mouth gaped open. Julian told him about The Stirring, starting with the avalanche and ending with him sucking the life out of Seraphina and being attacked by her brother.

"And that's not all," the Vampire muttered, lowering his gaze and inhaling deeply. He let the air out slowly before continuing. "Apparently, they are Gabriel and Phebe's kids. The twins."

"Holy crap. First, you found them? We've spent all of this time actively searching and they just fall into your lap on accident? And second, you fed on Phebe's kid?" His voice went up an octave on the last word.

"I had no idea who she was until their protector shifted. By the time he told me, it was too late. Gabriel and Phebe were there too. But they were too far gone after the car fell over the edge," Julian replied.

"Wait, wait," Thane interrupted. "Gabriel and Phebe wouldn't die from a car crash. It would take…"

"They weren't Therions. They were Human. I think that's why we haven't been able to find them. The legend about the Witches… it must be true. They hid them. Hid them as *Humans*," Julian said.

Thane was mentally processing. "Ingenious," he commented, while shaking his head.

"I never even got to talk to them. They died from injuries before I arrived on scene. And it's probably a good thing because I'd all but drained their daughter to one drop of blood. It tasted… different."

"Different? You shouldn't be able to drink her blood at all. It should make you sick." Thane ran his hands through his hair, matching Julian's frustration. "So then what?"

"Their protector wanted me to turn her, but I wouldn't. We took the twins to the Therion camp and Brock demanded that I do it. Said that the circumstances overrode the oath. That it was my duty to save her life."

"But you would lose your powers. You didn't do it, right?" Thane asked.

Julian didn't answer.

"Right?" Thane asked and demanded at the same time.

"She was barely alive. She looked so much like Phebe. I didn't have time to really consider any other option. I did it, and then I bolted," he said hanging his head and wringing his hands.

Thane knew Julian better than anyone. It was entirely out of character for the charismatic and cocky creature to be so tormented and distraught. But he could understand his anguish. Gabriel, Thane and Julian had been best friends—a bond so tight no outsider could ever infiltrate.

They were like gods, serving the highest power and ruling the planet. Gabriel and Julian were on the Alliance because of their lineage and Thane was a close ally. The Beta to Gabriel's Alpha. He wasn't privy to all of the council's secrets, but he did know the Witches hid Gabriel, Phebe and their unborn children, just as the Monk hid them all from each other.

Because Thane wasn't a council member, he and Julian were able to remain connected, but neither of them had seen Gabriel or the others in fifteen hundred years despite their best efforts to find them. Hidden as Humans, living on average anywhere from fifty to seventy-five years in each lifetime, the Graysons and their children had lived many, many lives. Never knowing what aged person they were looking for made it all the more challenging for Julian and Thane to ever track them, even with the invention of the internet and all of Julian's technology tools.

"I'm sure she's alive and I'm sure she's fine," Thane said, in a gallant effort to convince Julian and himself. "And maybe we should be looking at this from a different perspective. We finally found them! There must be a crack in the curse. And if you found them, there must be a way to find the others. And then Amelia. And then we can reunite the Alliance. With or without, your powers."

Amelia. I knew Julian's heart ached for her too. His sister was his best friend and closest ally. This was closer than they'd ever been to bringing her back. If he did lose his Vampire traits, or 'powers' as Thane liked to call them, Julian would see it as an even trade for freeing Amelia. Julian wouldn't believe this to be a coincidence. The odds of the Royal Therion family being in Colorado during this time, the Age of Aquarius and this close to the Snow Moon Eclipse were nearly impossible. Couple that with him being the one to 'find' them, albeit under tragic circumstances, would be unbelievable.

And then there was The Stirring, that feeling he could not shake, that had started earlier this evening in the command center. It was all connected. Everything always was. Julian should know that.

"Come on," Julian said to Thane. "Let's find out."

10. DEAD INSIDE

AFTER DINNER BROCK FORMALLY INTRODUCED ME AND MY brother to the rest of the Therion pack. They were a mostly friendly and polite group except for one male who was kind of odd and stand offish. He was new to the pack and just passing through, Brock explained.

After the introductions and some mingling, Brock took us back to his tent and offered up additional history that colored in Omega's earlier story. Apparently, since the Dark Ages when the Alliance was destroyed, the factions stuck to their own kind. Most Therions stayed hidden from the rest of the earth dwellers, in camps like this one in the woods made up of family groups all over world. Since every Full Moon drained their energy completely and forced them to shift into animal form for twelve hours, being around outsiders could get complicated.

There was a time when Therions were violently hunted, which also contributed to their modern aversion to living among outsiders. While technically immortal—a Therion's life span was limitless, and they were immune to disease—modern weapons could still kill one if shot in the head or heart. Also the Death Camas plant would make them extremely ill. When killed they reincarnate like Humans and become full Therions at age twelve. They could shapeshift into any animal they identified as, but when they chose it, they were stuck with it for that one life.

"Shifting takes an enormous amount of power from the sun, on clear days or during a Full Moon," said Brock.

"Resulting in werewolf legends?" I asked.

"Yes, I would imagine so," Brock said. "During a Full Moon, the sun and moon face each other, as Therions do when bonded with a Vampire. This creates an opposition—a healthy balance.

The sun throws its light out into the universe and the moon reflects it, allowing it to be seen in its greatest splendor. This opposition of two great luminaries suggests a powerful balance, a search for a mid-point between two extremes," he explained.

"Right now," Brock continued, "the sun in Aquarius seeks revolution and equality, while the moon in Leo represents the monarchy regaining."

"Monarchy, like our parents?" asked Steele.

"Yes," Brock said. "And the two of you. It is incumbent upon you both to restore your family's seat and reunite Arete 8. Since the Alliance was destroyed, the factions have unsuccessfully tried to find one another to reform it, at times getting close but never being able to fully reunite the entire council, mostly because your family line was so well disguised and so were the Witches."

Steele and I exchanged uneasy glances, neither of us quite prepared to be thrust into the Royal limelight or inherit these lofty responsibilities.

"Therions, Vampires, and Witches have been waiting a very long time for a special upcoming cosmic event," said Brock, as his eyes began to glisten, and he leaned in closer to me and Steele. "We have now entered the Age of Aquarius. It has been foretold that during this unique time, there will be an eclipse during the first Full Moon in February, the Snow Moon."

He paused and rocked forward, moving his hands back and forth on his legs, obviously giddy. His excitement was lost on us.

"Should that mean something to us?" Steele asked, reading my mind.

"This is a once in a lifetime event for us, that will reveal, for a very brief period of time, the location of all Alliance members," Brock said, his entire face lighting up with anticipation.

"How brief?" I asked.

"During totality, when the Earth comes between the Sun and the Moon and its shadow fully covers the moon, it will turn blood red for seven and a half minutes. That is when the dark force that hid us from one another will weaken on the astral plane and the lights of the Alliance members will shine."

It was too much information to take in all at once and I was suddenly hit with an enormous wave of exhaustion.

"This is all super interesting," I said, "but if it's ok, I think I am going to call it a night. Can we pick up this conversation tomorrow?"

Brock nodded. "Of course," he said.

I attempted to stand but wobbled over the side of the table as I did.

Steele jumped up just in time and caught me.

"What's wrong with her?" I heard him ask Brock.

"She needs blood," a deep voice replied from the door.

It was the Vampire who attacked me. I recognized him instantly but not the stranger he was with. Steele must have recognized the monster too because he placed me gently on the couch and lunged at the figure in the doorway with ferocity.

"You!" he growled, hands clenched into fists and already swinging.

The guy standing next to Steele's object of loathing caught the punch a millisecond before it hit the Vampire squarely in the jaw.

"Whoa there, bud. We're here to help," said the stranger.

Ignoring his words, Steele, ambidextrous since birth, swung with his other hand and hit the speaker on the side of the head. He stumbled back half a step, giving Steele a chance to attack the Vampire. A millisecond before the punch would have landed on his face, the Vampire dissolved into a cloud of black smoke.

Steele punched the air, taking him by surprise and causing him to fall forward. The Vampire materialized and helped Steele stand up, much to my brother's dismay. By now, Brock was up on his feet and placed himself squarely between Steele and the Vampire.

"Steele, stop," said Brock.

He placed his hand squarely on my brother's chest, calming him. I was barely conscious and fading fast. Brock took his hand off Steele's chest and turned toward our visitors. He extended a hand toward the Vampire's friend and shook his hand pulling him in for a hug.

"Good to see you, Thane," he said. Then he turned his attention to my attacker. "Jules, hello."

While I recognized him as my attacker I didn't remember all of the intricate details of his face. He was striking. Back in Florida I'd crushed on plenty of guys. There was only one who really stole my heart. A soccer player who was tall, dark, athletic and charming. Jules put him to shame.

He was tall, probably a little over six feet, with a lean, muscular build. His straight dark brown hair was messy and longer on top than in the back. His eyes were a brilliant purplish blue, almost neon with silver strands moving through them and his skin, while pale, was flawless. His chiseled cheekbones clenched and sent butterflies through my entire body. I wanted to hate him, but he was an absolute specimen of perfection.

"Hello, Brock," he said, cold eyes locked on me. "She is dying inside and out. She needs blood."

I am dying. This was becoming a regular occurrence. The words described exactly how I felt. Dead inside and out. What did that mean exactly?

"The best, fastest way for her to recover would be to drink blood. It is the only way to complete the process so that she can live," the Vampire said.

"You are joking right?" Steele snapped back. "Live? You already killed her! She is never going to attack someone and drink their blood!"

It didn't sound like the worst idea to me but I couldn't even gather the strength muster a reply.

"It doesn't have to be like that," Jules said softly. "We… share."

Steele looked perplexed, but all I could manage was a whimper.

"She's dying," Jules repeated. "This time for good. New Vampires can't go more than a few hours after being turned without blood. After the first time, she'll be able to go longer without it, but she'll die by morning if you don't let me help her."

As my eyes got heavier and harder to keep open, I noticed for a split second that his friend Thane looked nervous. I wondered why.

"It's a simple process," the Vampire said. "I transfer blood from my system to hers."

"And how exactly do you do that?" Steele asked.

"It's… kind of like mouth-to-mouth resuscitation," he said.

That woke me up slightly. My heartbeat quickened.

"Are you crazy? You think I am going to stand here and watch you make out with my sister under the guise of saving her life? There is no way that is happening," Steele said. "That's not happening," he said again, this time directing his comments to Brock.

The Vampire crossed his arms, tapping his fingers and giving Brock a look of annoyance.

"Steele," Brock replied. "There is nothing more important to me than protecting you and your sister. Jules is an original descendant. He knew your parents. He sat on the Alliance with them. He broke an ancestral oath when he attacked Seraphina but also when I asked him to save her, at tremendous risk to himself. I imagine he is here offering to help because he knows, as do I, that reuniting the council is more likely now than it has ever been before. I give you my word that you can trust him. Seraphina can trust him. Bloodsharing between Vampires is customary. It's an example of kinship. There is nothing... *weird* . . . about it. We need to let him save her."

I managed to make eye contact with Steele and silently sent him my approval. Then I looked at Jules, feeling the life force leaving my body. I was dying inside. Imploring him to hurry.

"You'll probably . . . um . . . want to give them some privacy," Thane remarked.

Brock put his hand on Steele's shoulder and led him toward the door.

"We'll be right outside, Sera," he said to me, but also as a warning to our cold-blooded friend.

Steele, Thane, and Brock walked outside. Jules slowly made his way toward the couch and sat down next to me.

"Hello again," he said softly and locked his gaze onto mine. "I am so sorry about what happened. I am sorry about your parents. I wish I could have saved them. But now I'd like to save you. Is that okay?"

I nodded once.

"I don't want to do anything you are not comfortable with. Like Brock said, bloodsharing is very normal for Vampires. It's an extension of our close familial bond with each other. Are you ready?"

I nodded again. He placed his hand under my chin and tilted it up towards his face. He hesitated slightly, looking into my eyes and sending shock waves down my spine. He leaned in and placed his lips onto mine. I closed my eyes.

I completely and utterly surrendered. Reality faded away and I was engulfed with the essence of peace, power, and knowledge.

You know that feeling at the end of summer when you're fresh out of the ocean right before sunset and you plop down on the sand to dry off? The temperature is perfect—in the high seventies with a slight breeze—just cold enough to give you goosebumps but you don't shiver because the sun is still shining on your skin? It's that feeling of warmth that envelopes you, surrounds you, and makes you feel happy and content, for just a split second. A feeling of completeness.

As Jules's lips pushed against mine, his mouth opened wider, and he shared a piece of his soul with me. This is what it's like in the space before time. The space before being reborn. A complete feeling of fulfillment, of omnipotence, of clarity into what you did right, what should have been done better, and what needs to be corrected the next time around. You see, know, and understand. You connect with a higher power and feel one with the air around you. I'm not sure how long it lasted but I never wanted it to end. And then in an instant. It was gone.

I opened my eyes and felt strong. Fulfilled. My skin tingled and tightened and my insides were on fire with sensations. I felt intensely connected to the creature sitting next to me that should have terrified me.

"Better, right?" he asked, like it was just a regular transaction for him.

"Much better," I said, staring up at him and realizing how beautiful he was.

"Great. You will feel energized and awake but then tired in a few hours. I'm not really sure how this will affect you, but I can tell you about most Vampires. We don't need much sleep but when we do sleep, it's like the dead. Plan to be out cold for a solid twelve once you fall asleep next. Over the next few weeks, your powers may develop, slowly at first and then quicker. You'll be faster, stronger, the top of the food chain. When the time comes, I will show you how to feed. I don't know for sure because of your, unique, um blood, but the share should tide you over for about a week," he responded.

I felt disappointed that I'd have to wait so long to experience that utter piece of heaven again and contemplated for one quick second faking sick. It was a fleeting thought.

"Let's go find the others. I'm sure your brother is anxious to see you alive." He stood up, and reached for my hand to help me up, while seeming to be relieved to be done with this situation.

When I stood up, it was more like a leap, and it surprised me. Every muscle and tendon in my body seemed to be alert and on full patrol, ready for action and working together like a flawless machine. I felt graceful but powerful, and ready to take on the world. I followed him outside the tent, and we saw the boys throwing around a football in the clearing. The sun was shining, and the snow was already melting, with small patches of grass peeking through. Steele rushed over to me.

"Are you ok?" he asked, grabbing my arms and inspecting me closely for any differences in my appearance but finding none.

"Yes! Feeling much, much better," I answered, glancing over at Jules who fit right into the mix with the others.

As we walked over to join them, Steele continued his inspection. "You look the same."

"You seem disappointed."

"I thought you'd be paler or all shiny in the sun," he said with a chuckle.

"I guess not," I held my arm out into the sun and closely scrutinized it myself.

There's no better way to solve a problem than by throwing a ball around together, Dad always used to say. He was right. We worked on lots of issues in our backyard either playing catch or kicking around a soccer ball. A wave of grief came over me as I remembered being with my dad and realized it would be a very long time until I saw him again. I longed to be able to send him a quick text or hear his deep, protective voice.

There was something about keeping your mind occupied with sports that made for clear vision and planning. For the next two hours that's exactly what the five of us did.

We discussed how it was most likely not a coincidence that we were brought together, and the opportunity at the upcoming Snow Moon Eclipse.

"So, you mentioned that the Alliance members' location is visible from the astral plane on the night of the Snow Moon," I said to Brock. "How exactly do we get to the astral plane?"

"That is another piece of the puzzle we are missing," Brock said.

"The priority needs to be finding Amelia," Jules interjected.

Jules and Thane told us how they'd been perpetually attending high school for the past seventy years in a futile effort to locate the Vampire named Amelia, another member of the Alliance They knew her body was hidden in the tunnels beneath the current school they were attending closer to the city, but they just didn't know exactly where. Sometimes they would get hired as teachers or coaches, other times they'd attend as students. Humans had short attention spans so every four years, they take a five or ten-year hiatus, travel the world, and change their appearance slightly to come back all over again as Freshmen.

"Talk about eternal hell," joked Steele.

"Vampires are patient," Jules said. "When you live forever, going into hiding or hibernation for a few decades to allow the Humans to forget you is kind of a nice break."

"Don't feel too sorry for us; we've enjoyed some pretty amazing places during those in between times," Thane added. "And if someone ever does recognize us, Jules can usually handle that."

"Not anymore," Jules said wistfully.

"We don't know that for sure," Thane replied.

Seeing the look of confusion on our faces, Thane continued. "Back when Arete 8 existed, if a Vampire turned another creature, the Triad Witches made sure their powers were stripped. It was the only way to deter it. When Jules was forced, or convinced, to turn you Sera, that curse would have been activated. That means he can feed, but other things like speed, compulsion, strength… all of those will begin to fade if the curse is still intact. Only time will tell."

He'd made a huge sacrifice to save me. I averted my gaze and felt a pang in the back of my throat.

"When your powers develop, you'll find that many Humans will invite you in with their negative thoughts, or actions," Jules said. "That will allow you to not only feed on them, but also control their emotions. It has been useful in the past if anyone questioned our place at the school."

"We keep a low profile and control and manipulate the students through technology," said Thane.

"I don't understand," I said, wanting to turn the conversation back to finding Amelia. "How do you know her body is under the school, but you can't find exactly where?"

Jules inhaled deeply and slowly exhaled.

"Don't relive it, just retell it," Thane counseled.

I could tell that whatever happened was deeply upsetting to Jules.

"Amelia was smart, but she was also lovesick. She watched her lover die when a Witch murdered him. He'd also been cheating on Amelia with the Witch, so he deserved it if you ask me. The Witch killed him because she had no further need for him and she beheaded him with the Blade of Black Tourmaline, the weapon he used as the Alliance's assassin. The Blade is one half of a mystical dagger. When it is combined with its other half, the Selenite Dagger, it yields a lethal blow to Vampires, Therions, Witches, and obviously Humans. Even a small scratch from the Blade will imprison a soul in its private purgatory, locking the soul inside it until it's cleansed enough to come out."

The story clearly pained Jules, so Thane picked up where he left off.

"Anyone who controls The Blade of Cain—that's its name when both halves are combined—is all powerful. The Alliance kept it safe, but the Witch managed to weasel her way into Amelia's boyfriend's pants and took it from him. Amelia knew the importance of keeping the Blade out of wrong hands. So when she saw the Witch kill her lover, she was probably distraught and pissed but also wanting to protect the Blade. She came out of hiding, saw it all happen and ripped the Witch to shreds. Knowing that the Witch's accomplice was near, she took the dagger and inserted it into her own heart, knowing that only an Alliance member could remove it. Since it was only one half of The Blade of Cain, it didn't kill her."

"What did it do to her?" I asked.

"She's in permanent stasis," Jules replied. "After that, the Monk – the Witch's father and her accomplice, destroyed the Alliance, and cursed us. He moved Amelia's body constantly so we could never track it and forged a partnership with an evil coven here in America to hide Amelia's body indefinitely with dark magic. We believe it's under the school because we traced the coven here a long time ago. There is an enormous dark source of energy underneath the school, along with a vast tunnel network that we cannot seem to unravel."

"Wow," Steele said.

I felt a tinge of jealously when Jules talked about Amelia and how he'd been trying to find her body in an intricate underground maze for over a millennium.

"You must really care for Amelia," I said. "Were you two, like, dating as well?" I asked awkwardly.

Jules laughed. "No, we weren't a couple. Amelia is my sister," he said. "It rips me up that while that half of a blade is stuck inside her, thanks to her idiot boyfriend, she's been paralyzed for over ten centuries, her soul locked in a perpetual tortuous purgatory, between the world of the living and the dead."

I was relieved at the revelation of the family tie but also heartbroken for this creature who was clearly tormented.

"Where is the other half of the Blade?" I asked.

"No one knows," Jules was quick to point out. "It was lost in the aftermath. Probably somewhere underground near Israel or Egypt, waiting to be discovered by an archaeologist."

Quickly getting the subject back to freeing Amelia, Thane continued.

"Ancient scripts reveal that only during the Age of Aquarius, during the Snow Moon totality, will the dark magic be lifted, and the path to the Blade will be illuminated."

"But even then, we'll need the crystals," Brock chimed in. "There are thousands of doors in the tunnels under the school. They are all locked with the Seal of Sephiro. We've found a lot of them over the years."

"Before some of us gave up," Jules said snidely.

Brock ignored him and continued.

"The only way to unlock the tomb will be to insert twelve holy gemstones, comprised of the Earth's earliest elements, into the seal on the correct door. Each faction in the Alliance guards their own powerful crystals. When all twelve are activated and linked together as one, and placed inside the door seal, they'll melt together to unlock the door and reveal the dagger's location…and Amelia."

"Gotta give it to that evil bastard," said Jules. "His convoluted plan was pretty smart."

Brock explained that each faction originally had three holy gemstones. Omega guarded one within his collar tag. The second, we figured out, was embedded in a ring given to Steele on his twelfth birthday, and the third Therion crystal was the gemstone I'd worn around my neck since childhood, given to me by my mother.

Jules had the three from his family line but had put his efforts of finding the others—from the Witch and the Human lines—on the backburner after getting frustrated from centuries of dead ends. With me and

Steele showing up like we did, and another three crystals now accounted for, it gave him a renewed sense of hope. Plus, the more crystals we linked together, the more powerful we became.

The plan was for Steele and me to enroll in high school with Jules to have access to his technology, and to link our six crystals together. It may help us target the entrance to Amelia's location. We'd enroll to keep up appearances and work with Thane and Jules to try and find the Witches and the Human descendants, along with their gemstones. Jules offered up his residence as a place for us to crash— apparently it had plenty of space and we'd get started on Monday. The idea excited me, but I also wished I could wake up from what seemed to be a bad dream and be back in my bed at home in Florida with my parents and my regular dog, like things were before.

Jules left us at the Therion camp for the weekend. As soon as they left, it was like a piece of me went with him and I could not get his image or his scent out of my mind. But the tiredness he'd alluded to, began to engulf me.

I excused myself and told Brock and Steele I was going to bed. Steele said he was going back for seconds on dessert and that he'd be right behind me. As I walked toward the tent, I felt eyes watching me from the forest. I turned but saw nothing. I shook it off and headed inside. Literally five seconds after my head hit the pillow, I fell into a deep sleep.

I dreamt of my mother. She looked so beautiful and happy. She was sitting on a throne in the middle of a calm turquoise ocean, floating like an angel. She took my hand and asked me to fly with her. I did. I thought I felt my soul leave my body as we flew over fields of flowers and majestic mountains, light and complete with an immense peace. She thanked me for choosing her as my mother. She told me that I was a gift to her from the universe. That she learned so much from me over many lifetimes together.

She warned me that every creature had its own agenda and about a great evil hidden within the Earth but also within each soul and implored me to remember that things were not always what they appeared on the surface. The ocean waves turned tidal, violent, and gray, our hands were ripped apart and I yelled out her name. She disappeared from my sight, and I fell deeper and deeper into oblivion.

11. SHINY THINGS

It filled me with joy to see the twins together with Julian. Although they had never met, and he had been separated from their parents for over a thousand years, their bond was clearly unbreakable. Steele hated him now, but I was sure that would change in time. It was their karma to be together, just like it was for The Blade of Cain, separated like the factions were. Separated, it was commonplace; connected, it was extraordinary.

When Arete 8 entrusted me with the Blade of Black Tourmaline, I knew it had the power to paralyze its victims if left in their bodies. I was carefully instructed to never use it in that way. I was to kill swiftly and reclaim the Blade, guarding it with my life. Mara was the one who told me of its companion, the Selenite Dagger.

Originally forged as one weapon that held enormous untold power greater than that of the Gods, it split when the first brothers did, with one half being claimed and closely guarded by the Therions and the other by the Vampires. But the Blade wanted to reconnect. It would try and find its mirror image unless forcibly kept apart.

Mara wanted that power, and she used me to try and find it. When Amelia stabbed herself, she not only plunged her soul into purgatory, but she also kept the weapon out of Mara's hands. Mara could use its power to awaken The Great Old Ones of The Third Air, and in their hands the world would be helpless - plunging into a deep and dark state of chaos forever.

Transforming that inherent dark and chaotic nature to be more like the light is the reason all creatures inhabit this world. Rising above inherent reactivity and behaving proactively creates a genuine spiritual transformation that connects to endless light and fulfillment. I watched the twins with Julian, and I knew I had made the right choice.

As I hid in the forest, I inserted a log into the path of an oncoming fox, making him leap over it. As he rose up, he brushed a branch on a nearby tree that moved so the sun shined through its leaves, hitting and illuminating the crystal in Steele's ring at just the right angle. It was enough to make him notice the ring at the precise moment in their conversation. I knew they would figure out that they had the gemstones for a reason.

It was also, at this precise moment, watching the Humans interact with the Therions, being assisted by the Vampire that something dawned on me. Mara's father Samael—the Monk—for all of his hatred, deception, and evil traits, had actually done us all a great service. Only by being separated from each other were we able to see the power in erasing the veils between us and finding one another to unite once again. Only in our despair were we able to find the light to lead us back to each other.

12. SYNERGY

Monday morning could not come quick enough for me. We'd had a pretty relaxing weekend in the mountains getting to know our new "family," learning some sparring moves from the Therions and playing with Omega in his dog form. We'd definitely be taking him with us to our new pad. Besides some distant relatives in Florida and California, he was the only true family we had left.

Jules asked Brock to drop us off at his house in the early morning to give us time to change into clothes worthy of our first day of school. Apparently, he had extras. Thank goodness because the only outfits we had besides the pajamas donated to us by the camp were bloodied and ripped clothes from the accident. Steele was less than thrilled about starting eleventh grade over again and wasn't exactly one hundred percent on board with our plan but I just couldn't wait to see Jules again, and if that involved school, so be it.

I barely slept the night before but felt fine and was awake before the sun came up when Brock came to get us. The Therions kept a few cars in a hidden spot down the mountain. We took a quick hike in the fresh air and passed a beautiful stream and frozen waterfall on the way. We hopped into a brand new four door black Jeep Wrangler and got underway. Apparently even though they lived on a campground with sparse surroundings, the Therions had amassed an arsenal of wealth and weapons over the years that they had hidden all over the world but was only accessible to their kind. Crystal magic kept the secret spaces camouflaged for only Therion eyes to see.

Steele hopped up front with Brock and I was in back with Omega. I rolled the window down for him to stick his head out in the wind. Before we left Florida, Steele got his driver's license. Life for him was good. We'd turned sixteen last February and were approaching our seventeenth birthday now, but I'd been a little lazy about taking the online course to secure my driver's permit, meaning I'd be delayed on securing a license.

Steele, of course, got his on our birthday. He was a pretty good driver too, learning from our dad who was a police officer. I knew Steele would probably prefer to be the one driving the Jeep right now, but he was in a sour mood and hadn't said much since we left the camp. I'm sure he would have preferred to stay in the woods avoiding reality for as long as possible.

And even though I tried my best to convey to him my belief that our parents were still with us spiritually, he was mourning the loss pretty hard. I missed them terribly too. My emotions just seemed more muted now, not shut off, but distant. I knew in my heart that we would see our parents again, and connecting with my mom in my dreams felt like she was still with me, guiding my path. I also knew they would want us to help reunite Arete 8. It was their legacy and our destiny.

The drive into town took about an hour. Brock took a windy route that evaded the spot where we crashed. I assumed so we wouldn't see it. We still went through the tunnel, the one we'd almost made it to just before the avalanche violently ripped away our simpler life. It seemed like a year ago, even though road crews still worked on clearing some of the avalanche snow off the roads.

The landscape was much prettier here than in Florida where the highways were straight and flat, and the only interesting things to look at were palmettos and maybe an occasional alligator on the side of the road. Here as we drove closer to town and the road passed over hills and curves, we could at times see the Denver City skyline, the Chatfield Reservoir, and everything in between. We entered the town of Emberglow and made our way through a few more winding roads before entering a gated community. Brock turned in. Jules had mentioned that his house was big, but he did not mention that it was enormous. After we drove through the black iron gates, it took ten minutes before we saw the house on its own private enclave at the end of a cul-de-sac. The view from the front yard was amazing—a lake and snowcapped mountains in the distance. You could even see Pike's Peak.

The back of the three-story home had a view of downtown Denver and the Rocky Mountain range. Sleek and huge windows dominated the front exterior with modern black framing and gray and white brick accents. A wrapped matte gray Range Rover sat in the driveway and one door of the five-car garage was open revealing a Tesla Model X plugged in to the wall inside.

"Guess being a Vampire pays well," Steele scoffed as we pulled into the half circular driveway.

Those were the only words he'd uttered on the entire ride.

"When you live a long time, it's easy to amass great wealth," said Brock. "Supernatural powers of compulsion don't hurt either. So, listen you two. Before we head inside, I just want you to know I trust Jules and I trust Thane. Thane is one of us, a lone soldier, once the Beta to your father, and bonded to Jules. Jules sat on the council with your parents which means he swore to uphold an oath to never hurt our kind. But know that he is still a Vampire. It is his nature to feed on negative energy, feed on the darkness that lives within all of our souls, and harness it, nurture it. Never forget that in your dealings with him. Thane exists to monitor his dark nature but it's important to know that Vampires, while allies, are dangerous."

I knew he was talking to me and me alone. Steele already hated Jules.

Brock walked us up to the front door and opened it like he owned the place. I wondered how often he had been here. Omega ran inside first. No one appeared as we followed him inside. We were greeted by an immaculate home that smelled like wildflowers. It was tastefully and perfectly decorated with high ceilings and modern touches like steel horizontal stair railings, grey washed wooden floors, an oversized white couch, and a ginormous television mounted above a white marble fireplace. The floor to ceiling windows revealed a sunrise like none I had ever seen. Beautiful amber rays illuminated the full mountain range in the distance, the Denver city skyline bordered by cotton candy clouds, and the great room. The home sat above all the others in the neighborhood with a huge balcony and outdoor kitchen, fire pit, and jacuzzi just beyond the sliding glass doors.

Brock yelled, "Hello? Anyone home?"

No one answered. We walked into the kitchen that had a gourmet cooking area worthy of a food network television star. It made me long for our home in Florida. Although not nearly as grand, it had similar interior finishes and reminded me of the happy place we'd gather for meals as a family. A place where Steele and I could talk about our days and the trivial problems we'd encountered at school or soccer or at football. Family dinnertime was sacred in our home. Our problems discussed around the dinner table seemed so grand just a few weeks ago and so trivial now by comparison.

Thane interrupted my daydream as he tromped up the stairs leading from the basement.

"Hey, hey," he said. "You're late! We need to get to school with some extra time today to get you two registered. Scarlett!" he yelled toward the upstairs. "Scarlett!"

I had no idea who Scarlett was. Thane told us to help ourselves to the bagels and croissants laid out on the kitchen island and Steele immediately grabbed one. The kid was literally always hangry. That's when I saw a tall, dark auburn-haired girl with bright silvery green eyes wearing a tight black dress and high-top sneakers glide down the stairs. Her long shiny locks were pulled up into a messy bun with a few loose strands framing her face. She was definitely more developed than your average sixteen-year-old girl.

I instantly felt self-conscious and pushed my unruly dirty blond mess of hair behind my ear on one side. My ridiculous outfit made me squirm in embarrassment. It didn't help that she was staring at me with an air of condescension and disgust.

"Oh, finally. The queen has arrived," Thane said. "Scarlett, meet Seraphina and Steele. You know Brock."

She stuck out her hand to shake Steele's hand and then mine.

"Hello, Brock. Seraphina, Steele, welcome," she said, not conveying much sincerity.

"Scar, can you show them their rooms and give her something to wear?" Thane offered. "Steele—feel free to grab anything out of my closet."

Scarlett turned to walk back upstairs, and we followed like little puppy dogs. Up two flights and we entered a loft that overlooked the great room. Scarlett led Steele into Thane's room to change and then led me to another room. How many rooms were there in this place?

"This can be your room," Scarlett said as she walked me inside a large space with light grey walls and clean modern furniture. "For now, let's try to find you something to wear. We're not exactly the same size," she said looking me up and down. "It may be a challenge." She walked me into another room with an enormous walk-in closet worthy of a supermodel. "Grab whatever you can find that fits. I'll meet you back downstairs," and she turned to walk away.

"Uh, Scarlett?" I said before she'd left the room. She turned back around to face me. "So, you live here too? With Thane and Jules?"

The standoffish red headed goddess turned toward me with a stare that burned into my soul. "Yes, I do. Did they forget to mention that? We're just one big happy dysfunctional and supernatural family working together to save the world."

And with that she glided out and left me alone with my fashion nightmare. I found a pair of black leggings that fit me okay and paired them with a long sleeve Vineyard Vines t-shirt that was buried in the back of the hanging shirts section. Not exactly her style. She'd probably never worn it.

My room had its own bathroom. Another familiar sign of home. I used to take so many things for granted. The fact that I had an amazing room full of all my favorite creature comforts all to myself, and that my parents never made me share a bathroom with my disgusting brother who never seemed to master his aim, and the creature comforts of a home filled with love. This room was awesome, but it felt sterile. Clean and new, but not homey at all.

On the bathroom counter was everything I needed to make myself presentable including some simple makeup and accessories, all unopened and new. I washed my face, put on some mascara and lip gloss, and ran a brush through my wavy, air-dried hair. I found a straight iron under the sink and plugged it in. I stared at myself in the mirror and barely recognized the girl I saw in the reflection. Something about my face seemed different. Off. My skin was clear, which was an anomaly and had a certain glow to it. My eyes were more of a sparkling blue with gold flecks rather than the blue green I remembered. My hair had a luster to it that I also didn't remember, and for the first time in a long time I actually kind of liked how I looked. One thought back to the raven-haired super model crushed my internal love fest and I heard Thane yelling for us to leave from downstairs.

A few strokes of the flat iron, mascara and lip gloss and I was ready to go. I met Steele in the loft, and he looked like a stud in jeans and a black hoodie with his hair spiked with gel.

"Well, you cleaned up nicely," I said to my brother.

"Right back atcha," he said with a wink. "You ready to start eleventh grade all over again?" he asked.

"Ugh. Let's go, little bro." I grabbed his hand and headed down the stairs.

Jules was standing in the kitchen talking to Brock, Thane, and Scarlett. My breath caught in my throat. He didn't even look at me. He said goodbye to Brock and headed out the garage door. Thane and Scarlett grabbed their backpacks from the mudroom and followed, leaving me and Steele inside with Brock.

"I have great confidence in what you will accomplish working together, but remember what I said earlier," Brock said, lowering his voice. "You two have suffered a great trauma. An enormous loss. Don't underestimate those emotions. Let them in. Sit with them. You will ask yourself why this awful thing has happened to you, and why bad things happen to good people, like your parents. Remember, life is like a beautiful tapestry.

Up close you see a disarray of color and patterns, an unpleasant and disordered image. But when you hang the tapestry on the wall and step back, you see the entire image. The camp is always open to you. I hope you will choose to be there with us for the Snow Moon. Take care, good luck, and know that we are just a short drive away."

We said our goodbyes and he led us out through the garage. I gave Omega a head rub and exited the house last.

On the short ten minute ride to school, Jules, Thane, and Scarlett tried to fill us in on the kids in our grade we should watch out for. The cocky quarterback, the school bully, the emo mean girl. They told us we'd likely be assigned an ambassador for the day to take us to all our classes and acclimate us to our new school.

We pulled around a corner and I saw the school's steeple towering above the hilltop. Valiant High School looked more like an Ivy League College with its clocktower and red and tan brick buildings spread over five city blocks. Jules explained the layout of the place. It was comprised of three main buildings—the arts building, the academics building, and the athletic building. Next to that was a huge football field and stadium with a state-of-the-art gym, locker room, and a media room overlooking the field. There was an additional baseball field, two more fields for soccer, and a golf simulator. It was one of the most prestigious private Christian Schools in the state of Colorado. I'm not exactly sure who was paying the tuition for Steele and me, but I'm glad it wasn't me.

We parked in Jules's assigned space and walked inside together with the exception of Scarlett who immediately went her own way the second she got out of the car. Registration was pretty uneventful as most of our classes from Florida were offered here. They sent off for our transcripts. Within twenty minutes, Steele and I had our ambassadors and were heading off to class. I told Steele I'd try to find him at lunch.

A girl named Avery was my ambassador. She was a bubbly cheerleader type who seemed nice enough. She handed me a flyer for a club called Students With Light and implored me to come to a meeting after school, explaining it was a new club that focused on working toward positive change. Today they were going to all pray for a football player who died in an avalanche a week ago over Thanksgiving break.

"Did you hear about that?" she asked.

I got a lump in my throat and my hands got clammy.

"Uh, yeah. I saw something about it on the news I think," I said.

"It's so sad. Jason Kessler was our star quarterback, and he was driving back from a ski trip with his girlfriend when the avalanche knocked their car over the side. She is still in the hospital but will be okay, but he wasn't so lucky. I heard they haven't even found his body yet. It's so sad. You'll probably see tribute signs up about his memorial coming up, and we're trying to get a really big prayer group together today after school."

I told her I would think about attending. I'd been so consumed about my life, I hadn't even thought about how many other families lost people in that accident. No one knew Steele and I were in it, and I thought it was best to keep it that way.

My first class was Science—Biology to be exact, my favorite class back in Florida. Avery introduced me to the teacher, Mrs. Vaughn. She was extremely welcoming and told me I could sit between my ambassador and a girl named Mia who instantly made me feel uneasy. She had shoulder length black hair that was obviously dyed, thick black eye liner that arched up into a cat eye, a nose piercing and a sleeve of black tattoos up her left arm, including one small teal tattoo on the inside of her left wrist that was a strange alien looking symbol. Unfortunately, Mrs. Vaughn also made her my lab partner. She was friendly but something about her was off putting, and it made me nervous. She smelled like a mix of lavender and vanilla with perfume that was entirely too strong.

"So, let's see, this first question is about exocytosis? Am I spelling that right?" Mia asked me, squinting at our lab worksheet.

"That looks right to me. Back at my old school, we learned about that last month, but I totally bombed the test," I lied, making a feeble attempt to be friendly.

"I always try to remember it like exo is like exit, going out. Endo is going in," Mia said.

"Oh yeah, good tip."

We answered the rest of our lab questions just in time for the bell to ring.

"What's your next class?" Mia asked me as we packed up our things.

"It's History," Avery announced. "So we'll see you there." She motioned for me to follow her out the door.

"Mia runs Students With Light," Avery told me as we walked through the hallway filled with students. "If she likes you, everyone will like you, and if she doesn't, well I'm sure you can figure that out. She's into some cool things too, like herbs and supplements so if you need any help staying awake studying or just something to relax, she's your girl."

"Oh wow, really? Like drugs?" I asked.

"No, not drugs, just herbs and things that are all natural. We have two more classes with her so you can ask her yourself if you want," she told me as we navigated through a sea of students.

History was boring except for a slight altercation that Mia had with the teacher. We were learning about the World and the West and specifi-cally about France during the 1700s. The teacher was telling us about the tribulations of Olympe de Gouges. When the teacher mentioned how rebellious she was and that she stood firmly against the vows of marriage Mia scoffed loudly.

"Is there something you'd care to share with the class, Miss Owens?" the teacher asked.

"Her name was Marie, and it wasn't that she was against marriage," Mia said coldly. "It was that her first husband died on the same day her first child was born, and she thought she was cursed. She was never the same after that, but turned her grief into advocacy and fought tirelessly for women, for the poor, for cleaner streets, and equality. She was wise beyond her years."

The class stared at her incredulously.

"You say it like you knew her personally, Miss Owens, but nevertheless I appreciate the color you have added to her story," said the teacher.

Mia rolled her eyes and whispered something under her breath and then glared at me. I felt a chill and looked away.

"Chick loves her history," said the kid next to me.

I was guessing this was a regular occurrence for Mia.

The rest of the day was pretty uneventful. As for lunch, I guess that's what tuition will get you. There were three places to eat: the Café, the Commons, or the Bistro. The Café was in the arts building with 'limited' food choices—an array of sandwiches, salads, yogurt, and these ridiculously amazing homemade potato chips. Mostly the nerdy arts kids ate in there, but it was a great place to gather if you wanted privacy and quiet. The Commons was a huge cafeteria on the second floor of the academics building with floor to ceiling windows and stunning views of the mountains. Large circular tables and booths held eight to ten kids each, and it was loud and chaotic with tons of food choices from hot meals to salads and sandwiches. Then finally there was the Bistro, cozy with round booths of varying sizes; it was also dark, with no windows, and hot since it was located in the basement of the athletic building. Kind of a weird place to eat, in my opinion, but the Freshmen loved it. Likely because it was the only place on campus to score a smoothie or milkshake. Most Seniors didn't eat on campus because they were allowed to leave and could usually be found at the nearby Starbucks, Whole Foods or Chick-fil-A, just a short walk away.

I didn't find Steele at lunch, so I headed to the Commons and sat with Avery and her group of very bubbly girlfriends who told me all about every boy in the grade—who was taken, who was available, and who wasn't into girls. We all exchanged phone numbers and they all added me on Snap, an app I hadn't been on since before the accident. It was only a few days, but I was sure my notifications were on fire from friends back home. I was never all that social, with more acquaintances than good friends but I did have one close girlfriend back in Florida, Alivia. I used Brock's phone to call her before we left the camp and explain what happened and that we'd be staying out here in Colorado with our "relatives." I had to make all new social media accounts because I didn't know what to say to my old friends, how to respond about the questions I knew I would get asked and how to tell them I wasn't coming home. I'd figure that out later, I guess.

The girls at lunch told me about the upcoming Winter Ball and had a very intense conversation between themselves about who they should try and hook me up with as a date, pointing and laughing at several prospects. I pretty much tuned them all out and retreated into daydreams about Jules. The way his mouth felt against mine. The way our hearts beat as one and the way time stood still while he was so close and intimate with me. And then I remembered how disconnected and nonchalant he acted toward me afterward. It was no big deal to him but it was life changing for me.

A text message from the devil himself ripped me out of my imagination. Instead of a love note, it was just a group text to me, Steele, Thane, and Scarlett.

don't rush to meet at car after school – I have a quick mtg with coach so will be a few min late

Thane texted back a thumbs up, and Scarlett texted the eye roll emoji—that one must have been her favorite. After a few minutes of contemplating my response, I texted back: *Thx*

No response from Steele. Shocker.

After lunch was Bible, then Language Arts and finally Geometry. After school, Avery walked me to my locker, and we said a quick goodbye. Even though she was only required to be my ambassador for my first day, she told me she'd show me around more tomorrow and I should plan to sit with her and her friends at lunch. I promised I would even though the quiet Café sounded like a much better option to me.

On my way out of the school I passed a classroom with tons of students clamoring to get inside. When I peeked inside the door, I saw a huge logo on the whiteboard. The words underneath it read "Students With Light." The logo was the same one I saw on Mia's wrist earlier in the day.

I got a whiff of that smell again. The lavender and vanilla mix and then she appeared right next to me, almost as if I manifested her out of thin air.

"Hey, Sera. Come on in. The meeting is about to start," she said, standing a little too close for comfort. "And we're giving out tattoos today!"

"Oh, I can't. I'll miss my ride, but maybe another time."

"Okay, well check out our online hangout group. It has all the meeting dates and times. Anyway, see ya later!" And she walked inside.

I brushed off the encounter deciding any group that included her was not for me.

On my way to Jules's car I passed the soccer fields and saw a team of girls juggling and warming up. It made me long for normalcy. Soccer was always my safe haven. I'd been playing since I was three years old and before we left for vacation, I had just been moved up to highest level club team in Tampa and just made the Varsity team at my High School. After the accident and my phone was demolished, I never bothered to reach out to anyone back home to give them my new number. Brock had emailed my coach and teachers, posing as our uncle, and told them what had happened and let them know we'd be enrolling in school out here.

Seeing these girls train made me long to be back out there. I made a mental note to email the coach later tonight and ask if it was too late to try out for the school team.

I walked on over to the parking lot and before I rounded the corner to where Jules was parked, I saw Steele in a hidden corner of the school talking to a couple of boys who were lurking near the dumpsters. As soon as I decided to check it out, Steele felt my presence and walked toward me before I reached the group.

"Hey," he said.

"Hey. What's up? How was your day?" I asked.

"It was fine, I guess. I'm going to get a bite to eat before heading back to the house. I'll just hitch a ride and meet you there later."

"With who? Those randos?" I asked.

"Those randos are fine. And the less time I spend in that Vampire's mansion the better," he said, walking away.

I grabbed his arm. "Steele, don't. We are stronger together. Don't be weird. I don't want to go back there by myself."

He pulled his arm out of my grasp.

"It's fine, Sera. I'm just going for a bite to eat. I'll be back to the house in a few hours." And with that he went back to join his new 'friends.'

He was so frustrating sometimes. He was my closest ally and my biggest annoyance all at the same time. He also tended to go into a very dark place when things weren't going his way. Back in Florida, there were a few times when Mom and Dad had to take him to see a specialist about his dark thoughts. He'd been diagnosed with OCD but could usually manage it by eating clean and taking supplements, rather than having to go on medication like so many others. At times though, usually when he was under stress, he'd see a psychologist and an occupational therapist which helped a lot. Mom was super against him taking medication and would always say that the side effects from the medications the doctors wanted to prescribe were worse than his actual symptoms. If he lacked sleep, ate junk food or missed his daily supplements it would make the dark thoughts, OCD and those tics come back. I don't know what I would do if his symptoms began to emerge again. I shook the thought off.

As I walked back toward Jules's car, I noticed him walking toward it with someone. He caught my eye and waved. When we met at his Tesla, he introduced me to Coach Quintero, the school's athletic director.

"Nice to meet you, Seraphina. Welcome to Valiant. Do you play any sports?" he asked.

"I played soccer back in Florida and was missing it seeing those girls warm up over there," I replied.

"Oh, wow really? You're small for a soccer player. Did you play club soccer, school or both?" he inquired.

"Both. I played Varsity last year and was about to move to the ECNL team at TBU," I said.

"Wow, Tampa Bay United? That's a great club," he replied. "But you should know though that soccer here in Colorado is very competitive. Even so, you should come out to practice this week—it's tomorrow, Thursday and Friday right after school."

With that, I thanked him, and he walked away. He seemed nice enough, but man did I hate hearing people tell me I was small. Like I didn't know that already. I'd heard it my entire life. In soccer especially, size did not matter. Unfortunately there were plenty of coaches who only valued size. Sure, I may be 5'4", but I was also scrappy, fast, and skillful with great reflexes. I could volley a ball into goal better than anyone and was a top scorer on my team. I'll never forgot once in middle school when the PE coach put me in as Goalie, I had a ball passed back to me and I took it and dribbled around every player on the field and scored. That certainly made an impression.

Thinking about the sport I loved put a smile on my face. I had my first feeling of hope that maybe things would be ok.

Just when I was starting to break a smile, Scarlett walked up and said, "Finally, you're here. Let's go, I'm starving."

We waited about five more minutes until Thane showed up, then we headed back to Jules's house. When we arrived, Omega greeted me with his trademark tackle and snuggle and it made some of the stress from the day dissipate. It was hard to forget that he could at any moment turn into a dude. It made all those belly rubs seem kind of weird. Now I definitely saw him more as a cute little brother than a snuggly pet.

Scarlett excused herself saying she was going to change and head out to grab a bite to eat. Jules told me to make myself at home, grab any kind of snack I wanted from the kitchen, and he let me know that him and Thane would be downstairs in the basement working and that I should join them later to start planning our strategy and next steps. He was anxious to link our crystals together, and so was I.

I dropped my backpack off in the mudroom and headed upstairs with Omega, ready to have some time to myself. I plopped down on the queen-sized bed with a white down comforter and realized immediately how drained I was from the day. Omega hopped up next to me. I looked into his steel blue eyes and still couldn't believe the precious pup that I grew up with could change into Human form whenever he chose. He seemed to know what I was thinking and sneezed, which I thought was a chuckle. I wasn't really tired and didn't want to sleep but I was mentally drained and exhausted from meeting new people, arguing with Steele, and being in this new strange place with strange people...or creatures.

I stared out the window and peered toward the majestic mountains where snowflakes were starting to fall. They looked magical, angelic, and just plain perfect. Each flake hit the rooftop below my window and dissolved instantly, only to be replaced by a new one. It was mesmerizing. The flakes got larger and larger and fell faster and faster and I couldn't take my eyes away.

A text message tore me from my snow trance. It was Thane asking when I'd make it down to the basement. I'd been staring at the snow for hours. Feeling refreshed I grabbed a hair band out of the bathroom, threw my hair up in a ponytail and headed downstairs to join the others. Omega followed.

At the bottom of the basement stairs was a large great room set up like a movie theater with raised seating, a huge flat screen, and projector. I walked through that room into a bar with a countertop and drink wall, then into a full second kitchen before I saw lights on in the back bedroom and heard voices.

The room beyond it was full of technology that rivaled the CIA's. There were about twenty computer stations with large monitors, two stand up desks, a couch against the back wall, and two leather recliners. A spiral staircase led to a second loft level with even more desks and computers. Every work station was filled with people furiously typing away on keyboards. Thane kicked back in a recliner with a laptop, while Jules worked at a stand-up desk. Who were all these people? And when and how did they get here?

"Alright, everyone. Time to take your dinner break. I need this room for a few hours," Jules said as I walked in.

The workers gathered up their things and were all gone within thirty seconds, leaving the room to me, Omega, Thane, and Jules.

"I'm guessing this isn't a homework club?" I said with a nervous giggle.

"Yeah, not quite," Thane said, then motioned for me to sit down.

"So, since we are going to be working together, all toward a common goal, we are going to entrust you with what is going on here," Jules said. "But before we get in to all that, our first business item is to order you and your brother some clothes. Use my Amazon log in and get whatever you want. I'll let you work on that while I finish up some other tasks with Thane."

What a relief. No more stealing from Scarlett's closet. As I searched for clothes, I listened in to Jules and Thane's conversation. My hearing skills had definitely improved since my near-death experience. They were chatting about whose social media accounts they could manipulate, which students were off balance and why the school's umbra was shifting faster than usual toward gray. I wasn't quite sure what that all meant but I was amazed at how much private information they could glean from staring at the news feeds of the two thousand students and staff at Valiant High School. I loaded up the shopping cart and was about to hit purchase when I noticed the total exceeded $5,000.

"Ugh, Jules," I said hesitantly. "I'm done but the total is a little over the top. I feel like I'll need to get a job to pay you back."

"Seraphina, I almost killed you," he said, looking up only briefly from typing and staring at his screen. "And I am a millionaire ten times over. Get whatever you want," he said.

I hit the purchase button.

"Great. Now to the business at hand," Jules said as he grabbed his computer out of his work station and walked it over to a larger monitor, and clipped it in. "How much do you know about Arete 8, or the Alliance, as you've heard it called, your family's role on the council, and what happened to us?"

"Well, Brock and Omega told us about the council, and how it was formed from the original descendants of the first inhabitants of this planet. Two Vampires, two Therions, two Witches and two Humans. There was a power play of sorts and the council's assassin turned against them but wound up getting double crossed himself and being murdered. Amelia, your sister, loved him and murdered his killer but then her father, a powerful sorcerer or monk dude took his revenge on the council by destroying it and separating the family lines, hiding them magically from each other for eternity so that they would never rule the earth together as a united council again, or something like that?"

"Nice summary. More or less, yes, you have the gist of it," Jules said. "We guarded ancient secrets, prevented world catastrophes, and forged an uneasy but necessary alliance to keep true, unharnessed evil and chaos at bay and dormant. Before the invention of computers and modern technology, it was easy to keep our existence secret. It was easy to stay hidden even when one of the factions exerted violence on another which is in our nature, but we cleaned it up and worked together to mend our differences."

"Ok, I'm following," I said, pulling the handle back on the side of my chair and reclining it backward to kick up my feet. "Go on."

"After our assassin was killed and Amelia daggered herself, and the council was cursed, the world descended into darkness. What history books call the Dark Ages. We couldn't find one another and many of us went into hiding, afraid of what would happen without our alliance of peace. But then in the age of technology, those of us who managed to survive, got a glimmer of hope. We have mastered computer science. Our team has access to every technological device on the planet. We manipulate the world now online and that knowledge, that we've been able to garner from being immortal and learning this technology has brought us closer than ever before to finding the members of the council and reuniting it once again."

"That is alarming and fascinating at the same time," I said.

He continued without skipping a beat.

Your family was hidden as Humans. The four of you have lived a number of lifetimes since the Dark Ages. The original Witches have also been reincarnated time and time again. When they cast spells, they are much easier for me to sense, but this time around I can't track them as well. I suspect they're not using magic currently. I have found a few suspects on social media who may be them, but I haven't pressed it until now because without any new crystals, we were stuck. The Human descendants, with pure lineage from Adam and Eve, are much easier to find as they are, in this day and age, all over social media and easy to track through ancestry websites. The only challenge will be finding Humans who have no idea of their family history and are blissfully ignorant. But we'll cross that bridge later. Once we have all the crystals, and we know Amelia's location, we can open the door, remove the Blade of Black Tourmaline, and reunite the council."

Jules seemed different retelling the story, locked in his own mind as if the movie of his existence was playing out behind his eyeballs. His eyes turned a dark and stormy shade of silver, and he seemed like he was in a trance.

"I know this quest is super important, but would you be able to do me a favor, unrelated to saving the world?" I asked.

"That depends on the favor," he answered.

"After the accident, I lost my phone. I'm sure it was destroyed. But I had a ton of old photos on there. Of my friends, my family, my mom and dad. I'd love to get those back. Is that something you could help me with, with all of this technology?" I asked.

"I'm sure I could, yes. It would take some time to retrieve them off the cloud," Jules said. "But it's doable."

"That would be really awesome," I said, smiling.

Having that connection to my family was important to me. Memories I cherished and really wanted to have back.

"I'll work on it. But now, our first step is to connect your crystals with mine," Jules said. "Do you have them?"

"I do." I removed Omega's crystal from my pocket. "This one is Omega's, mine is around my neck, and Steele's is in his ring. He gave it to me before school this morning, I guess knowing he wouldn't be here."

"Or not caring to be," Jules said, extending his hand.

I handed them all over.

"All twelve stones are needed to unlock the door that hides Amelia's body. When they are all linked together, they harness great power. Linking yours to mine should reveal more details to us. I have a computer simulation we can use."

He dimmed the lights and put on a pair of black mesh gloves and began to move his hands to activate the computer screen, projected on the wall. A giant hologram seemed to appear in front of the wall forming a grid with twelve holes. Behind the hologram grid on the projector screen was a map of the world and on the ground below the hologram was a corresponding gem holder. He took our family gemstones and entered them into place, next to three others already there. It partially illuminated the holographic grid and parts of the map became brighter while an even larger part of the grid became visible. He motioned with his hands to turn the hologram left over the map, and then right, and he enlarged it.

"There!" Thane said.

"I see it," Jules responded.

"See what?" I asked.

"Right there," he motioned with his magically technological gloves to a spot that was glowing much brighter than the others. "Two Human crystals in Hawaii and one in the Turks and Caicos. Incredible." "That has never shown up before," Thane said.

Something caught my eye on the map in America. It was faint but I had a hunch to inspect further. "Can you enlarge the grid more, and zoom in so that we can get a closer view of California?," I asked, greedy for more to be revealed.

He did as I asked and we could see two more energy hot spots, glowing, albeit duller, near the coast of Northern California.

"I'll be damned," Jules said.

"That has got to be the Witches," said Thane, "right?"

"I could never find them," said Jules, "After they stopped using magic, it was..." his voice trailed off and Thane picked up right where Jules left off.

"It was like looking for a bristle on a broomstick?" he chuckled. "See what I did there?"

Jules rolled his eyes and I giggled.

"This is fantastic," Jules said. "Now if we can just figure out how the Snow Moon Eclipse will light the way to Amelia, we'll be set."

"That's in like nine weeks?" I asked.

"Yes, it's the first Full Moon in February. If we can gather the three Human crystals, find the Witches and get their three crystals, we'll be able to unlock the door. Even if nothing happens during the Snow Moon, I will spend the rest of my life trying to open every damn door in every tunnel underneath that school to find Amelia," said Jules.

Realizing I left my phone upstairs I asked to borrow Jules's for a quick google search. He tossed it to me.

"The Snow Moon is on February 11," I announced. The notifications on his phone were coming in at a breakneck speed, mostly in Instagram.

"You have an Instagram account?" I asked Jules.

"I have an everything account. I am a social media hacker. That means, I have to be on every form of social media," he said.

I opened the app and looked at his account. Jules Blakewell, Vampire. Not very subtle about it.

He had thousands of followers even though there was not one photo of his face, only shots of the back of his head, beautiful landscape pictures, and videos from high above the ground, like drone shots.

"Your profile says you are Vampire!"

"Well obviously," he retorted.

"Vampires are very in these days," Thane followed up.

"The best way to hide is in plain sight," Jules continued. "Humans are obsessed with our kind, to an unhealthy extent, I might add. But clearly, most people either assume I am being facetious or want to date me."

Oh, wow, the ego on this guy. Time for a subject change.

"Let's make a plan to find the Witches and the Humans while we're waiting for this mystical Snow Moon," I said.

"Starting with the Witches, now that we know the general area is Northern California," Jules said as he hopped on his computer. "I can narrow it down to a few families. Thane, can you finish up the simulation?" he asked as he looked at his watch. "I've got to run."

And with that the Vampire dissolved into smoke.

"Ugh sure, Jules." Thane said to the space where his friend had once been.

"Where is he going?" I asked Thane, trying not to sound as interested as I was.

"Let's just say Jules has a very busy social calendar," Thane said laughing.

13. ONLY
EMPTINESS REMAINS

THE CREATURE SLOWLY AND METHODICALLY INSPECTED HIS treasures from the night's escapades. An antique ring still splattered with blood from the finger he sliced off, a lock of hair from the immoral being whose neck was broken instantly, and a high-end diamond encrusted watch ripped from the victim's wrist after his decapitation. Satisfied that he'd wiped these retched souls from the planet so they would never be able to return, he smirked. Purged inside the dagger meant their souls were locked, never able to be cleansed. Even if they did escape and came back in this lifetime or the next, the vigilante would most likely find them again and again until they'd learned their lesson.

Before each of them lost consciousness and slipped into the cursed afterlife, they saw their distorted reflections in the glowing dagger and his shimmering blue and silver eyes. The last words they heard fell from his lips: *Nam-tar, Tesh, Kur.*

14. LOVE YOU'RE BORN TO FIND

THE DAY COULD NOT HAVE BEEN MORE PERFECT.

On the way to school, the magnificent Rocky Mountains stood tall and whitecapped beneath a perfectly clear blue sky. In Florida, fifty-eight degrees would be freezing, but here in Colorado with such low humidity and the sun shining, the temperature was awesome. My dad would have called it a blue bird day, exactly the kind of weather my mom loved for skiing. Dad preferred blustery days and fresh powder, but Mom loved the sun and being able to ski with her jacket unzipped and to enjoy après ski cocktails on an outside patio. How I wished to go back in time to one of those moments.

After school, I headed out to the soccer fields. I was excited to play but I loathed meeting new people. A group of girls were gathered in a tight circle whispering, and when I walked up they stopped instantly. Two of them threw some plastic bags into their backpacks quickly. So quickly that I couldn't see what was inside. I plopped down to switch out my sneakers for cleats overhearing a girl named Amber, who was in my Bible class, bash the coach, bash some of the players and lament tryouts.

"I don't even want to try out," she said, slipping a shin guard into its sleeve. "I hated this team so much last year."

Two of the girls caught me staring and glared back at me.

"Uh, hi," I said. "I'm Sera."

"I'm Mollie," said one of the girls who had hidden the contraband, her voice oozing with fake sincerity. "You're new to Valiant, right? And a junior?"

"Yeah. My first day was yesterday," I said.

"Cool, well welcome. I'm a junior too, and so are Amber, Grace, Cecily, and Quincy."

The girls she mentioned waved as she called them out by name.

"Where are you from?" she asked, even though I had the feeling she already knew.

"Florida," I replied.

"Oh nice. My grandma lives in Florida," said Amber.

"Yours and everyone else's," I said, which got me some laughs in return.

"Good luck today!" Mollie said as we headed for warmups.

I played horribly. These girls were really, really good, and I just couldn't get into the right frame of mind. I was so self-conscious and worried that every time I got the ball I either lost it to someone else immediately or passed it to the opposing team. I never played at my best when I was either stressed or had to go to bathroom, and now I had both sensations. All the while the coaches stood on the sidelines, taking notes.

Then to add insult to injury, I had to wait in the parking lot for like thirty minutes after practice for Jules to pick me up. I texted him after the first ten.

Hey, practice is over

After no reply for five minutes, I texted again.

hello? r u coming?

Another five minutes and I started to get mad.

???

Then finally I saw the dots, meaning he was typing. Then they stopped.

"Omigod, this is ridiculous!" I said aloud to no one in particular.

I tried calling. It went right to voicemail. Then finally, he responded via text.

There in 5

What an ass. I got angrier and angrier as fifteen minutes rolled by and he still hadn't arrived, leaving me alone in an empty parking lot. Finally, his Range Rover pulled into the school. There was someone in the passenger seat I didn't recognize but I also couldn't really see inside because his window tint was so dark.

He screeched into the field parking lot and barely missed me as he pulled up inches from my feet. He rolled down the passenger side window to reveal some random blond girl sitting next to him. His hand was in between her legs.

"Sorry, Sera. hop in the back," he said as he unlocked the doors.

So this is why he was late? I got into the back seat without saying a word. We rolled out of the parking lot, and he introduced the girl in the front seat as Julie.

"Julie and Jules," she giggled.

At the first stop light he leaned in and nuzzled her neck, moving his hand even further up her leg.

I think I am going to throw up, I thought.

"Don't be rude," he said to me.

"Rude about what?"

"I heard what you said."

"But I didn't *say* anything." Right? I questioned myself. Had I mumbled it under my breath?

His brow furrowed for a second, but he leaned in and kissed Julie with so much tongue that I gagged. *He is really such an ass.* Just as I thought the words, he turned to glare at me.

"What the hell?' he said out loud.

"What's the matter, baby?" Julie crooned, trying to turn his face back to hers.

The light turned green. The people behind us honked. Jules didn't move. A full ten seconds passed before he snapped out of it. "Nothing. Sorry, babe."

I put in my ear pods and listened to music for the rest of the short ride home. When we pulled into the driveway, Jules said he'd be downstairs for a few hours, but that Thane was ordering in pizza for dinner. I got out of the car, slammed the door shut and retreated to my room.

A few hours later when I smelled the pizza I sauntered down to the kitchen. Thane, Jules, Steele, and Scarlett had already started eating without me. Julie was nowhere in sight. They were deep into conversation about finding the Witches and their crystals but then Steele got bored or annoyed when I arrived and headed upstairs. The rest of them continued their conversation.

"If they are who you think they are," Thane said to Jules, "Seraphina can help with that." "How?" I asked.

"Well," said Thane, "You play soccer, right?"

I nodded, thinking to myself that I *used* to play soccer.

"We've been deep diving into the girls we think are our Witches. They play soccer too. There is a showcase coming up in Half Moon Bay where they live. If Jules can convince Coach Q to bring the Valiant teams to that event, you can make contact. They post about their team all the time. Jules knows their jersey numbers, positions, and team schedule."

I made a mental note to never post anything on social media again.

"She has to make a team first," Jules said.

What the hell is his problem?

Thane pressed on. "Get yourself on the soccer team and Jules will handle getting Coach to go to the tournament. Then, you make contact. You'll know if it's them. The minute you see them you'll be drawn in, and when you make physical contact there should be a spark that you both will see and feel."

I remembered the spark I felt at the Therion camp when we joined hands with the others. "Okay, so I make the team, Jules convinces coach to go, and then what do I do if it is them?"

"Just um…make friends, ask questions. We'll figure that part out later," Thane said.

Oh, great plan. I already hated making new friends and now they were asking me to make two on a competing soccer team, but make sure to touch them and tell them they are magical Witches who need to reunite with us to save the world? Sure. No problem.

"Let's just take it one step at a time and see if I even make the soccer team, okay?"

"That won't be an issue. I can make you a highlight reel and send it to Coach Quintero. Even if he doesn't want you, I can compel him to get you on the team. Want to be captain?" Jules asked, kidding, sort of.

"No thanks. I'd rather do it on my own."

Snow drifted past the windows and dark clouds scudded in to block out the sun. That was Colorado for you. One minute it was fifty-eight and sunny and the next minute it turned to blizzard conditions.

"You may have to put your tryout plans on hold," said Thane. "Looks like tomorrow may be a snow day."

We never had snow days in Florida, obviously. How cool. Just then the house alarm signaled that someone was here.

"It's Devyn," Jules said. "The others will be back soon anyway, so why don't you call it a night and we'll regroup in the morning. We'll be down in the basement if you need us."

All night? What happened to Julie? I exited the kitchen and headed back upstairs. The was a huge picture window in the stairway that framed the heavy snowflakes as they fell in slow motion. A snow day sounded amazing.

I found Steele on his bed, headphones on, eyes closed, and reeking of smoke. I ripped the headphones off his head.

"Are you for real?" I yelled.

"What the hell, Sera?"

"You have got to get it together, Steele! You reek of pot!" I screamed.

"So? It's legal here, and besides, I don't answer to you. You're not my mother. She's dead remember?" His voice was snarky, but too calm.

That made me even angrier.

"And how do you think she would react to the way you're dealing with it? Do you think she'd be proud? What about Dad?" Tears burned my eyes.

"GET OUT OF MY ROOM." He grabbed the headphones out of my hand and jammed them back on his head. I stormed out, tears rolling down my face, and slammed my bedroom's door.

I tried to sleep but tossed and turned all night. At four a.m. I got a notification on my phone from the school that classes were canceled. I had a second notification from Brock inviting me and Steele out to the camp for the day to watch some event they had going on. He said he'd swing by around 9 a.m. to pick us up, not really giving any option for us to back out. Maybe it would be a good distraction.

I had been so upset with Steele that I forgot to eat anything and when I rolled out of bed I was starving. The aroma of bacon and eggs lured me out from under the covers and I threw on a pair of sweatpants I found in the closet and headed downstairs. When I got there, Steele and Scarlett chatted while sitting next to each other at the breakfast bar. *Well, isn't that cozy.* I walked up feeling like I was interrupting something which made me even angrier.

"Good morning," I said as I grabbed a piece of bacon off Steele's plate.

Steele eyed me. "Good morning, Queen Seraphina Paige." It was the nickname he always used to call me whenever he thought I was acting uppity or snooty.

Guess he was trying to tell me I was being a snob for disapproving of his new friends and his choice of extracurricular activities.

"I'm surprised you're up so early, 'your highness,'" I said, using air quotes so the pot irony wouldn't be lost on him.

He rolled his eyes and shoved another piece of bacon in his mouth. Scarlett watched our interaction like it was a dramatic movie on Netflix. Her eyes darted back and forth as we took turns jabbing each other.

"Well," he stated, "Brock has texted and called me about a thousand times since six a.m. so it was kind of hard to ignore him. I guess we have a camping date today."

I was surprised his phone woke him. Usually, Steele slept in on the weekends until around noon.

"Oh yeah, he texted me too. We have about thirty minutes before he's here," I said, and I attempted to grab a plate and fill it with the last of the scrambled eggs from a platter on the counter.

"You don't mind if I take the last of them, do you?" I asked Scarlett.

"No, that's fine. Eggs aren't really my thing. I mean, I can eat them in a pinch, but I much prefer other forms of sustenance," she replied.

"So, you bloodsuckers eat real food then?" Steele asked her, clearly feeling no sense of tact this morning.

"Why don't you ask your sister?" Scarlett answered.

"I haven't really had any real side effects yet," I said.

"Hmmm," she replied, eyeing me up and down. "That'll change soon," she said. "To answer your question, yes, we can eat real food. It's like eating without flavor or fat, though. It doesn't really satisfy us, but it will hold us over until we can feed on blood. Now a raw, bloody piece of filet or even raw sushi would do just fine. After about a week though without real blood, and we'd need to feed or it can get messy around here," she said with a venomous wink.

Hmmm. I never really liked red meat much growing up but all of sudden a bloody filet sounded pretty appetizing to me, too.

"You know what I mean, Seraphina?" she asked as she stared deeply into my soul.

I looked away, feeling uneasy. Something about the thought of feeding on blood made me excited and energized. I grabbed one last piece of bacon, paying special attention to its flavor, and excused myself to go get dressed.

Brock arrived right on time. He texted us to announce his arrival and honked the horn without bothering to even come to the door. I met back up with Steele in the foyer. There was no sign of Scarlett, Jules or Thane. I scribbled a quick note to the boys to let them know we'd be gone for the day and then we headed out the door with Omega on our heels.

Brock was giddy with excitement. In preparation for the upcoming Snow Moon, the Therions held power trials. Every year the Snow Moon was a grand event, even if it wasn't as special as this one which coincided with the Age of Aquarius and the eclipse. It was still always an annual event that allowed pack members to move up ranks and sometimes assume key leadership roles. The trials were a series of adventure races and tests of skill and wit, which narrowed down the top three Therions. Those three would compete in one final trial that would determine the top 'dog' if you will— who would lead the pack into the next year.

For the past ten years the same three Therions had held the executive leadership positions and the competition wasn't even really close, Brock told us. He consistently placed first and held his place as commander, his second chief was named Noah, and third captain was named Nila, a female warrior who gave Noah a good race every year. Therions aged much slower than humans so the top three would likely hold their spots for three or four decades at a time. After we pulled into the Jeep's secret hiding spot, Brock hopped out and grabbed two pairs of snow boots for our hike to the camp and two super thick parkas out of the trunk.

He threw them to us. "Alright, let's go!"

It was more animated than I'd remembered him being the entire first weekend when we met.

The short, brisk hike was invigorating. Something about being out in the bright white freshly fallen snow, with the sun shining and exerting my muscles was extremely therapeutic. Omega adored being in the snow, running through the trees and sprinting through the fluffy drifts, and basically leading the way. As we neared the camp, I had the uneasy feeling of eyes watching us from the forest again. I looked at Steele and even though we hadn't said two words to each other on the hike I knew he felt the same when our eyes met each other. Omega didn't seem bothered by it all, so we brushed it off.

When we turned the last corner before the grand clearing where the camp was, I was amazed at the transformation that had occurred since we were last there. The clearing had been turned into a giant obstacle course with a huge, mechanical looking contraption in the center, comprised of wooden slides, rope swings, giant climbing walls that connected to wires, and a huge moving target platform as thin as a gymnast balance beam in the center about ten stories up in the air. It was like a Ninja Warrior set on steroids. There were Therions in Human and animal form all over the course, practicing their moves, jumping from ropes, and sparring in the treetops. Human forms versus wolves, wolves versus mountain lions, and even a couple of bears and foxes. Brock must have noticed our amazement.

"There are all types of Therions. They choose a form early in life and the only rule for the competition is that they must choose their human form or Therion form before we begin and then they must remain in that form the entire race," he said. "Changing is exhausting though so it's not really advisable to switch during combat anyway," he added.

"How do they know what form to pick?" Steele asked, perking up for the first time in three days.

"That's all part of the competition. Choosing the form is one of the key battles in itself. It can be integral to success or failure," Brock said. "You know Steele and Sera, as members of the Royal Family, although Human, well sort of," he said looking at me with embarassment, "you are more than welcome to take part, even though you can't shapeshift," Brock said, almost teasing. "We can take precautions for your safety."

"Uh, no thanks. I'm happy to spectate," I said.

"Seriously? Heck yeah. I'm in!" Steele said.

Testosterone made boys do the stupidest things.

"Don't come crying to me when you get a splinter," I said.

Just then I felt the eyes on me again and looked into the trees. That's when I saw them. The most stunning turquoise eyes watched us from inside the forest. One set of eyes turned to two, and they crept out of the shadows and into the sun. wo incredibly beautiful wolves—one white, one black and gray—and a Therion in Human form. The wolves had glowing eyes that I couldn't look away from. They came closer to us.

"That's Noah, Cayla, and Hunter," Brock said to us. "You didn't get to meet them last time you were here, but they are anxious to meet you," Brock said, with a hint of uneasiness in his tone that I could tell he was trying to disguise. Then right there before our eyes, Noah and Cayla started to shake, their forms blurred, and with a flash of white light they transformed into Humans. Noah was tall, muscular, and blond with a floppy surfer haircut. and bright turquoise and golden eyes. Hunter, the one who came out of the woods in Human form, was a handsome shorter boy with shaggy light brown hair who looked like he could be a high school quarterback. He looked familiar to me, but I couldn't quite place where I had seen him before. Cayla was an incredible beauty with long, dark wavy hair, dark eyes, lean muscles and a big toothy smile. I liked her immediately. Noah, on the other hand, made me feel strange. He felt familiar, like I had met him before even though I knew I hadn't. He came up and shook my hand.

"Nice to finally meet you, Seraphina."

Our hands sparked. We both felt it and he smiled, holding my hand even tighter. It felt, warm, good, like home.

"Nice, to uh, meet you too," I said.

Brock told us that the games would start after lunch and that we should feel free to hang out and mingle, eat whatever we liked, and be back at the clearing in about three hours. Cayla asked us if we wanted to come eat with her and some of her friends. We agreed and followed her along to the food tent. Hunter and Noah excused themselves to go get ready for the games but not before Noah made sure to let me know to cheer for him.

"I'll be the biggest, whitest wolf with the turquoise eyes," he said, staring at me like we were the only two people here.

"I will, I promise," I said breaking eye contact and nervously tucking hair behind my right ear.

At lunch we met McKenzie, Miley, and Mason—Cayla's best friends. Cayla and Steele seemed to be getting along just great. He was flirting with her, and she was definitely into him. She gave us the run down about everyone who'd be competing today, who would be in what form, and who had any chance of beating the current leadership. No one thought Brock was touchable, there were always a few that challenged Noah but unlikely that he would be unseated, and Nila was the one who most of the male Therions thought they could beat. Yes, she was a bad ass, but the guys always thought they could take her. She'd held the spot for five years, trained constantly, and was ripped.

No one knew what form Brock would be taking this year, but he's dominated the competition in both forms. Noah always chose wolf and Nila usually chose her animal form, mountain lion. Steele bragged about throwing his hat into the ring this year.

"We've never had a regular Human take part in the games. Not that you are a regular—you know—Human but I would be careful," Cayla warned him.

"Thanks for the concern, but I think I'll be okay," Steele said in the manliest voice he could muster.

"Steele, can I talk to you for a minute?" I asked and didn't really wait for an answer as I grabbed his hand and pulled him over for a side bar. "These are supernatural creatures that can transform into beasts and literally train for this all year. I know you're strong, but I don't think—"

He cut me off. "Sera, it's fine. I am crazy fast, I have great reflexes and, apparently, have the soul of a Therion trapped inside this human body. I'm not going to overdo it. I'm not even really going to compete. I'm just going to run through the course for fun. I'm sure they'll give me a safety harness or something. It's fine. I'll be fine," he said sincerely.

I reluctantly agreed and we finished up our meal and did nothing but have fun for the next couple of hours. It had stopped snowing, the sun was shining and it felt great to be out in the middle of such a beautiful natural area of the mountains. The evergreen trees, all perfectly dipped in white, made our surroundings look like a winter wonderland. We followed Cayla and her crew on a hike through the woods along a half frozen stream that opened up to a grand lake. Parts of it were covered in a thin layer of ice but most of it was still liquid. We skipped rocks. When Steele and Cayla disappeared on their own, the others asked me all about my life, what it was like to be a pure Human, and if I'd noticed any repercussions from being drained and turned by a Vampire. It was the first time I'd really talked about that with anyone but out here in nature with people who were starting to feel like family, I could open up about it.

"I do feel different, that's for sure. I've always had heightened senses, but ever since the accident, it's off. It's like something inside me has shifted. I can sense things from very far away, movement, smells, sounds. It comes and goes. I can sense things in people too—if they have good intentions or bad. Steele and I have always been able to tap into each other's thoughts but now it's stronger. I can literally let him inside my head, and I can go into his. There's also the desire for... blood," I said letting the last word trail off softly. "I don't need as much sleep and I can eat real food but when I collapsed, it felt like I was dying all over again. All I wanted was blood. I couldn't think about anything else. That, and him."

I wasn't sure how my new Therion friends would react to me talking about a Vampire, but I had to share my feelings with someone, and it kind of just slipped out.

"You mean the hot Vampire?" Miley asked.

I nervously laughed, still unsure of how they would respond.

"He's actually cold," said Miley. "They can be tricky, you know, Sera. You never really know what they can and can't force you into," she continued carefully.

I told them about how gentle Jules was when we bloodshared and how the world stood still for those short moments in time.

The others sat quietly, listening to me talk and absorbing every word. When I finished talking, Mason looked at the girls and said, "We should tell her."

"Tell me what?"

Just then Cayla and Steele came out of the forest, catching the last part of our conversation. Cayla looked furious.

"That is not our call," she said tersely to the others.

"She should know. They both should," said Mason.

"Okay, someone needs to spill the tea," said Steele.

"It is up to Brock to tell you about the prophecy. When he feels the time is right," said McKenzie.

"Guys, seriously, tell us," I said, almost as a command.

And inexplicably, they obeyed. Cayla began to talk.

"Our tribes have been hidden from each other since the Dark Ages. Since then, a prophecy has passed down, and more information is revealed with each Snow Moon. It centers around the hidden twins, you two. The prophecy states that in the Age of Aquarius when the Royal Alphas die, their children will retake the throne and reunify the Alliance by first reuniting the Therion tribes."

"I'm not really sure what that means," I said. "What Therion tribes need to be reunited?"

Cayla continued. "Our kind is spread out all over the globe. We've lived in separate tribes all over the world for thousands of years. We tend to gather where the spiritual energy is the highest—near the oceans, mountains, crystal deposits. Humans poach or hunt us in animal form, so we've mostly retreated to camps like ours to live in peace. Some of us live among Humans though, denying our true nature and trying to fit into the real world, but since we're forced to turn every Full Moon, those cases are few and far between. We've been waiting for the two of you for so long."

Miley picked up where Cayla left off.

"The Age of Aquarius is a time of great change. The last 2,600 years has been the Age of Pisces, a time when patriarchal power led by masculine rules, logical thinking, structures, and boundaries. As we transition into the new age, we find ourselves shifting to a matriarchal culture. That shift in itself will elevate chaos. Systems are crashing, rules are changing, and the divine feminine power is rising. Power that Phebe possessed; power inherent inside you Seraphina. This divine feminine essence is part of every woman. It's about connecting to the goddess within and releasing your power to allow you to unify the tribes. The Age of Aquarius will last for about 2,100 years but we're hoping you can figure it out a lot sooner than that," she said with a giggle.

"Figure what out? I'm confused," I said.

"Figure out how to reunite our packs under one strong, central leader, bringing peace and unity back to our kind," said Miley.

"No one figured our savior would be half vamp though," said Mason, earning jeers. "What?" he said, throwing his hands up in the air.

"That does make things a bit more complicated, but I'm sure Brock will help figure this all out. I will let him fill in the rest of the details," Cayla said.

The others looked at her like she left out one integral piece of information.

"Oh jeez, fine!" she exclaimed. "So, there is one other little thing about the prophecy. Apparently, you unify the tribes by completing the betrothal promised centuries ago to... Noah."

"I'm sorry...what did you say?" I asked.

"In the beginning, like the very beginning, the earth was divided into two nodes—North and South. Your family represented the North and Noah's family the South. Only by bonding the families can our tribes truly be reunited. It's never been done before though, even when the Alliance was intact. The power of unification would make us strong enough to fight the moonlight and allow us to avoid forced Full Moon transformations. So to create a power surge, your parents and his parents betrothed the two of you. It was an ancient tradition though, forged like a kazillion years ago. It was before the curse and before the Witches turned your DNA. It obviously means nothing anymore."

Mentally processing the story we'd be told, Steele and I sat in silence for a minute.

"Are you guys… okay?" Cayla broke the silence.

"Yeah, I'm fine," I said. "You're right. It's just an old legend that doesn't mean much anymore. Let's go. The games will be starting soon, right?"

"Follow me," Mason said.

There was a buzz in the air. Spectators gathered and the competitors warmed up and stretched. Brock motioned for Steele to join him. I took a seat on the sideline with the spectators and noticed Steele and Brock deep in conversation. Brock put a safety harness on Steele, handed him a pair of gloves, and gave him a drink out of a strange silver goblet. Brock wasn't Dad, but he was a good guy.

I felt a pang of sadness wash over me as I thought about my dad. I missed him so much.

Brock announced that the games were about to begin and everyone grabbed hands, forming a giant circle around the course.

"It's how we start the games," Cayla whispered, seeing the bewildered look on my face. "Kind of like a blessing and protection spell."

Brock made an announcement in a language I did not understand, and then the twenty competitors left the circle and lined up on a wooden platform. As Brock walked by, he painted something different on each of their arms—a symbol made from what looked like black mud.

"That's tourmaline dust mud," Cayla said. "It's made from Black Tourmaline crystals, and it protects them and connects them while competing."

Then Brock began to chant. It was that same strange language again and the spectators all joined in. As they chanted, I felt the surge of powerful and beautiful shared energy and an unspoken bond of friendship and family. The chant came to an end, and we all dropped hands.

The obstacle course seemed to wake up. Wooden beams crackled into motion, water flowed into holes in the ground, ropes floated into the sky, and platforms shifted into place.

About ten feet in front of each warrior was a pole with a flag at the top of it, each in a different color. Beyond the poles was the entrance to the forest with a marked course running through the trees, which came out on the other side near a mountainous cliff with a lake at the bottom. Beyond that were platforms and ropes that had to be navigated to get competitors to the last part of the race. At the very top platform on the highest level of the course were three glowing orbs that seemed to float above the course. One silver, one blue, and one gold.

"Pretty amazing, right?" Cayla asked.

"Yes, that's incredible," I replied. "What is it?"

"We are all connected, Sera, and when we focus on and harness that, it's powerful. It's like a hundred times stronger since you and Steele found us. We use that power in many ways." She smiled at me mysteriously.

Three enormous black wolves walked up on to the platform with the competitors and howled in unison. That must have been the sign to start because the race began.

"It's kind of like capture the flag," Mason said. "Only it starts with the flag and ends with the orb. After the first obstacle of figuring out how to get their flag, they have to run the marked course—about five miles through the forest—and then come out to the obstacle course. The first three to ascend the platform and grab the glowing balls are the winners."

The competitors ran to their poles. All of the Therions in their animal forms tried to jump up onto their poles and climb to grab their flags but they kept slipping down as they were smoother than a regular tree would be. Steele ran up to his pole and stared at it for a minute before he began to shove it. Three big pushes and it fell to the ground, allowing him to easily pick up the flag. The crowd went wild and cheered him on. The other Therion competitors continued to try to run up their poles but one by one realized what Steele had done, looked shocked, and then quickly maneuvered to do the same with their poles. But Steele had a huge running start into the woods.

After a few more minutes all of the runners disappeared into the forest and the crowd erupted in cheers.

"Wow, he's fast," said Cayla, clearly smitten.

"He is crazy fast," I said. "My mom used to say he had Fred Flintstone feet."

Cayla looked perplexed. I laughed.

"It's just an old TV show she used to watch," I muttered, knowing the reference would be lost on Cayla and realizing I had tears in my eyes as I said it. "He's good at every sport and was the star football receiver and a great soccer striker in Florida. She—my mom, I mean— used to love to watch us play sports."

"I'm so sorry, Sera. It must be so hard for you guys to have lost your parents and now be in this weird new reality." Cayla grabbed my hand and squeezed it, sending a feeling of love coursing through my body.

"Thank you," I said, and I closed my eyes to fully receive the love she was sending my way.

Then I focused on the sounds around me and realized I could hear the runners in the woods. I zoned in on Steele's gait and heard him, pounding the pathway and pushing branches and obstacles out of his way. The skilled footwork he learned from soccer helped maintain his lead. Other runners—on the course at a ground-eating pace—were Therions in animal form closing in on him. A few mountain lions, a few wolves, and a fox. I shared that information telepathically and knew he got the message. They should easily be able to beat Steele with four legs and animal speed, but nevertheless he had kept the lead. Strange.

"Are you listening to them?" Cayla asked, picking up on what I was doing.

"I guess I am," I said, sounding just as surprised as she was.

"You must be tuning in to your Vampire hearing. Every time you feed, your Vampire nature and powers will grow. How many times have you, um, fed?" she asked.

"I actually haven't fed at all," I told her. "Jules shared blood with me when I first turned, but I haven't had any since. I'm kind of trying not to think about having to feed at all."

I tuned back into the forest and into Steele's mind and watched through his eyes as he moved obstacles out of his way with his feet. He pulled something out of his pocket and put it into his mouth. What was it? As runners began to come out of the forest, I noticed that a mountain lion and a wolf were neck and neck with Steele as they approached the obstacle course. They leaped onto the course ahead of him with ease and began working through the obstacles. Steele was close behind with a superhuman strength I had never seen in him before. He jumped from platform to platform performing each obstacle like he'd practiced for months. His instincts and reflexes were on fire, and he was close behind Noah and Brock, at times passing them both. I wondered to myself what would happen if he beat Brock? Or Noah? Or Nila? I brushed the thought aside and watched him climb up the side of the mountain to the obstacle where he'd have to jump into the water below, he clipped the safety harness onto the pole and stood there, examining the fifty foot drop. He froze.

Others moved past him and leaped into the water below, continuing on the course to the final challenge. Steele didn't move. I was afraid this might happen. He was terrified of heights. I tried to enter his mind for some positive reinforcement, but he pushed me out.

"What's he doing?" Cayla asked. "He's letting everyone pass him." Another two competitors dove into the water below. I ignored her and tried to enter his mind again. No luck. He's so stubborn.

Steele had been afraid of heights his entire life. One summer when we were about ten years old and were visiting Colorado Springs all he wanted to do was go cliff jumping in this place called Paradise Cove. He talked about it over and over again and insisted we make the two-hour drive from our hotel. Finally, when we got there and completed the two-mile hike out to the jump spot, he and Dad climbed up to the lowest diving ledge. There were like five different places people were jumping into the water, but they picked the easiest one for their first jump. He froze and wouldn't make the jump. There was a long line of people behind them waiting to jump and he just stood there, unable to move.

Dad tried to encourage him, the people behind him and down below were cheering him on, telling him he could do it, but he didn't move. He started to cry. Dad asked him if he wanted to see him jump first and when he said that he did, Dad made the jump into the water below. The crowd erupted into cheers and started chanting Steele's name for him to follow Dad. It didn't work. He stood there for what seemed like forever until he finally just turned around and climbed back down.

I felt so bad for him. He was mortified and didn't say one word for the entire ride home even though Mom tried to impress upon him that he just wasn't ready, and it wasn't a big deal at all. Even though he was six years older now, I still saw that same little scared boy standing up on the ledge not being able to jump. What would he do? Would he climb back down in front of all of the Therions and forfeit the rest of the race? He closed his eyes. He started to waver and sway back and forth. What on earth was he doing? The swaying got faster, and I got scared. At least he had the harness.

Just as quickly as the thought gave me peace of mind, I saw Hunter. He was floating, up toward the landing.

"Do you see that?" I asked Cayla.

"See what?" she said.

I assumed Hunter was heading toward Steele to save him, but when he arrived at the landing, he unhooked the safety harness. Steele didn't seem to notice.

"What are you doing?" I yelled.

Hunter looked at me, perplexed.

"Steele!" I tried yelling at him mentally.

He was going to fall and without his harness he was going to hit the rocks.

He began to tip to the side. Before I even knew what was happening, I plunged into motion. His arms flailed as he tumbled off the platform, but somehow I was there before he hit the ground. His body thudded against mine, forcing the breath out of both of us. My legs buckled and we hit the forest floor.

But wait…how? I covered the hundred yards between us in less than a half of a second. The crowd was silent. Steele opened his eyes and realized what happened. Everyone stared at us, mouths wide with shock. He jumped out of my arms and ran into the woods. Cayla followed. The other competitors shook off their disbelief and continued on the course to the last obstacle before grabbing the orbs.

Hunter floated back to the ground, and I stormed toward him, fuming. He stared at me blankly. That's when it hit me. I knew why he looked familiar. I had seen the same face on tribute flyers all over school. He looked just like the quarterback who died in the avalanche, Jason.

"Who are you? And why would you do that?" I screamed, attracting attention from the crowd but not caring.

He tilted his head to the side and examined me closely. "It's what *you* are, that is the real question."

15. LAW OF ATTRACTION

ALL OF THE COMMOTION DISTRACTED THE CROWD, BUT IT DID not, for the most part, distract the other competitors, who were dead set on finishing the race. Brock finished first, Noah second, and Nila third. No change to the power formation this time around. After the last of the competitors finished the course, the platforms and ropes returned to their original lifeless forms, energy drained from them, and the spectators mulled around, congratulating the winners, and buzzing about the crazy events of the day.

Brock noticed my ambush of Hunter and as soon as he finished the race, he and Noah made their way toward us. The raised tone of my voice was beginning to attract a crowd. Brock asked me and Hunter to move our conversation inside to his tent.

"What is going on here?" Brock asked once we were all inside.

"I saw him unhook Steele's harness just before he fell," I said. "I also don't think he is who he says he is. He looks exactly like a football player from Valiant who died in the avalanche."

"I'm sure this is a big misunderstanding, Sera. How could that be possible?" Noah said.

Seriously? He was just flirting with me a few hours ago and now he is questioning my eyesight?

"I am telling you," I said, making sure to make eye contact with both Noah and Brock. "I saw him. He…he floated from the ground over to the platform. I watched him do it! I also have a photo on my phone of the flyer with the kid who died on it," I said, raising my voice and fumbling through my photos to find it.

"Hunter, is there any truth to this?" Brock asked.

"Yes," Hunter replied. "She is correct about both things."

"See! I told you!" I exclaimed.

Take that Noah!

"Who are you? And why would you do that? Start talking," Noah demanded.

Hunter took a deep breath.

"First, I stole a body from the avalanche. It must be the boy you speak of. And second, I had to unhook the harness. He cheated," Hunter responded.

How would he have known that?

"He cut the course and he took a performance enhancing stimulant while running through the forest," Hunter continued, with zero emotion in his voice whatsoever.

I could feel the color drain from my face, and I wasn't sure how to respond. Noah filled the void. "What are you? And what do you mean, you *stole* a body?"

"It is my job to protect the balance," Hunter replied. "Steele cheated. In response, Karma caused his harness to malfunction. Sometimes the results of our actions are immediate, sometimes they are not. This time it was."

"What are you talking about?" I asked. "How would you even know if he cheated or not?"

"I see everything. I am a solder of iL Separatio. I must maintain the balance. Of energy, everywhere I encounter it," he said. "Normally I exist on the astral plane but in this case, I thought I would take physical form to meet you and your brother. This is not the way I had intended to introduce myself to you, but perhaps it is the way it was meant to be."

I tried to mentally register what he was saying.

"I am also not sure how you saw me. No earthly creature has ever been able to see me enacting balance," he continued.

Brock looked suspicious, with his arms crossed and one eyebrow raised. "iL Separatio is a legend. It's rarely spoken of, and no one has ever seen it. Since the beginning of time," he said.

"It is a well-guarded secret that an entity exists between good and evil. Very rarely iL Sep will claim a new soul for his army to carry out balance, or Karma as many call it, throughout the world," said Hunter. "I was claimed a very long time ago. Now, I'm here to help reunite Arete 8. It is that important. Even in physical form, I must correct the balance when I see it shift. It is not something I can prevent. Every action has an equal or opposite reaction. Good attracts good, and bad attracts bad. It is not something I invented. I only guard it and maintain it."

We sat in silence, each of us mentally reviewing what Hunter was trying to explain. After about a minute of all of us staring in silence, I spoke up but couldn't make eye contact with any of them. "He did cheat. I saw it too."

"I don't lie," said Hunter. "What I did also sped up your Vampire powers. This was the first time you've seen them emerge, correct?"

"Yes," I answered. "I mean from time to time my hearing is better and my instincts and reaction times are all heightened, but I've never been able to move that fast until today."

"You are becoming a unique creature, Sera," Brock chimed in. "Your physical appearance still looks Human, which is in itself odd after being turned. You have Therion DNA and apparently you see things no other creature can."

"There is a reason this is all happening now," said Hunter. "It is the upcoming totality. The Snow Moon Eclipse. I cannot interfere besides counseling you on the shifts in balance, but I can help as much as I am able, to reunite Arete 8."

16. FROM FRIENDS TO THIS

AFTER HUNTER'S REVELATIONS, ALL I WANTED TO DO WAS FIND Steele, but he'd disappeared. Noah agreed to help me look for him. Maybe Cayla could ease his embarrassment and talk some sense into him? Lord knows he wouldn't listen to me. He wouldn't even let me in to his head. I replayed the scene over again in my mind. Sure, he was humiliated I had to catch him, but what was I supposed to do? Let him fall to his death?

As we walked through the woods in silence, I looked at Noah's face. He busted me staring at him and gave me a huge smile. His gaze sent a warm feeling through my soul. I unconsciously walked closer to him.

"I'm sorry your first experience at the games didn't turn out how you expected."

"Yeah," I responded. "This whole Hunter, Karma, balance thing is interesting, right? I mean, how he can say that putting Steele's life in danger was like a good thing? That he had to do it. I just don't know if I believe him."

"I know energy balancing is real, that is for sure," Noah started. "And iL Separatio is a term I've heard of, but no one has ever really known if it was real. The soldiers of iL Sep thing are definitely a new concept. I do believe in Karma, and it is interesting that it can take form and actually enact Karma on others as a being."

We walked in silence for a bit, both registering these new, big concepts.

"Well, the competition was very cool, actually, and at least I guess we found another piece of this really weird puzzle. I just hope that Steele can regroup and recover," I said.

"I can sense that Cayla is with him, and she will help him. His Human DNA will shield him from his true nature and power. As Therions we are not prone to many of the most common human fears like height, death, the dark."

"How about spiders?" I giggled.

"Oh spiders are gross," he joked back. "Kidding aside, he is going to have to fight his human nature and uncover his Therion power underneath the surface. As Humans, you are all fighting unknown battles beneath the surface. How Steele fights that battle will determine if he wins the war. If he leans into the darkness, it will attract more darkness. Only light can push it out," Noah said.

"Let's hope light wins," I told him. "Can I ask you something?"

"Of course, anything," he said.

"What exactly do you think I am?" I inquired.

I still felt Human and, with the exception of a few new abilities, I expected to feel more dead, I guess, being a Vampire. I could tell Noah was trying to prepare an answer that wouldn't upset me.

"It is very rare for a Vampire to turn Humans in modern times and during the days of the Alliance it was forbidden. Your Therion soul coupled with your Human DNA though has made you something else, something different, something special. Something that we have never seen before.

If you're open to it, Brock could draw some blood and examine it to find out more."

He must have sensed my angst at the mention of studying my blood. He turned toward me and put a hand on my shoulder.

"Just a thought and there is no rush, of course," he assured me.

I definitely wanted to change the subject.

"Congratulations, by the way," I said.

"Thanks. Running the course is quite a rush," he said. "Hey, I know you want to find Steele, but would you want to take a little detour? There is a waterfall I'd love to show you."

I hesitated for about a half second before agreeing and we headed into the woods. We made some small talk along our hike as Noah asked me about my childhood, hobbies, and my brother. I learned that although he looked to be about eighteen years old, he had actually lived about 130 years so far in this lifetime. He was born in California and moved to Colorado fifty years ago after he met Brock. He had an easygoing way about him that made me feel extremely comfortable. With Jules, I got so flustered. He made me feel things, intensely. With Noah I didn't get butterflies in my stomach or the insane desire to kiss him, but he was warm, tender, and sincere.

He was extremely handsome but a little goofy. His blond surfer boy hair occasionally fell into his eyes as he walked, and he'd casually throw it back or run his hands through it to get it out of his face. He had a cute, crooked smile and big, white, perfectly straight teeth.

As we walked over icy streams and through the meandering path mostly covered in snow, he would occasionally run his hand through the cold water and then stare at it, like the water was some sacred potion. When I asked him what he was doing he told me there was so much beauty and magic all around us but that most people didn't take the time to appreciate it. As Therions, he told me, they drew power from the elements and from nature. Water, snow, grass, earth, were all powerful substances that could be drawn upon for strength. And when sunlight merged with these elements, the energy was even stronger. Think sparkling snow when the sun hits it, dew on the morning grass illuminated by the rising sun.

Our time together flew by, and I felt like I could tell him anything. Kind of like my bond with Steele when he wasn't being annoying. Finally, after walking for what seemed to be hours, we arrived at the payoff. A sparkling turquoise blue lake at the top of a mountainous clearing that was gleaming in the soft sunlight. Two small waterfalls were dumping out into the lake from the higher elevations and as the sun began to set, the water shimmered as if it were on fire.

"Oh wow," was all I could muster.

"It's breathtaking, right?" he said as he grabbed my hand to assist me taking the final steps to the top of the lake.

"Yes, it is," I agreed, and I felt the spark in my hand. I could tell he felt it too.

"Seraphina, that spark is you tapping into the nature magic around you. Connecting with me will amplify it, but that's all you. As a Human/Therion/Vampire, it's hard to know what your gifts will be but connecting to nature will definitely help you harness whatever your unique powers are."

"How do I connect though? I didn't realize I was doing anything," I said.

"In time, you'll learn. For now, just try to clear your mind and focus only on the beauty around you. Ground yourself with the natural elements. Take your shoes and socks off and stand directly on the earth or put your hand on sparkling snow. You'll feel the magic stirring and you can draw it in and use it how you need."

We sat together on top of the lake for a while sharing more stories and connecting to the nature magic that was so strong here at this spot. Just when I was feeling the most at ease, he brought up the one topic I really did not want to discuss.

"The others told you, about our…um, families' past commitments to each other." Before I could reply, he went on. "Look, I just want you to know that those promises were made a long time ago, in an ancient ceremony during an ancient time. They obviously don't apply to us here and now, in today's modern world. So just know that I want to be your friend," he said.

I didn't know if I should feel relieved or rejected.

"Thanks, Noah. I'm cool with being friends, too."

He nodded. Whew, I was glad for that awkwardness to be out of the way.

"The sun will be setting soon. We should head back for dinner and to make sure your brother is ok. I bet he's back by now," he said, standing up and offering me a hand.

I agreed and we trekked through the woods back to camp.

When we arrived, Steele was sitting with Cayla all cozied up by a big bonfire. It was like a party with Therions in both Human and animal form hanging out in clusters all over the clearing. Omega ran up to Noah and me as we made our way into the camp and just about knocked me over. He nuzzled against Noah, and it was clear that the two of them liked each other. We walked over to the food table and grabbed a huge helping of veggies, rice, and fresh fish that was being put on the table directly from the fire. I wondered how I would break the news to Steele about Hunter, but for now, he was nowhere to be found and all I wanted to do was enjoy the evening. The next couple of hours were peaceful, relaxing, and enjoyable as we hung out and got to know our new friends. Noah never left my side and our connection deepened. It was a pretty amazing evening.

17. SIPPING ON EMOTION

We got back to Jules's house late, around eleven p.m. On the ride, Brock and I filled Steele in on Hunter. Steele was skeptical.

"You're telling me some dude, the one named Hunter, who looks like a high school jock, flew up to me and unhooked my harness because I cheated?" he asked.

"Karma is a universal energy," Brock explained. "So it makes sense on some level."

Steele told us he never saw or felt anything odd when he was on the platform besides extreme anxiety. He admitted to taking the drugs to boost his speed. I didn't even have the strength to yell at him. Brock said we would have to fill in Jules and Thane about Hunter and asked that we wait until we were all together. We made a plan to meet the next day after school.

We thanked him for the day and headed back inside. My head spun from learning about iL Separatio, meeting Noah, the time we spent together and the betrothal. Then, like he was thinking about me at the exact same time, my phone dinged with an incoming text.

Really enjoyed hanging with you today. Have a good night.

I texted back immediately.

Me too. Hope to see you again soon.

I couldn't get his scent and the betrothal story out of my mind, but even so, when I thought about seeing Jules, my stomach did flip flops and my face flushed. Why did that jerk make me feel like this? I shook the thought out of my mind.

We went inside and the house was dark besides one light on in the basement, but all I wanted to do was go upstairs, take a shower, and relax in my room. I said goodnight to Steele, and we headed toward our rooms. He slammed his door and as I headed toward my room, I heard music and strange noises coming from Scarlett's room. I thought I would peek in and say goodnight.

If I'm being honest, I wanted to find out what the heck she was doing in there. The door was cracked open and I pushed further, mouth open to say hello, when I saw them.

My heart stopped.

Scarlett and Jules. Her back against the headboard. His body on top of hers. Her hands on his face. His on her waist. Mouths pressed together. She must have sensed me standing paralyzed in the doorway, because she opened her eyes and looked right at me. She seemed to smile then, never taking her mouth off of his, and skimmed her hands down his chest.

I couldn't move. I couldn't talk. And, ridiculously, I couldn't look away. It felt like an eternity passed before Jules opened his eyes and pulled his face from hers. He sighed, satisfied.

Mortified, I muttered, "Oh my gosh, I'm so sorry... I didn't mean to . . ." and I turned around and walked out before ever having to make eye contact with him.

I went straight to my room, closed the door, and plopped down on my bed and began to sob. I buried my head into my pillow to stifle the sounds of my crying. I don't know why I was so upset. It's not like we were dating or anything. We were barely even friends. It was completely irrational for me to be upset but nevertheless my feelings betrayed my logical mind. I tried to drift off to sleep but couldn't.

I tossed and turned for a couple of hours. Around two a.m. my door creaked open. I rolled over to find Jules standing in the doorway.

"Have a minute?" he asked.

"Sure, come on in," I said, hoping there were no tear tracks on my face. I sat up and tried to smooth my hair down nonchalantly.

"Seraphina," he said, shifting his weight hesitantly. He took one step into the room and shut the door behind him but didn't come any closer. "I feel like we've gotten off on the wrong foot."

"Well you did kill me," I said sarcastically, trying to lighten the incredibly awkward mood.

"Right. Noted," he said, smiling. He took another step closer. His expression turned serious.

"Look, you should know that I am a creature of habit. Not all of my, um, habits are what Humans would consider virtuous. How I live my life is really none of your concern. And second, don't be embarrassed by what you saw earlier. Bloodsharing is a normal, natural part of life as a Vampire. You experienced it yourself. We weren't doing anything you should be ashamed of walking in on. I hope you're not upset."

He thought I was embarrassed at walking in on them. Well, that's good, I guess. And what he did with me looked nothing like what I saw in that room.

"I tend to get overwhelmed with my work and my habits, if you will, and I frequently forget to, um, eat, so Scarlett hunts for me from time to time and shares," he told me. "We do it all the time. That's most likely not the only time you'll see us together like that, and as a Vampire now yourself, you should get used to seeing it and doing it yourself."

Hell no. Not with you. I mean, maybe with you. But only because I think about you all the time. And I'm so hungry. Maybe he'd bloodshare with me right now? The logical part of my brain hit the brakes on that train of thought. I'd just watched him, quite literally, suck face with the girl who sleeps across the hall. Jealousy and lust were clouding my judgment. He didn't owe me an apology. He didn't owe me anything, really.

"How often do you think I should, you know, feed?" I asked him.

"I'm not really sure what your tolerance level will be as I've never encountered a creature with a Therion soul and Human DNA who has been turned into a Vampire," he chuckled. "But I would imagine you'd probably want to hunt about every other week to keep your strength up. Would you like me to show you how?"

I nodded. He motioned for me to come over to the sliding glass doors that led to a balcony outside my room. I had never truly paid attention to the backyard at night before. It was just as beautiful as during the day only completely different. The entire valley below was lit up, sparkling. From this vantage point I could see the thousands of houses and businesses in the city below, the Denver Broncos Football Stadium and the full downtown Denver city skyline illuminated.

"This view is awesome," I said.

"It is." He put his hand into his pocket and pulled out a crystal. He placed it into my left hand. "Take this and close your hand around it and feel every facet of the stone. It will help," he said. "We feed on people who invite us in. They do that with negative thoughts and actions. Or we feed on people who are dying and are past the point of recovery. Tonight, we'll focus on those who invite us. Now look into the homes, businesses, and cars below. Watch for the shade or color emanating from each of them. We call it an umbra. Ground yourself to the stone in your hand. Connect to your senses. Watch with your emotions."

I looked into the homes below but didn't see anything except some flickering lights, television sets blaring and people mulling around inside their homes.

"It's not working," I told him.

"You have to reach an alpha state," he said. "For Humans, it's the place between wakefulness and sleep; the moments just before sleep. It's when your conscious mind is connected to the universe. It's when many people come up with great ideas, inventions, or new innovations. Humans can only sustain it for a few moments, but Therions use alpha state to transform into animals and Vampires use it to feed. We can stay there longer. As a little bit of both, it should be easy for you to get to. Concentrate on the stone, turn it to reflect the moonlight, watch how it glistens, clear your mind, focus on the noise coming from the homes and cars below, and you'll get there. Try again."

I tried to clear my mind but standing this close to him made it challenging. I could smell him, feel the cold heat from his body, taste him almost, and it was definitely making it hard to focus. I closed my eyes and turned my thoughts to the crystal in my left hand. It felt warm. I encouraged the warmth to travel through my hand into my arm and into the rest of my body.

"You'll start to see their umbras," coaxed his deep voice. "Only Vampires can see umbras. They all mean different things but right now I want you to focus on the black or gray ones. Can you see them?"

I closed my eyes and listened to him carefully and then opened my eyes again. I could see them now. Black and gray shadows almost oozing out of some of the homes below. Some were much darker than others.

"Yes, I can see them," I told him.

"Good. Now find the darkest one. The one that calls to you."

I surveyed the thousands of homes and saw dark shadows flowing from many of them, but one in particular called to me. It looked to be about ten miles away as the crow flies, and just to the west of downtown.

"I see it."

"Good, Sera. Me too. Let's go," he said.

He grabbed my hand, holding the crystal between our palms and squeezed. The strangest feeling came over my body. A tingle spread from my head to my toes, and my skin began to quiver, and then get blurry.

We dissolved.

We became the shadows that called to us. Our physical bodies dissipated into the sky, and we flew across the landscape. Within seconds we reached the home we'd been staring at from our balcony. We landed inside a bedroom, where a middle-aged, overweight man snored in the large bed.

Our form was more physical now than when we were in flight but not completely solid. Jules sat down on the bed next to the man and pulled me down next to him. He grabbed the man's arm and pulled it toward his mouth, showing me what to do. I grabbed his other arm. As his arm moved closer to Jules's mouth, he opened it and long white fangs protruded from his teeth. He bit the man's arm and began to suck on it. He motioned for me to do the same. Something felt so sensual about the smooth, silent action that I was completely mesmerized by the feeling. As I took the man's other wrist and moved it up toward my mouth, I felt my own fangs emerge. I couldn't turn off the urge to taste him and my mind was in a complete frenzy. I *needed* his dark, smoky blood. When I bit into his wrist, I felt a small pop where the skin broke and then deliriously delicious liquid slid across my tongue. It was exhilarating.

The man's blood filled me with adrenaline and satisfaction. After about thirty seconds, Jules released the man's arm and mentally implored me to do the same. I followed his lead, although I didn't want to stop. I did want to please Jules, and that urge was stronger. He wiped a droplet of blood from my mouth with this thumb, and took another small crystal of out of his pocket. It took every ounce of willpower in my entire being to not kiss him. I silently begged him to want me in the same way, but he was all business. He placed the second crystal on the puncture wounds and softly rubbed the holes. They disappeared. He handed the crystal to me, and I did the same to the other arm. The man, blissfully ignorant, let out a snore and turned onto his side. Jules grabbed my hand and we dissolved into smoke, heading to the next home full of dark umbra. We continued hunting and feeding, moving from home to home, until the night began to fade into day.

Satisfied and full, we ended back where we started on the balcony of my bedroom. The sun peeked above the skyline, shining its angelic rays on the mountains. We sat together in silence as we watched the sunrise. I still had so many questions.

"What would happen if someone woke up as we were feeding?" I asked.

"They can't see us. It would just feel like a nightmare to them. As we feed on them, we mostly take their blood but a small portion of ours enters their bloodstream as well. It makes them feel bound to us. If you ever see a Human that you've fed on during the day, they will be compelled to do whatever you say. So, if they wake while you're feeding you just tell them to forget and fall back asleep. It's very rare but sometimes they do wake up, frightened, and then quickly fall back asleep with coaxing. After we've fed on them, our darkness stays with them forever, making it even more difficult to find the light. It's like a self-fulfilling prophecy. Darkness begets darkness."

I thought about what he was saying. Giving in to darkness only invited more darkness in.

His gaze held mine, quiet and intense, offering me answers to any questions I might have, but I wanted more than words. I longed for him. I silently begged him to lean in, to brush his perfect lips against mine, but he just sat there, still as a statue. Could I make the first move?

Julie and Scarlett's faces popped into my head. What was wrong with me? I broke our staring contest and looked out at the sparkling lights. After about five minutes of silence, I thanked Jules for the evening lesson, and he told me I most likely wouldn't have to feed again for a few weeks. I was curious and somewhat sad that so many people called to us with their dark umbras. I asked him if it was always that way.

"Since the dawn of time creatures have given in to their dark thoughts, feelings, and impulses. No matter how happy someone seems on the outside, everyone battles these urges," he told me.

He handed me the crystals and explained that one would help me identify people's umbras, and the healing crystal would give me strength and protection during the day when our powers were weakened by the sun. "Don't try to feed during the day," he explained. "And since we leave for school in an hour, I'll let you get ready."

And with that he disappeared and left me to my thoughts.

18. USE THAT RAGE

AROUND LUNCHTIME, BROCK TEXTED ME, STEELE, THANE, AND Jules about the need for an immediate meeting today after school. When we returned to Jules's house that afternoon, his Jeep was already in the driveway. I was anxious to hear how Jules and Thane would respond to Hunter's claims about being Karma.

"So what is this meeting about exactly?" Jules asked as we pulled into the driveway.

Steele and I remained silent.

"Uh, hello? Anyone?" he said.

"I am pretty sure he wants you to meet someone," I said.

"And if he's telling the truth, you will not like him. At all. That is for sure," Steele chimed in. "I can only imagine the bad shit you've got coming to you."

Jules brushed off Steele's remarks and we all headed inside. Brock and Hunter were waiting at the kitchen table. They stopped talking as we walked in.

"Don't let us interrupt," said Jules. "And of course, come in, make yourself at home."

We all grabbed a seat at the table.

"Why is there a dead football player at our kitchen table?" Thane asked.

"He is the reason we're here," Brock said. "This is Hunter."

"Hello Julian," Hunter said to the Vampire whose face was completely white, whiter than usual, like he was looking at a ghost.

"It's Jules," the Vampire responded back.

"I've always called you Julian," Hunter replied.

Jules steadied himself on the table with his hands. He took a minute to stare at the dead teenager, mentally trying to reconcile his outer appearance with the name Hunter.

"Amantes," Jules said, the growl in his voice the only warning of the violence he was about to unleash. He lunged, hands outstretched, ready to strangle the life out of Hunter, or Amantes—or at least this version of him. But instead of super speed, Jules's movements were clunky and strangely awkward. He surprised himself when his body fell on top of the table instead of on top of the adversary he was trying to attack.

"What the hell?" he said, trying to compose himself.

"Your powers are fading," Hunter said to Jules. "It is the consequence for turning a Therion."

Jules's nostrils flared and he made a feeble attempt to show his fangs, but nothing emerged. He slammed his fists down on the table.

"What did you do to me?" he hissed.

"I didn't do anything to you. You did it to yourself," Hunter said.

"How did you get here? Why are you in that body? And just because it has been a millennium does not mean I have forgotten what you did to my sister," Jules said.

"Jules, Hunter, enough," Brock said. "We have a lot of ground to cover."

"His name is Amantes," Jules said.

"That is correct," Amantes said. "Hunter was the name mortals called me."

Brock explained Amantes's backstory, what happened at the Therion competition, and why he looked like the deceased quarterback from their high school.

"Julian, I never had the chance to apologize to any of you. Mara tricked me with dark, twisted magic. I have been working as a soldier of iL Separatio since the moment of my death. What I wouldn't give to be able to see Amelia again and explain to her what really happened."

Jules inspected his face closely, as if trying to examine the soul inside.

"And just to be clear," Thane said. "You are not the one messing with Jules's powers?"

"Not really," Amantes said. He explained his role in balancing energy but that ultimately Jules's actions coupled with the Witches' curse led to the universe stripping him of his powers. "As you lose them, she will gain them."

I shifted in my chair wishing I could shrink myself.

"Every negative experience is an opportunity to grow, Julian," Amantes continued. "It's how you react to it that makes the difference. Use your rage to strengthen your resolve."

"How long until they are completely gone?" he asked.

"I'm sorry, I'm just not sure," Amantes responded.

Jules walked to the sliding glass doors and stood there, staring out the window.

We filled Amantes in on the plan to find the Alliance Witches and the Humans and their crystals. We all agreed that since he looked like a student everyone thought was dead, he should stay far away from Emberglow. He would hang with Brock at the Therion camp for now.

"Time is not on our side. We need to reunite Arete 8 in order to defeat The Stirring," Amantes said.

"I feel it, too," Jules said.

"When the armies of God and Lucifer separated the forces of darkness, and hid them, they weakened them but did not extinguish them," Amantes warned. "The darkness in this world emboldens The Third Air and the Great Old Ones hidden in this planet's core gain strength. Only by reuniting the Alliance can they be kept at bay. Otherwise, all earthly creatures will fall to their dark desires."

19. NUMB

I COULDN'T SLEEP AT ALL THAT NIGHT. THE ENORMOUS RESPON-
sibility that sat on my shoulders was exhausting. On top of that, I knew
Jules resented me for 'stealing' his powers. I didn't even want them! I didn't
want to save the world from darkness, and I didn't want this bizarre new
reality. All I wanted was to be normal and go back to my life in Florida.
Speaking of normal, I was hoping to go back to soccer the next day and
show the coach that I deserved to be on the team.

As we headed into school, we walked right past Coach Quintero. I
told him I planned to be at tryouts again and hoped he wouldn't tell me
not to bother coming back. To my relief, he invited me to come back out
for practice every day this week, starting this afternoon. I agreed and was
in a pretty good mood thinking about that on my way to English class. A
quick stop at my locker revealed a piece of paper sticking out of it. It was a
hot pink flyer with an invitation to the Students With Light club that was
meeting today at lunchtime in the Commons. I was about to throw it in the
trash can when Mia came up behind me and grabbed it out of my hand.

"Hi there, Seraphina. Hope you can make it to the meeting today. We're onboarding the new members and we'd be happy to squeeze you in," she said, more as a demand than a request.

I was not a club person. And there was something about Mia that turned me off. Despite my misgivings, I told her I would try to attend, secretly hoping if I tried out one meeting, it would get her off my back. I also had a new fascination with the recently deceased football player and had a new calling to pray with his friends. I walked off to class. While I was sitting in English, listening to the teacher drone on about Beowulf and the essay we'd have to write over the next couple of weeks, I tried entering my alpha state in an effort to examine some of my classmates' umbras. It was easy to get there before but now I couldn't see a thing. No smoke signals coming from anyone. I remembered Jules's warning telling me our powers weren't as strong during the day and I wondered if that was contributing to my failure. Out at the Therion camp though, I felt immensely powerful during the day when I caught Steele. That was a question I would ask Brock or Jules about later, if he would even discuss it with me.

I daydreamed about my incredible evening with my Vampire mentor. Even if he did lose all of his powers, he would still have his good looks. Then I remembered seeing him with Scarlett. I shook the image of them blood sharing out of my head just as the bell rang signaling the end of English.

When I saw Avery in Biology and she begged me to meet up with her and the girls for lunch, I was actually relieved to have an excuse to miss the gossip session.

"I think I am going to sit in on the Students With Light new member meeting to see what it's all about," I told her. "You should come."

"Maybe," she said, "but I'm already a member and we have the same lunch as Ethan today. I'm hoping he'll notice my new jeans," she replied with a giggle.

I promised her I would try to find her if the meeting got out early.

At lunchtime, I grabbed a quick smoothie from the Bistro and made my way over to the meeting. There were about ten students in the corner of the Commons where Mia was welcoming people to grab a seat. There was a sign in sheet to fill out before entering and when Mia saw me, she smiled and handed me the clipboard.

"I'm so glad you could make it," she told me. "Sign in here and grab a mark to place on your arm for support," she told me.

"A mark?" I asked.

"Yeah. Cole is handing them out. It's just a temporary tattoo that our members wear to show support for the cause and for Jason. Even if you don't decide to join, it's a way to show solidarity," she said.

I filled out the form and walked over to Cole who was handing out small pieces of paper with the logo on them. Three triangles that intersected with one another forming what looked like the letter "W" with a circle around it. It looked like the kind of tattoo I used to hunt for in the crackerjack boxes Dad would buy me after soccer practice. I grabbed one with no intention of putting it on my arm and shoved it into my back pocket.

Mia started it off by welcoming the new members, giving an update on events they had coming up, and listed the various committees people could join. Cole talked about his experience the day of the recent school shooting, how he'd played hockey with one of the kids who was killed, and why it was so important to prevent future violence in our schools. Most of the kids in the room already had the tattoo on their arms. As the meeting was about to come to an end, Mia called on me specifically.

"I'd like to offer a special welcome to Seraphina, who recently moved here from Florida," she told the group as my face flushed. "Seraphina, why don't you go ahead and put your tattoo on to show your support for our group?"

My face got even hotter. What was she doing?

"That's ok," I said, with all eyes on me. "I'm not sure I am going to join just yet. I really just wanted to pray for Jason today and get a feel for the group."

"Well, like I said before," Mia retorted, "Even if you don't join as a full member, you can still show your support for the cause and for Jason, right? It's important to have as many Valiant students wearing the mark as possible, so that we can be an example for others."

What was with this chick?

"I don't see how falling in line like a herd of sheep is really setting a good example for anyone," I said before thinking.

"Excuse me?" Mia hissed.

"I'm sorry. This is just not for me." I picked up my backpack and bolted out the door. I could hear whispers behind me, but I didn't care. I was never one to respond well to authority in any form or fashion. And Mia demanding that I not only join her club but also brand myself was not something I was willing to do.

That afternoon I headed to the soccer fields with the girls getting ready for tryouts. It went pretty well this time around and once I relaxed. The team saw what I could do with a soccer ball and everyone was super nice. I scored a hat trick at the scrimmage and started to feel more normal than I had in a really long time, sweating and dribbling in and out of players. There was no better feeling than scoring a goal.

As I was heading to Jules's car after practice, I looked down at my phone and almost ran into Mia.

"You know texting while walking can be hazardous to your health," she said, as we bumped into each other.

"Oh, wow. I'm so sorry," I said, tucking my phone in my pocket.. "I really should watch where I'm going."

"Don't worry about it," she said, making direct eye contact with me. "And look, we've had a bumpy start."

She moved closer to me, never even blinking once.

"I see you're trying out for soccer. I have a ton of supplements that can up your game. I normally sell them, but I'd be happy to give you a few samples as a peace offering. Would you like some?"

"Supplements? Like what?" I asked.

"They're all natural. Just some herbal blends I've perfected over the years. Most of the athletes here use them. And from what I see, you could really use to put on some muscle."

This girl was really something else. I wanted to punch her. I looked over and saw Jules walking out of the academic building, making his way over.

"There's my ride. I'll think about it," I said, and started to walk away.

She grabbed my arm.

"I really hope you will, Seraphina," she said as she squeezed my arm and continued looking directly into my eyes with her steely glare.

I snapped my arm away. That bitch had slapped a tattoo right onto my arm.

"Don't touch me, Mia," I said as I ripped the paper off my arm before it had any time to soak in. I tore it in half and dropped it on the ground as she glared at me. I turned and walked away quickly, making a mental note to check her umbra sometime soon.

I met up with Jules at his car.

"There is something really off about that girl," I said to him.

"She just your typical school bully," he said.

Just as I was about to open the car door, I heard a rumbling coming from the other side of the parking lot. I looked over and saw Steele with a bunch of other boys speeding through the school parking lot on dirt bikes.

"Oh Lord, that boy is going to be the death of me," I said.

"I thought I was."

I ignored his sarcastic tone and watched as the group of six on dirt bikes did donuts in the parking lot and left as fast as they entered. *How on earth did he even get a dirt bike?*

"Never underestimate the power of the male ego," I said.

"The ego is the Devil's strongest tool. The bigger the ego, the darker the umbra. That has been my experience. I guess he won't be needing a ride home?" Jules asked somewhat rhetorically.

"Let's just go, please," I muttered as I got into the car sulking.

As Jules squealed out of the parking lot—*hypocrite much?* —I told him about my run in with Mia. He said she'd been pushing the student body pretty relentlessly about getting her so called "light" tattoos and that most kids at the school were on some kind of her supplements.

It wasn't just at Valiant either. She had partnered with some other student ambassadors to expand the club and her 'business' into other area high schools. I wondered what her end game was. It certainly wasn't altruistic, and something wasn't sitting well with me. Dad always taught me that if it didn't feel right, it probably wasn't. He also loved to say suspect everyone and trust no one. Jules's voice snapped me out of my thoughts.

"Did you make the soccer team?"

"Not officially, but I am pretty sure I'll get a call from Coach Quintero tonight about it," I told him.

"Good, because you need to be on the tournament team over Winter Break. I already talked coach in to registering for it," he said as he pulled into the garage.

After he parked, we both sat there for a minute longer, tension filling the car. We both knew we had to talk about it.

"I'm really sorry about everything Jules," I started. "I am sure you probably hate me right now."

He didn't say a word. So I continued.

"I don't even want these powers. If there was a way I could stop it from happening, I would do it in a second," I said, gaining the courage to put my hand on his knee.

As I did, the strangest thing happened. I felt as if we were being pulled into an invisible room, with an incredibly strong force that I had no control over whatsoever. We were still in the car but removed from it, almost on a different plane of existence. My senses were increasing, my eyesight and hearing were intensified, and an energy of strength pulsed through every muscle in my body. It shocked me and I removed my hand. It stopped.

"What was that?" I asked. "You felt that too, right?"

"I did, yes, and I don't know," he responded. "Try it again."

I touched his leg again. This time, nothing.

"That is odd. I have never experienced anything like that," Jules said. "But I feel weak, or somehow drained by it."

"That's weird. It made me feel stronger," I said.

He threw his hands up. "I'm sure it must be related to some power I am losing or our unique connection to each other. On that note, I know it's not your fault. It's mine. I made the choice to turn you and I will face the consequences."

That ended the conversation, and he left me in the car alone.

Later that night around midnight as I was in my room studying and Jules and Thane were in their bat cave manipulating the world through social media, I got an urgent text message from Tyler, one of Steele's new friends. Apparently, they were at a rave in downtown Denver, and Steele was about to be arrested for getting into a fight.

"Oh, for the love of God!" I said to no one. Tyler texted me the address of the police station and I ran downstairs to ask one of the boys for a ride downtown. Jules volunteered, hoping his skills at manipulation might come in handy. I'd never seen him use that particular skill set and if it was one I would inherit, I was eager to see Jules work his magic.

Turns out the forty-five minute ride to the police station was a good opportunity for Jules to give me another lesson in being a Vampire.

"Since you'll be taking, or getting more and more powers every day, you should probably know more about them," he said. "You may have noticed that your senses come to life at night, are magnified by the moonlight, and drained by the sun. Although since Therions are fueled by the sun, that may not be the case for you. You'll have to let me know. Monitor it. You should probably keep a journal. During the New Moon, we are fueled by the star light, during a Full Moon, we are fueled by its glow. You should never feed on these occasions, or you may not be able to keep your prey alive."

"I can feel it," I said. "It's like the darkness is a part of me. It gives me strength, I can see better at night, and I want to be outside, grounded to the power."

"Yes, exactly. All earthbound creatures can harness power from grounding themselves. We ground ourselves to the darkness or moonlight, Witches use nature, and Therions use the sun."

I sat quietly in the passenger seat appreciating this shared knowledge and not able to break my stare. His voice was incredibly soothing and spoke to my soul.

At the police station the desk clerk let us know that Steele was being charged with battery and held on $1,000 bond and was still being processed. He didn't just get into a fight at the rave party. He broke some poor kid's leg with a kick to his kneecap.

Jules leaned closer to the officer, put his hand on his shoulder, and asked him to skip the processing. It was imperative Steele be released immediately. Without missing a beat, the cop repeated exactly what Jules had said and excused himself to go retrieve my brother. Jules had fed on the guy last month. I would definitely have to learn that trick. Steele came out just a few moments later, escorted by Officer Friendly and turned Steele over to us. He reeked of alcohol and smoke. He'd definitely have to show up at a later date for his trial, the officer said, and if the other kid wanted to press charges, he could be facing community service and a mark on his permanent record.

"You have got to get your shit together, Steele!" I said once we were back in the car.

"Seriously Sera. Shut up. I don't want to hear it. I'm tired. And you're not my mother. She's dead."

He put his sweatshirt hoodie up over his head and leaned into the window.

"You are literally such an ass. Whatever! Throw your life away. End up in jail. Is that your end game?"

Jules just drove and didn't intervene. When we got back to the house, Steele got out of the car, slammed the door, and headed inside to his room. It was almost two a.m..

Jules grabbed my arm as we walked inside and looked me right in the eye.

"Seraphina, I'm not one to give advice. Really, ever. But I think you have to let him figure this out on his own. I think you're making it worse."

"Gee thanks, what a pep talk," I muttered. "I don't understand. He was so happy with Cayla out at the camp, and he was making friends."

"I think he'll come around, but he has to get there on his own. Maybe what happened tonight will wake him up. I didn't want to compel his way out of the situation because I think the consequences will be good for him. But I did want to hurry the process up for us," he said with a wink.

Us. There went the butterflies again. I silenced them.

"Thanks for going with me tonight. See you in the morning," I said as I hurried upstairs.

20. UGLY SCAR

Being introduced to Seraphina and Steele didn't relieve me of my duties. Karma is neither good nor evil. It is just. It is patient. Usually, it takes its time, but sometimes it can be immediate. Time and space cloud one's judgment so that the act and the punishment are not connected immediately, making it more difficult for creatures to understand. When you complain for no reason, the universe will usually give you a reason to complain. Earth dwellers have a hard time with that concept and keep inviting chaos and misery into their lives like a never-ending downward spiral.

When we are born into this world, we have every possibility open to us, the ability to make choices. Karmic corrections will occur so we don't always have control over what happens to us, but we can control the way we respond. For Humans, like Steele, when your soul returns to this Earth, it can come back in a variety of forms—an animal, plant, or even an inanimate object. Conversely the spark of light in a leaf or a rock can become a Human soul if the spirit evolves. You may be born as a leaf or rock to experience something specific in that incarnation that you couldn't learn any other way. Maybe your correction is to spend a lifetime watching others enjoy life when you took it for granted in the past. When you come back as a Human you must correct your past actions, both in this life and in past lives and sometimes that correction is immediate; other times is can take years or even lifetimes to adjust. I would have to speed up that process for Steele. I needed him to be ready.

21. CRUEL WINTER

I FELL ASLEEP AND DREAMT OF WITCHES, VAMPIRES, AND Therions. I woke in the middle of night feeling uneasy and sweating. I'd been having these weird sweating spells recently, but this time I sweated through my sheets.

I went into the bathroom to wipe my face down with a cold washcloth. The face staring back at me in the mirror looked tired and flushed. I was agitated and hot. It was strange since Jules's body was always so cold. I pulled my hair up into a ponytail and swore I could see my veins bulging out of my neck. Admittedly, I didn't know everything about Vampires yet but if I was one, I didn't understand how my blood could be so hot. I thought Vampires were cold and dead.

I turned on the shower and intended to let the water calm my body and my blood. Before stepping in though, I headed out to the loft area for some fresh towels and sheets. As I opened the linen closet door, I heard something. A strange yet familiar sound coming from Steele's room. The door was cracked. Maybe he was having a nightmare. I almost ignored it and headed back to the cool shower that was beckoning, but I tuned my ears in like a radio station, dialing in on the sound. I'd heard it before, but it wasn't registering. Then it hit me. Someone was feeding inside that room. I burst inside to see someone straddled across his body, sitting on top of Steele sucking on his neck.

It was Scarlett. She noticed me but it was too late. The rage and heat that filled my body boiled over and I moved in record speed to Steele's bedside. I grabbed her by the hair, ripping her away from my brother, and threw her against the wall. Before she could steady herself, I leaped on her again, and slammed her head into the floor. Rage engulfed me. All I wanted to do was rip her head off.

"What the hell are you doing!" I growled at her.

She gained her bearings and struck at me with precision and speed that matched my own. Her nails ripped into the flesh on my face, and I grabbed her wrist as she tried to pull it away. I flipped her over on her side and cracked her wrist backwards feeling her bones crunch beneath my grasp.

Jules and Thane came barreling into the room to break us up. Thane pushed me to one side of the room while Jules hauled Scarlett to the other. Steele was still sound asleep oblivious to the battle taking place. Jules and Thane pulled us outside in super speed mode and shoved us downstairs to the basement.

"Someone tell me what happened," Jules said, still holding Scarlett away from me.

"That demon bitch was feeding on Steele!" I screamed, and broke free of Thane's grasp and lunged at her again. "I am going to kill you," I told her.

"Thane, get a hold of her!"

"I'm trying!" he yelled.

He couldn't hold me. The anger brought incredible strength. It coursed through my every cell. I broke free of Thane's hold with every intention of ripping Scarlett's head clean off her body but a millisecond before I could reach her, Jules and Scarlett dissolved into smoke. I screamed.

I wanted to follow them, but I had no crystal to assist with the transition. Even if I did, I didn't think I'd ever have been able to reach the relaxation point necessary to transition into alpha level. I turned my aggression toward Thane. Just as I was about to pounce on him, he pulled a crystal of his own out of his pocket and ran toward me slapping me hard across the face. It paralyzed me.

"Seraphina, this will only hold for a moment. You need to calm down. I think you are experiencing Winter Wolf Syndrome. Female Therions that identify with wolves go through it every winter. You have every right to be angry, but you cannot kill her. That anger is something else. It's not you. We don't kill Vampires. It is against our natural order and code. Can you calm yourself?"

How dare he attribute my anger to some stupid syndrome, like PMS. I wanted to break loose so badly but I couldn't move. I felt his hand cool on my head and felt the pulsating energy of the crystal entering my body. I heard what he was saying and understood it but could not reconcile it with my rage. That was the last thought I had before feeling the injection on the back of my neck.

When I woke up, it was pitch black. My eyes wouldn't focus on anything. I blinked. Nothing. I blinked again harder. Still nothing. I did a mental assessment of my body. My legs felt heavy. My hands felt restrained. They were tied down to something and hurting. I couldn't lift them even to scratch my face, which was itching. My hair matted to my forehead. I no longer felt rage or hot, but my memories of the night's events came back slowly. I still couldn't believe what happened. I heard someone open a door and light creeped into my consciousness. The next thing I knew the top of whatever container I was in began to open and I saw a fuzzy image opening the lid. Wait, was I in a coffin? The scent told me it was Thane, but I had to blink a few times before my vision returned.

"Hey there. Let me help you up," he said.

I sat up and realized it was not so much a coffin but some sort of glass chamber. The room was filled with them. A quick glance had me guessing there were about thirty.

"It's a cryo chamber. It's for super-fast healing and calming. Should definitely help with your um, symptoms," Thane said.

"I'm not sure what you mean," I snarled, more annoyance than rage.

"Well, that was quite a show you gave us earlier when you almost killed Scarlett. She wasn't hurting your brother, you know," he said.

"How can you say that with a straight face? She was *feeding* on him," I said slowly for emphasis.

"That she was," he said slowly, mirroring my tone. "But Seraphina, Vampires are creatures of habit. They feed on those who invite them in. You know this. You've done this."

I instantly felt betrayed that obviously Jules had shared the story about our evening feeding encounter with Thane.

"Steele is headed down a path that is inviting darkness," Thane continued. "It's his choice. He is the only one who can reverse it. He must exhibit his own free will to change the narrative, turn a new direction. You understand that right?"

"I understand it, but I don't have to condone his safety being sacrificed right inside his own home," I said. "We should be able to feel safe here."

"You know better than most that it doesn't matter where the Vampire lives, they will find those who invite them in. If it wasn't Scarlett, it would have been someone else. I'm surprised you weren't called to it."

I thought about that for a minute. Why didn't I get the feeling about Steele's umbra? Maybe I had chosen to ignore it. Or had I felt it and not listened? We sat in silence for a few minutes.

"Where am I?" I asked finally.

"We're in the sub-basement. I had to inject you with a sedative. It was the only way to counteract the WWS."

My look of confusion led him to continue.

"Winter Wolf Syndrome. I am thinking your Therion DNA must have been heightened, or even triggered when Jules turned you. WWS is a trait of Therions in the wolf family. It's kind of like PMS only instead of monthly it's annually. You'll feel especially territorial, hot, you'll get enraged easily, you'll have exceptional strength and speed, and you'll want to kill pretty much everyone around you for no apparent reason," he said, throwing his hands up in the air. "I know, I know, you had reason to be angry, but that was something different. In wolf packs, some female wolves are known to kill their own family members during the winter months when it comes on randomly. Anger completely clouds your vision. I've never seen a Therion in Human form have it to the extent that you did but nothing about you is exactly normal. Your eyes even turned crimson."

I remembered it clearly now. I couldn't focus on anything except the rage. It encompassed my entire being. I would have killed Scarlett for sure. Thinking about it more clearly now, I was angry, but I didn't want to kill her.

"Where is Steele now?" I asked.

"He's fine. He's upstairs, still sound asleep and will probably sleep better than most nights with her venom residue in his veins," he replied.

"And what about Scarlett?" I asked, not wanting or being ready to see her just yet.

"Jules asked her to go stay with Devyn for a bit, to give you some space."

That was a relief.

"It's seven a.m.," he continued. "If you're up for it, Jules wants to brief us about the Witches in California."

"Sure," I said. "Just help me out of this coffin. Umm…cryo chamber."

Back in the control room, Jules stood at his desk with the glow from the computer lighting up his face. I was still angry at him for helping Scarlett but also enthralled by his handsome features. He acted like nothing had happened and began to brief Thane and I about the sister Witches I was to seek out in California next week at the tournament. I wasn't even on the team yet. They both played for one of the opposing teams in the top bracket. One was goalie and the other played striker. I would be playing them in the afternoon on the first day of the tournament, if I made the Varsity team. Their lives were like an open book on social media. Pretty weird for Witches if you asked me, but what did I know?

One was tall and thin, with long, wavy red hair and a beautiful, radiant face with bright green eyes. Her sister was shorter and darker skinned, with shoulder length almost black hair and looked kind of emo from her online profiles but also very pretty. She'd be even prettier without the black lipstick and eyeliner, in my opinion. Their names were Rachael and Hannah, the exact same as when their earlier selves were on the Alliance.

The only thing Jules didn't understand was why there were only two sisters when there should be three. In order to be strong enough to sit on Arete 8, they would need to be Triad Witches, meaning they were born as a set of three with powerful energy coming from their connection to one another. But there was no record of any third child within this family. Jules still thought they were our best chance.

If they were the Witches, and our contact created a spark, I'd try and get them alone and tell them about our quest to reunite the Alliance, find Amelia, and save the world.

"What if they think I am crazy?" I asked the boys.

"You can't grow up with that kind of Witch power and not know it," said Jules. "They will know they are Witches, and Witches are very proud and particular about their genealogy and family legacies. Them thinking you are crazy is the last thing I am worried about."

"What is the first thing you are worried about?" I asked.

"That you will accidentally rip their heads off," he said.

I rolled my eyes.

"Can't you guys come with me? Why don't we just all hop on a plane and head out there together?" I asked.

"I don't want to ambush them," Jules said. "If they feel too many supernatural creatures coming near them they may spook."

"Or even worse, attack," said Thane.

"I also need to stay here, near Amelia," added Jules. "You'll be in good hands with Quintero, so I'm not worried about babysitting you."

"Well, I can't go to California worrying if Steele is safe. If I go, you both need to give me your word that you will keep Scarlett far away from him and keep an eye on him."

"I'm not sure how great a guardian I'll be," said Jules. "I can feel my strength dissipating every day. But I know Thane will. Right, Thane?"

"Yes, absolutely. Promise," he said, making a cross on his chest.

The next day after school was tryouts. To my surprise, when I arrived out to the fields, I saw Amantes. We'd warned him to stay far away from Emberglow, and yet, there he was. After closer inspection though, I noticed he was hovering, and was not in the physical plane. He put his index finger up to his mouth, and said, "Shhhh." It was clear that no one else could see him.

Once practice started, he continually got in my way. He tripped me, blocked my shots, and pushed the soccer ball to the side of goal. Every, single, time. I couldn't even complain about it, or the girls would think I was crazy. While he focused mostly on me, he knocked down a few of the others too. He maneuvered himself at just the right angle between Amber and another player that Amber took a hit so hard that she fell down screaming in pain, holding her knee. The coaches thought she tore her ACL, one of the worst but most common soccer injuries. If she did tear it, she'd be out for a year after surgery. Not that I'd ever wish that on anyone, but I did remember that it was Amber, who just a few days ago, was complaining about the coach and the team and having to try out. Amantes hovered above her as she was checked out by the trainers.

I tried counteracting his maneuvers by enacting my new Vampire or Therion strength, but it wasn't working. I got pummeled time and time again. I scored two goals out of pure grit but certainly not because he was getting out of my way. I wondered what Karmic recourse I was paying for and made a mental note to ask him about that later. Just a few minutes before practiced ended, his form dissipated into the wind. Nevertheless, I stuck it out and by the end of practice had two bloody knees, sore ribs, and a big scratch on my face. They had already started to heal when Jules picked me up.

"What happened to you?" he asked when I got into the car.

"Let's just say Karma is a bastard," I said and sulked the whole ride about high school girls, universal energy, and my life right now.

When the placement email came out that night, I'd be slotted on the JV team. It was infuriating. I could still go to the tournament with the lower team but since that team would be in a different bracket it would make it all the more difficult to find the Witches in the higher level group. Jules tried to make me feel better by offering to take out some of the Varsity players to make room for me on the team. Like literally take them out. And while I was flattered, I told him no thanks. I'd play JV, kill it, and show them why they made a mistake.

The rest of the week blurred by and before I knew it, it was Winter Break, and we were getting ready to head out to California for the tournament. I'd barely said a word to Steele since the incident and I still felt guilty about it. I didn't know how to talk to him, and that indifference led to a fight brewing between us. He continued to make bad choices, skipped classes, had become entrenched with the dirt bike crew, and was drinking and partying heavily. I thought about getting Brock involved or calling Cayla, but I was just too consumed with my own drama to get on him about it. He was barely ever home.

Between fighting the constant pressure to get tattooed every single day, to battling the girls at soccer, to trying to get in top shape for the tournament, to keeping my grades up and studying the Witches I was supposed to meet and recruit, I was at my limit and completely overwhelmed. But as I was packing to leave the next morning, I heard Steele walk into his room and close the door. This was as good a time as any, I guess. I texted him first.

Hey. Can we talk for a minute?

Within seconds he texted back.

idgaf

Just as pleasant as ever, I thought, contemplating giving up. Maybe he'd be nicer in person.

I walked up and knocked on his door.

"Come in," he grumbled.

I cracked open the door and saw him sitting on his bed watching a replay of a video game on his phone.

"You know they track everything you watch on that stupid app, right?" I said.

"What do you want Sera?"

"How's Cayla?" I asked, genuinely interested in whether they were still talking.

"I wouldn't know."

"Okay, well, I just wanted to let you know that I am leaving in the morning for California for a few days."

"That sounds like a you problem," he said without looking up from his phone.

I ignored his tone and continued, "I have the soccer tournament and I'm going to track down the Witches. I wanted to say goodbye and tell you not to do anything stupid while I'm away."

I couldn't help it. I tried to play the loving, seven minute older sister, but for some reason the antagonist in me always slipped out with him.

"Get out of my room," he barked back.

"I'm serious, Steele. You have been acting like an idiot lately. What is wrong with you? Do you think Mom and Dad would be proud of you? Drinking? Partying. Hanging out with the dumb ass crowd you're with?" I lectured.

It was hard for me to stop once I started in on him.

"What do you think is wrong with me Sera?" he said. "I have no real friends here, we're surrounded by freaks of nature, my tics are back, and I miss Mom and Dad. I miss everything about our old life. This school sucks. Everything here just sucks. Even the weather!"

I didn't know how to respond. Everything he said was true. Except for the part about the weather. I actually preferred it. I weighed my response carefully.

"I know, you're right. About all of that," I said. I cracked my knuckles not knowing how to console him.

"Why don't you spend the break, out with Brock and Cayla—"

He cut me off. "I don't want to be with Brock and Cayla. You just don't get it! Get out!" he screamed.

"Great talk," I said, as I stormed out.

Well that went well. I retreated to my packing and thought about what Mom and Dad would really think about the whole situation. I knew I could do a better job at getting through to him. I'd make it a priority to do that when I got back.

22. IT'S NOT ME, IT'S YOU

THE FLIGHT OUT TO CALIFORNIA WAS BUMPY, TURBULENT, AND loud. Our first stop in San Jose was a team lunch and then off to the hotel to unpack and hydrate. Our first game was tonight. I'd have to find the Witches after tomorrow morning's game. A quick look at the schedule revealed that they would be playing on the next field over.

My roommates were Isabelle, Madi and Daniela. I got along with them fine except for Daniela was a spoiled, bratty, pain in the butt. It was manageable and was nothing I didn't deal with on my last team and every team since I was four years old. And compared to Mia and the bitches on Varsity who laughed and whispered about me every time I saw them, these girls were fine. We picked our beds and changed into our uniforms and then had about an hour of down time before the game. I was just chilling out on the bed when Jules texted.

I see you made it to the hotel. How's it going?

Oh boy. He's tracking me. Micromanagement at its finest. I was also flattered and happy he cared enough to check my location.

Uneventful so far. Keep you posted. Gtg. I texted back.

I was so conflicted about him. He made me feel things I had never felt before and it made me nervous. But I knew he had serious evil running through his veins. I mean, wasn't he a kind of demon? But I also knew that I shared those traits with him now too. Was I evil? What was I? If I let myself think about it too long, I'd have a crisis of consciousness. I wasn't sure what I was anymore. Born Human but part Therion and now part Vampire. Not to mention that my new powers came and went with absolutely zero control. I couldn't control anything. I didn't know how to tap into all of the DNA running through my veins. Secretly I hoped the Witches would maybe help me with some mystical spells to figure out how to cope with who I was now. But I didn't even know if they'd like me. They'd probably think I was just a lowly JV loser.

On the ride to the fields in the team van, I noticed a few girls passing around pieces of paper to each other and then putting the small tablets into their mouths. They were trying to keep it hidden from our chaperone driver.

"You want one?" Daniela whispered to me.

"One what?" I asked.

"It's just a little something to get hyped before the game. Like caffeine only way better," she said.

"But what is it?" I pressed.

"It's just some herbal thing. Honestly, it's fine. Like every athlete at school is using some combination of it. Mia makes them," she said.

"Mia?" *Oh Lord.* I had to contain my eyeroll. "Uh, no thanks, I already had a bunch of coffee this morning so I'm good."

"Ok, your loss," she said with a shrug

We won the first game 3-0. I scored one goal and had one assist. When we got back to the hotel, we had a team dinner and went to bed. My roommates all took another hit of a different kind of Mia's 'herbs,' this time to help them sleep. I declined again.

At closer inspection, the herbs were embedded in a small piece of thin white paper. Each one had a symbol on it, marking what they were intended to be used for. Some to stay awake to study, others for an extra athletic boost, and even others who wanted to de-stress. They said she was like the school Witch. How ironic. I made a mental note to share this news with the others when I got home.

I wanted to look over the dossier about the soccer Witches one last time but I didn't have much privacy. So instead, I mentally went over it in my head. Hannah was the dark-haired girl who played goalie. She didn't post as much as her sister did online and she seemed to be really into getting good grades. It didn't seem like she had a boyfriend, and she surely wasn't as much of a party girl as her sister.

Rachael was the red head. She was very into herself and posted quite a few bikini beach shots on social media. Jules had intercepted quite a few racy snaps between her and several different boys. She was adventurous, loving to surf huge waves at Mavericks—a place known around the world for its enormous swells. Mostly everything about Rachael online showed her on the beach, either surfing in a wetsuit or posing in her string bikini. I hated girls like that. It was probably a mix of jealousy that I never felt confident enough to show myself in a bikini on social media but also just general annoyance that anyone could be so vain. Hannah and Rachael. Sugar and spice. Got it, I thought, as I allowed myself to drift off to sleep.

The alarm went off at 5:45am, and I hopped up anxious for the morning to begin. A lot was riding on this game and my ability to make friends, which by the way, was never my strong suit. Everyone was counting on me generating a magical spark with strange girls I had never met but was supposedly connected to on a higher level.

As soon as our van pulled into the soccer complex, I scanned the crowds for their high school team. After we got to our field and dropped our backpacks, I had an immediate feeling that they were near. I sensed their presence like when there is someone standing right behind you, and you can feel them there. Their high school warmed up on the sidelines. I looked closely at each player and checked them off one by one, but no one fit their description. Weird.

Our coach yelled for us to start warmups, so I laced up my cleats and headed onto the field. And that's when I saw them. They were on the JV team we were about to play! That's why I didn't see them earlier. I was looking on the wrong team. But that made no sense. I knew from the research that they both played Varsity. Not that I was complaining because this twist of fate was quite fortuitous for me.

I thought back to tryouts when Amantes seemed to sabotage me. There are no coincidences, Mom used to say. Everything happens for a reason. I guess I was meant to make the JV team. I looked around for a hovering presence but Amantes wasn't here.

Neither of our teams had taken the field yet since the game before ours was still going on. Rachael and Hannah were behind the opposing goal doing warm up drills. We started on our own drills, and I formed a plan about how to bump into Hannah before the game.

The prior game ended, and both of our teams headed out on to the field for warmups. Hannah moved into goal and Rachael was shooting on her. We warmed up on the opposite goal. During our shooting and passing drill, I deliberately shot off target in their direction, barely missing their goal. I wanted to get this over with as soon as possible.

"What was *that?*" Daniela asked.

"Oh wow, my bad," I said. "I'll go grab it."

As I ran to get my ball, planning on somehow touching one of them in the process, one of the other girls on their team kicked it back to me. Ugh! That was a fail. Guess I'd have to wait for the game. I'd have to tackle Rachael or somehow get into the goal box, maybe on a free kick or a penalty.

The first half of the game was scoreless. A few free kicks were called but nothing that got me anywhere close to either girl. I kept trying to make mental contact with them by staring but they were completely oblivious. Second half rolled around, and I knew I was running out of time. Then our team got a free kick right outside the box. This was it. I would crash the box right as Izzy kicked the ball and grab Hannah by the arm even if it got me a foul. And then, just as the plan formed in my head, the coach subbed me out. I looked over at him trying to silently beg to stay in, or even use any powers of compulsion I may have recently acquired, but no such luck. I sat on the bench for about ten minutes before I got to go back in.

When there was only fifteen minutes left in the game, we got a corner kick. I usually loved to get right inside the box on set plays and sneakily volley the ball in as soon as it came my way. This time though, I stayed out of the box, closer to Rachael, planning to run into her when everyone else was focused on the goal.

I maneuvered my way slowly toward her and just as the ball was kicked, I ran toward her and grabbed her arm. The shock wave was palpable. So much so that it knocked me backward onto the ground.

"What the hell are you doing?" Rachael screamed at me, unphased by the touch.

"Oh, I um…" I staggered to my feet.

"Back off, bitch," said Daniela to Rachael, coming to my rescue. "She tripped."

The ref didn't notice but what was disturbing was that Rachael was completely nonchalant about the encounter. Maybe these weren't our Witches after all. It didn't seem like she felt anything at all. But why did I feel the shock?

The game ended in a draw and since it wasn't the finals we didn't go into overtime or penalty kicks. I'd get one more chance at the end of the game to confirm whether they were the correct descendants when we high-fived. We lined up and walked past each player and when Hannah approached, I made sure to not only give her a high five but to also grab her hand a little bit longer. It hit me again. This time the wave was more controlled, channeled, but I felt it, nonetheless. No reaction from Hannah at all. When I got to Rachael, she moved her hand away, apparently still annoyed at the stunt outside the box.

Although I felt the connection, the other girls did not. I wasn't sure what to do next. Maybe they were Witches but were closed off to it or something? Or maybe they were Witch descendants but not the exact ones from the Alliance? This was so frustrating. I sulked over to my backpack and left with my team.

We had one more game that afternoon that we won, securing our spot in the final the next day. That night I texted Jules to tell him about my colossal failure and I could tell he was annoyed with me.

You're wrong. It's them. Try again, he texted back.

Tears welled up in my eyes. I didn't get it. Why was I not able to connect with them? It didn't work, and he was being such an ass about it.

As I rearranged my soccer bag the next morning, a piece of lavender tissue paper fell out. Hmm . . . where did that come from? On it, words began to form slowly, one at a time,

I know who you are. We don't want to be involved. H & R.

I covered my mouth with my hand to halt my gasp. My hands began to tremble, and I felt weak. I stared at it for what seemed like forever. I felt relief but also agitation about the content of the message. Maybe they didn't realize who I really was. Maybe they thought I had bad intentions. Or maybe they didn't know how close we were to reuniting the group and also the consequences that were coming if we didn't. Thank goodness I would have one more opportunity to see them at today's final game. I thought about calling Jules but then thought better of it until I accomplished the goal.

Let him sit there and wonder for a bit longer.

23. FALLING

STEELE IS HEADED DOWN A PATHWAY TO DARKNESS. THERE was nothing I could do but help enact the Karma that was due him. By purposefully breaking that boy's leg in the fight he put in motion forces that would come back to him ten times worse. It is the nature of the universe. What you put out, positive or negative, comes back to you times ten. For Humans, it may not come back in this lifetime. It may lie in wait for the next one or even the one after that, whenever the lesson will be needed the most.

One of the corrections for people who use a lot of negative speech is to suffer trauma to their mouth. If they take this life for granted or poison their bodies and tarnish their souls, they may be reborn as a rock. This is like an indefinite prison sentence, a form of purgatory in which the person can remain for however long it takes to regain their appreciation for life and humanity.

So, what I had to set in motion now was for Steele's own good. It was a blessing. He had to correct his soul.

24. WE ALL FALL DOWN

WHEN WE GOT TO THE FINAL, I TOLD COACH Q I WANTED TO chat with someone on the other team, that I knew from back in Florida. He agreed, I think feeling sorry for me, which is what I had hoped for. I made a beeline for Hannah since she seemed like the more reasonable one.

"Hi, are you Hannah? I think we might know each other?"

"Nope don't think so," she said and looked away.

"Actually, I am sure that we do, and I'd love to tell you all about it right here in front of your whole team," I said, shooting a significant look at her teammates warming up nearby. "Or we can take a quick walk?"

She looked at her teammates who had noticed our somewhat tense interaction, and I could sense she was mentally weighing her response. Rachael was also staring at us trying to catch every word.

"Um, yeah. Okay. One sec," she said.

She ran up to her coach and said something really quick and then motioned to me to start walking with her toward the bathroom.

I caught up to her.

"Did you put that note in my bag?" I asked, knowing we'd have to get to the conversation quick and skip the pleasantries.

"I was responsible for it being there, if that's what you mean," she said.

"I don't understand. We should be on the same side. I need your help, if you are who I think you are," I said.

"Look, I know who you are, and I know what you're trying to do. Rachael and I do not want to be involved. We don't cast and we can't help you," she said in a whispered tone.

I grabbed her arm. I felt the surge and I know she did too.

"That makes no sense. I can feel that you do, that witchcraft is flowing through your body. Help me find what we need to reunite the council and then if you don't want to be involved, we can find some other Witches. But we need your crystals and your help finding the others."

"Please do not touch me again. And hands off Rachael. She can't feel what you and I feel. And I'm truly sorry," she said, this time with more sincerity. She looked me straight in the eyes and said, "It is non-negotiable for us. We cannot and will not be involved. I wish you the best of luck, truly."

And with that she ran off back toward her team. Rachael met her a few feet before she reached the others. And even though she was more than a football field away from me, I heard Hannah clear as day. She laughed and said, "That was weird, she thought she knew me from somewhere. What did I miss?"

I was so frustrated. I'd failed and was dreading telling Jules. I debated mentally whether I should wait until after the game or just shoot him a quick text now. I grabbed my phone and noticed about a million text messages from Jules and seven missed calls.

Where are you?

Pick up the phone.

I'm not kidding.

It's urgent.

Dammit Seraphina, TURN ON YOUR phone.

Instead of listening to the voicemails, I called him.

He answered.

"What in the actual hell, Seraphina."

"Well, a happy hello to you too," I said.

He wasted no further time on banter. "Steele is in the hospital. He was in an accident. I am coming to get you to bring you home. I'll be at the Half Moon Bay Airport, the Eddie Andreini airfield in about an hour. Meet me there."

I felt a wave of queasiness take over my body and almost collapsed.

"Is he ok?" I asked, feeling heat flush my face and wave of nausea making me dizzy.

"It's not fatal but it's not good. He's pretty banged up and not in a great place mentally. I have to run; I'll explain everything on the jet."

And with that he hung up.

"What jet?" I thought to myself.

I ran over to Coach and told him what happened and that I had to leave before the game. He called me an Uber and since I'd already packed I grabbed my stuff out of the van.

"Jules's family has a private jet. I put the directions to the hangar in the Uber app and they should drop you off right on the runway. I'm so sorry Seraphina," Coach said. "I'll see you when we return and know that I'm praying for Steele."

A black Uber pulled into the parking lot and as I got into the car, I noticed Hannah staring at me with a confused expression on her face.

At the airport, the driver dropped me off in front of a sleek black jet. Jules walked out to meet me. On the ride I was able to put together bits and pieces of what had happened from social media posts, and I knew that Steele's friend Tyler had died in the same dirt bike accident that landed Steele in the hospital and that the police thought alcohol or drugs were involved.

"You look awful," Jules said when he saw me. "Come on. Let's get you to your brother."

25. BLIND BUT STILL ALIVE

ON THE PLANE, JULES TOLD ME WHAT HE KNEW OF THE INCI-dent.

Steele and his band of bad boy friends had been drinking. After driving way too fast on a curvy road at three a.m., Steele's dirt bike hit a bump unexpectedly and swerved, accidentally hitting Tyler's bike. Tyler spun out of control and into a tree, knocking him off the bike, and killing him instantly. Steele barely survived and was in critical condition with a pretty nasty leg injury and a crushed right eye socket. He'd need surgery for both.

I heard the words but didn't really process them. My mind was elsewhere, trying to mentally connect to my brother and tell him I was headed his way. I couldn't lose Steele. Not after my parents. It wasn't fair. Why was this happening to us? What did we do to deserve this? And now Steele would have to live the rest of his life knowing he killed his friend. I didn't think he would ever get over something like that.

As if reading my mind, Jules said, "Sera, you should be prepared for his mental state. I saw him just before they sedated him this morning when he found out Tyler was dead. He wanted to die as well. He couldn't bear what he had done."

I was lost in a cloud of my own thoughts the entire flight from Half Moon Bay to Centennial Airport. As we drove over to the hospital, it felt like I was watching someone else go through the motions. I think Jules could tell I was lost in my own mind. He barely said a word to me on the drive.

When we got to the hospital in Emberglow we were met in the waiting room by the doctor. He was tanned like he just got back from a vacation but looked tired, as if he'd been up all night, which I was guessing he had.

"Hello, I'm Dr. Stone," he said. "You must be Seraphina, Steele's sister?"

"Yes, how is he?" I asked.

"Physically, he will survive. He's very lucky. He has comminuted open fractures affecting both the upper and lower portions of the tibia and fibula bones in the lower right leg," he said. Seeing my confusion, he dumbed it down for me. "Comminuted basically means the bone was broken in multiple parts. It wasn't a clean fracture, which is not great. When we go in surgically, which we're scheduled to do later today, we'll have to repair all the pieces, set them all back together, most likely with some steel rods, and make sure it's stable. Additionally, the fracture broke through the skin which could lead to a high degree of infection, not just to the skin but to the bone itself. That's when you can start to have complications. Multiple bones breaking through the skin requires a lot of surgery to get the bones back to where there are supposed to be. It's not likely but there is the possibility of amputation. We also have to repair his right eye and he may be visually impaired, but that could improve with time. It's likely he will never play competitive sports again, but with luck and prayers and rehabilitation, he'll be okay."

I was totally numb. "Amputation?" I asked as if it were the only word I heard in his super long, detailed speech.

"That is the last resort," he assured me. "We will do everything in our power to save his leg and his eyesight. I have to get ready for another surgery, but it would be good for you to be here when he wakes up. It's important to be surrounded by family and friends. Are there other family members you can call?"

That's when the flood gates opened.

"No, it's just me," I managed. Brock's face popped into my head, and I added, "We do have an uncle nearby I can call."

"Give him a call. The more loved ones the better," the doctor said.

I regained my composure. "Can I see him now?"

"No, I'm sorry, he's heavily sedated and will go right into surgery prep. Then, he will be in surgery for several hours. I can have the nurses text you when he's out."

Brock showed up at the hospital an hour later. Noticing my physical and mental state he convinced me to go back to Jules's house with him for a shower and some food. Knowing Steele wouldn't be out of surgery for a few hours I implored the nurses to text me with any updates and said I would be back soon.

After I had cleaned up and changed, I joined Jules, Thane, and Brock at the kitchen table. Omega my trusted, sweet pup who sensed what had happened, stayed right by my side, waiting for me to finish changing, following me back downstairs to talk with the others, and eventually laying down with his head resting on my foot. He knew I was struggling to cope with the recent developments, and I knew he probably was too. Jules ordered pizza with a side of blood bags, telling me a bit of both would do me well. Apparently, he kept a stash on hand in the basement refrigerator for times when we couldn't feed or share, but it tasted terrible. I ate and I drank reluctantly, sitting in silence, rubbing Omega's soft fur with my foot, and lost in my own thoughts.

Finally, Jules broke the silence. "What happened in California?" he asked.

I told them the story about the Witches and their strange reaction to me. They took in every word without interrupting.

"We've got to find a way to change their minds," said Jules. "Maybe now that you've made the initial intro, we can all go there together and put on some serious pressure."

"I don't know, something about how she reacted made me think they had a good reason to stay out of it."

"We don't want to push them away even further," added Brock.

"We can put this on hold until we hear about Steele's condition," Thane said.

"Based on how he acted when he first arrived at the hospital," Jules said, brow furrowing. "It may be time to bring him into the fold."

"What does that mean?" I asked.

"We can talk about this later," Brock said giving the others a look of death.

"No, I want to know what you mean. Now."

Brock sighed deeply. Omega sat up and put his paw on my leg as if to reassure me. I motioned for him to jump on my lap but because he was so big, only his two front paws and body would fit.

"When you two arrived at the campground, a shift occurred," Brock began. "You knowing about us and us knowing about you. You and Steele are royalty to us. And while we have had various leaders over the ages, now that we are aware of your existence, the throne must pass to one of you.

When Jules bit you and then brought you back to life, we believe it also unlocked your Therion gene, giving you access to not only your Therion traits, but also your new Vampirism. That makes you very powerful and the natural choice to lead us, however you are no longer pure, meaning you would either have to fulfill your legacy bond with Noah and rule our kind together or we'd have to awaken the gene in Steele. If he wins at our annual competition, he would be found fit to rule in his purest sense. We'd still have to figure out a way to unite the nodes but the transition from Human to full Therion may give him a higher purpose, help him get over what happened, and turn things around for him. But it is a long journey, and he has to come along as a willing participant."

"How exactly do you awaken his Therion gene?" I asked.

"Well, we've never done it before. We need help from the Witch line that cast the initial spell, but we can start the process with our heirloom crystals and a ceremony to awaken his DNA."

"And for me to assume the throne, since I am *unpure* now," I said giving Jules a look of disgust, "I'd have to what, get married to Noah or something? I hardly even know him! Not to mention I am only sixteen!"

"It's more of a symbolic union," said Brock. But we can talk about that later. The most important thing now is that Steele recovers physically, and then we can work on the mental part. Even if we just start the DNA activation process, it may help shift his umbra, and we can always stop and go in another direction. He can say no all the way up until we find the Witches, which I know you will."

A call came in on my phone. It was the hospital.

"Hi Seraphina, this is Nurse Briggs at UC Health. Your brother is out of surgery."

"Oh, that's great, how did it go?" I asked.

"The surgery went well. We were able to save his leg and his eye. He's breathing better, but, um, he's being restrained in the ICU."

"What do you mean, restrained?" I asked, feeling nervous.

"Once he began to wake up and realized what had happened, that his friend had passed, he became violent and tried to injure himself. We had to sedate and restrain him. You can come see him, but I wanted to prepare you for what you would see."

I swallowed hard and tried to process what she was saying. "Okay, thank you. I'm on my way."

I ended the call. My friends with the super hearing obviously heard every word because they were unsure of what to say. You'd think creatures that had been around since the dawn of existence, would have something comforting to say, but no such luck. I broke the silence, with, "Come on. Let's go to the hospital."

Omega looked at me with longing eyes and I knew he wanted to come.

"Can we bring him?" I asked to no one in particular.

"Well if he shifts to a Human, yes," Jules said.

"It's getting dark. That would deplete his energy," said Brock.

"I'll convince them to allow a dog," Jules said with a wink.

"Great, thank you. I think it will be good for Steele to have him there," I said.

On the way there, Thane asked me if he could speak with Steele alone before I went into the room. He had to say something that he thought would help. I agreed, almost relieved because I didn't know what I would be able to say to my brother to make him feel ok about the entire situation.

When we reached the hospital, we were told only one person could go in at a time. Brock, Jules, and I stayed in the family waiting room and allowed Thane, accompanied by Omega, to go in first. The nurse was all too accommodating to Jules's charm. I sat on the couch, closed my eyes, and tuned my hearing to follow their footsteps through the hallway, and home in on what he was about to say. I heard him open the door and walk inside.

"I want to be alone." Steele said immediately.

"I'm glad to see you're out of surgery," said Thane. "I brought a friend."

Omega trotted over to Steele.

"Hey buddy," he said groggily.

"Your sister is waiting outside, and she really wants to see you, but I wanted to talk to you for a minute first," Thane said.

I heard the scrape of a chair that Thane must have pulled up near the bed.

"I am a captive audience," Steele replied.

"Look, dude. You've been through a lot. It is totally understandable what you're feeling. Over the years, I've been through a lot too. I've lost a lot of people, a lot of good people. And sometimes, it's been my fault. That grief you're feeling," he paused, and his swallow was audible. "I know what that is. It is a deep dark hole. I know what it's like to lose friends, brothers, family, and I've had lifetimes to wallow in regret. Over those thousands of years, I've learned something that I hope may help you shift your perception right now. Those people you've lost—Tyler, your mom and dad? They wouldn't want this for you."

"I did this to Tyler. I might as well have shot him! I couldn't save my parents. I let Sera be turned into a...a monster. How could you possibly know what *they* want? It's not like you can ask them!"

"I don't need to, Steele. I've been one of them."

"What are you talking about?" Steele asked.

Thane took a deep breath in. "About fifty years ago I was living a different life, going to high school for the hundredth time and bored as hell. I got into a crazy crowd. I really bonded with one kid in particular. His name was Stanley. He was goofy and wild, and we partied pretty hard together. We bought matching Chevy Camaros—his blue, mine black.

"One day we'd smoked a little too much weed, mixed it with some alcohol and decided to go drag racing in our separate cars through the mountain roads. I was showing off, feeling invincible and high and going about a hundred miles per hour around Red Mountain Pass. His car accidently rubbed into mine. He spun out and hit a tree, and my car flipped about ten times and fell over the side of the road, exploding. I ended up dead, or what seemed like dead, on the side of a ravine. Mangled and burned to the point that no one would have ever believed I would have been able to survive those types of injuries. When Brock found me, he took me back to the campsite to help me heal but everyone else in my Human circle thought I died, and I let them. I wanted to be dead."

"Wow," Steele said. "Man, I'm sorry, that sucks."

Thane sounded anguished retelling his story.

"It's safe to say I had my share of bad days. But you know what helped me get through it? Stanley. He lived. He crawled out of his car, with two broken, crushed legs, and tried to come save me but the flames were too hot. And I would have done the same for him if I'd been conscious. He lost both legs that day and lived with a wheelchair for the rest of his life. What's even worse is that morning, he'd tried to convince me not to go. But I kept drinking and pushed him to as well. He said we shouldn't drive in our condition, but I pressured him to go. Called him a coward. Bullied him about being cautious. And you know what, he was very lucky to make it out alive that day, despite of me. Some of my darkest days at the Therion camp, I didn't think I would make it. I begged Brock to kill me. The only thing that gave me hope was knowing that Stanley was spared. Watching him, with help from the pack, and seeing that he was okay, that he used the event to speak out to teens about drinking and driving. He grew up, got married, and had kids, and told them I was one the best friends he ever had. He only thought of me with fond memories, and kindness, and love. He forgave me and I knew I had to forgive myself. And I know Tyler would forgive you too. He would not want you to injure yourself or hate yourself for what happened to him."

Steele began to cry. "I'm such a moron. I don't know why I've been acting this way and I know I should move forward but I can't. I go to school and see all of these stupid kids going on with their lives and playing sports and talking about all of this trivial crap while my parents are dead. It's not fair. My life is completely upside down. My sister is a Vampire, my only friend is dead, and you know what? The world keeps spinning like nothing ever happened. People forget, the world keeps going. Nothing stops. I can't forget. I can't keep going."

As I listened in, I was completely torn up. I had been so wrapped up in my own crap that I failed to notice how lost my brother was and how helpless he felt.

"Not to throw a movie quote at you but it truly is the circle of life. Everyone dies. No one is immune. It's what you do while you're here that decides what your next life will be," said Thane. "Yes, the sun keeps shining, birds keep chirping, the world keeps spinning. But their legacy and the light they created, lives on forever in the hearts of those who knew them. And in small, sometimes unrealized ways that can reverberate throughout humanity for generations to come. You've traveled with the souls of your parents throughout many lifetimes. You will see them again. Time is a construct of only this physical world. You have the rest of eternity to be with your parents. What seems like a long time to you now—fifty or sixty years here on Earth—is a blink of an eye in the upper Realm."

Steele regained his composure.

"Sometimes, Steele, most times actually, bad things happen for a reason. You can choose to see the reason and learn from it and help others learn from it. Or you can allow yourself to succumb to the darkness. It's your choice. It is always your choice. I've talked with Brock, and he's agreed to have you come back and live at the camp with him and the other Therions. Learn their ways. Learn more about yourself. They will help you heal faster there too. I'll give you some time to think it over."

With that, Thane stood up and left the room with Omega following close behind.

26. ICE IN MY BONES

THEY TOLD ME TO STAY AWAY FROM EMBERGLOW. BUT I WANTED to help them, make them understand. When I entered the hospital the results of my actions were all around me. The child I had saved, the teen with a broken arm, the drunk driver who killed a family, and the first responder who so selflessly helped others.

Humans are strange. They are given glimpses of the truth all the time through art, culture, and literature. Briefly, they see the light and it sometimes catches on, but it always fades away just as fast as it flared.

Clues are even given in the most widely read book on the planet—the Bible. The Hebrew word *timshel* appears in the Cain and Abel story in the book of Genesis. It means "thou mayest," which means, you may. And if "thou mayest," then it should follow that "thou mayest not," as well. It is a choice.

When Cain was seduced by the darkness and used the Blade to end his brother's life, he made a choice to give in to his weak, dark impulses. The Blade of Cain, while mentioned symbolically as a metaphor throughout the ages, was in fact an actual relic, that possessed all of those evil, impure impulses of Cain's empty heart after his fall. After the murder, just as the blood of the brothers was spilled, like the Constellation of Gemini, the Blade split as well, into light—White Selenite, and dark—Black Tourmaline. In this existence, iL Separatio's soldiers ensure balance so that if a person goes too far in one direction, the scale slides to reestablish balance. Within every good deed, exists a seed of bad, that may flower when watered, and vice versa.

I entered the waiting room where Seraphina, Julian, and Brock were sitting, making sure they were by themselves. Julian saw me first.

"Oh for fuck's sake. Why are you here?" he said to me.

"I want to help," I said.

"Dude, what are you wearing? You look like a hoodlum," Julian said.

My brow furrowed and I wasn't sure what he meant. I had carefully selected the clothes I was wearing—jeans and a black hooded sweatshirt with the hood up to avoid this body being recognized and sunglasses.

"Did you do this to him?" Seraphina asked.

"He did this to himself," I answered. "Balance must be—"

"We know! We know the line. We understand the concept," Julian said.

"You are blinded by your egos. If you would let me speak, I can help you."

"Let him speak," Brock said.

"The only way I can help you is if you choose light. That sets off a reaction I must perform. You can choose whether to triumph over sin or to indulge in it. This ability to choose one's fate is the key. Free will allows you to make the choice to be sinful or not. Choices result in consequences, but the choice always exists, nonetheless."

"So you're saying by making positive choices, we can change our reality," Seraphina stated.

"Yes, exactly," I said. "Just as Cain sinned in the Bible, all earthbound creatures sin. What most people don't understand is that as much as they have inherited Cain's curse, they have also inherited his ability to redeem himself, at any time, just by making the choice to do so."

"Do you even have feelings? Do you care that you helped put my brother in the hospital?" Seraphina asked.

"He's Karma, Sera," Julian added. "He has no feelings."

"That is not true," I said. "I do have feelings. But my responsibility comes first. If you would just listen to me, and follow the rules, this would be so much easier."

27. FRAGILE STRENGTH

AFTER SOMEONE ELSE WALKED INTO THE WAITING ROOM AND
interrupted Amantes, Brock took the liberty of escorting him out of the
hospital and back to the Therion camp as surreptitiously as possible. I
thought a lot about what Amantes said. It made sense and I made a con-
certed effort to try and be more positive in everything I did and said.

It was my turn now to go see Steele. This would be a great first step. I
told myself I would go in with love and not a lecture.

When Omega and I went into his room, it took me by surprise. He
looked dreadful. His face was swollen and black and blue. His leg hung on a
sling with metal rods coming out of it in about ten different places. He had
the covers pulled up all the way to his shoulders on one side, but his right
hand was sticking out and there was a restraining belt across his chest.

He was sleeping. Looking at him lying there so peacefully but so beat
up, restrained, made tears prick my eyes. My sweet baby brother was going
through so much. He was lost without our parents, and I felt like a total
failure not being able to be there for him the way he needed.. I sat by his
bedside, with Omega laying by his side for what seemed like forever before
he finally began to stir. When he opened his eyes, our gazes locked.

I smiled at him. "Well, hello there."

Tears spilled down his cheeks. "I'm so sorry, Sera. I'm so, so sorry."

I put my hand on his cheek and rubbed his hair.

"It's okay, Steele. We're going to get you help. I promise."

He nodded. I could feel his sadness, confusion, and inner turmoil. I understood it too.

"I'm not-I'm not going to hurt myself. They can take this off," he said nodding toward the chest strap.

"Let me text Jules. He'll, um, *convince* the doctor."

On it. Jules texted back.

While we waited for the strap to be removed, we talked about memories of growing up in Florida. About some of our friends and playing soccer on Anna Maria Island beach or running over the John Ringling Bridge with Mom and Dad. As kids, we hated doing it, but looking back, they were good times.

"Once you're completely recovered, let's go back and run that bridge together again."

He nodded and winced with pain. I wasn't sure if it was because his medication was wearing off or because his heart ached.

The floodgates opened and I told him about the conversation with Brock and Thane about Steele or I assuming the Therion throne.

"I can't do it unless I bond with Noah and I have no interest in that," I told him. "I think for the time being, maybe you should go stay at the camp with Brock. Learn about our past, who you really are. I think you'll feel more connected to Mom and Dad there. I'll visit you on the weekends. I want you to get better, stronger, and find peace. Be happy."

He agreed. Just then a nurse came in to remove the restraint. *Nice going, Jules.*

She was in and out in about two minutes. Steele stretched his arms enjoying his new freedom and as he did, I caught a glimpse of something on his inner left wrist. It was a turquoise mark. The Students With Light tattoo. It looked like it was irritating his skin though, with some raised red skin around its outline.

"What is this?" I asked, grabbing his arm.

"Oh, Mia was relentless about me getting one, so I caved."

"There is something odd about her. Something dark. I can't really put my finger on it, but I don't believe the crap she's peddling about that club being a 'force for good." I rolled my eyes for emphasis. "She's also selling drugs, disguised as herbs."

"Yeah, I've tried those too," he said, embarrassed. "It's fine, Sera. I'm sure it'll come off in the shower or something," referring to the tattoo.

"I don't think you're going to be taking a shower anytime soon," I said, looking him up and down. "At least not without the help of a nurse or two." I gave him a suggestive wink.

"Oh, you know I could pull a nurse, even looking like this," he joked, and I couldn't help but laugh.

He probably could. He'd definitely been blessed with rugged good looks and had even modeled a bit back in Florida for extra cash. With his big, brown puppy dog eye, long lashes, chiseled facial features, and thick eyebrows, I'm sure girls would still find him extremely attractive. Even black and blue.

"Yeah, doubtful!" I joked. "Ok, I am going to let you get some rest. I'll be back after school."

28. WATCH YOUR BACK

Everyone at school buzzed about Steele's accident and Tyler's death. Most kids either avoided eye contact with me or brought it up immediately, telling me how sorry they were about Steele and asking when he'd be back at school—a question I didn't have the answer to. At the end of the day as I headed to soccer practice, Mia cornered me in the hallway.

"Seraphina, I'm sooo sorry about Steele. How is he?"

"He's doing okay, considering," I said, picking up my pace to get away from her.

"You know," she said, stepping right in front of me. "I can make you an herbal remedy for stress or even something for Steele to ease his recovery."

"No thanks," I said, getting more annoyed by the second and shouldering past her.

"Suit yourself. We'll pray for Steele and Tyler at our meetings this week and it would be amazing if you'd join us for that. Maybe lead the prayer?" she asked all syrupy, while trying to keep up with my increased pace.

That was it. I'd had it.

"Look Mia, take the hint. I'm not interested. You may have most everyone else at this school fooled into believing in your 'herbs' and this light club of yours but I'm not buying it. You're too pushy, and there's something odd about the whole thing. I'm just not into it and I'd appreciate it if you would just leave me alone about it. I'm not joining, I'm not praying, and I'm certainly not getting a tattoo or taking any herbs from you."

"You don't have to yell," she said to me in a whispered, angry tone.

I hadn't realized that my voice was attracting onlookers. I felt even more emboldened as more and more students began to stare. Heat rose into my cheeks. Rage seeped into every atom in my body. This time was only slightly different than the episode with Scarlett only because I recognized what it was: Winter Wolf Syndrome. But even though I recognized it, I had no control over it.

"I'll use whatever tone I like," I growled, walking toward her, voice even louder. "The rest of your weak little friends may hang on your every word and follow along like good little sheep, but I am not a follower."

Sneers ensued from the crowd, egging us both on. Mia didn't back down. She got up even closer to my face. "Suit. Yourself. Sera," she hissed. "We don't want your kind anyway. Your toxic energy makes me cringe."

Just as I had completely lost all control over my will power to keep my anger at bay, I shoved her to the ground, hard. She smacked her head against the wall as she fell. By now an even larger group of students had gathered and were taking photos and videos with their phones. She screamed in pain but hobbled back up to a standing position.

"You will regret that," she said storming toward me.

That's when Jules flashed in front of me like a blur, slipped something into my pocket and grabbed my arm. It was too fast for the human eye to catch but I saw it almost in slow motion. I instantly calmed down. I could see clearly. I could also see that a large group of students had even gathered on the upper stairs to watch the drama unfold, but they were frozen in time.

It was just like what happened in the garage, allowing Jules to talk with me privately in our own little reality. It took us both by surprise.

"Are you doing this?" I asked him.

"I-I'm actually not really sure." He seemed truly shocked that we somehow existed in a time bubble separate from the other students. "Besides that time in the car when you touched my knee, this has never happened to me before."

He remembered specifically that I touched his knee.

"Like ever? In your thousands of years on this planet?" I asked.

"Like ever," he said, mocking me. "We stopped time. Regardless of how or why it's happening, we should use it to our advantage. Look, Sera, don't let her get inside your head. Push her out. Tune in to your reflexes. Summon the moon and feel its peaceful power. Let it flow through you. Do not react to her," he said as we seemed to circle each other. Then, he let go of my arm and it instantly ended.

I gathered my composure, and just as I did Mia was coming at me, quickly. She raised her arms to shove me back, but I moved to the side, making her falter, and embarrassing her even more. Our fight had attracted attention from a school administrator who headed our way with a school resource officer. Students scattered like mice as they approached, I gave Mia one last stare down and walked away.

"Ms. Grayson and Ms. Owens," said the assistant principal. "My office, now."

Jules approached the school official and looked her squarely in the eyes. "This is all just a misunderstanding," he said. "They have worked it out and are free to go."

"Mr. Blakewell, go back to class. This does not concern you."

Jules opened his mouth and then stopped with a dazed look on his face. His compulsion didn't work. Before he had a chance to try again, she continued.

"Or you can meet us in the office as well if you like."

I stepped in.

"Ms. Fisher," I said, attempting to mimic exactly what Jules did. I looked her straight in the eyes. "He's right. This was all just a misunderstanding. It's all fine now. We can just forget about this and go back to class."

"Yes, Ms. Grayson, Ms. Owens. Since this was all just a misunderstanding, we can just forget about this and go back to class."

Mia watched the interaction closely, squinting her eyes suspiciously.

"Great, thank you," I said, motioning for Jules and Mia to leave. We went our separate ways, not wanting anything to jinx what had just happened.

On the ride home, I got about a hundred texts and snaps about the fight. There were already several memes circulating of me pushing Mia down. It was embarrassing for me, but probably more so for her.

"Both times that has happened, my powers have weakened and yours have gotten stronger," Jules said, trying to dissect the situation. "If I had to guess, it's some sort of psychic connection due to our blood sharing, and my decision. It enables you to drain my power."

"Do you think Mia noticed what happened when I compelled Ms. Fisher?" I asked.

"That depends," he answered. "We need to do some more digging into her background and these herbs she's pushing. If she's a practicing Witch, she probably knows there is something supernatural about you, and about me, for that matter."

Despite that feeling, it didn't stop Jules from scolding me about getting so angry again, and this time with onlookers and phones. I was actually proud of myself for not killing her.

Upon arriving home that afternoon, Omega jumped up to greet me. He felt like a warm, cozy blanket and the welcome brightened my day.

I had an idea I wanted to run by Jules. He was rummaging through the pantry trying to find something to eat.

'What do you think about us secretly sending someone into that Students With Light group to try and figure out what she is up to?' I thought.

"You mean like a spy?" Jules asked, out loud, without skipping a beat.

"You heard that?" I asked.

"Sure did."

"Let's try it again," I said. "I'm thinking of a color."

"Blue?" he asked.

"Hmm, no." I replied. "How about now?"

"Violet?" he asked.

"What kind of color is that?" I said, exasperated.

"I'm guessing that wasn't it."

"I feel like you're not trying," I said.

He ignored me.

"Regardless, I think sending in a spy is a terrible idea." He waited about ten seconds before adding,

"Who would you suggest? It's not like we can create a new student who Mia has never met before and even if we could, you could never be sure they'd be trustworthy and also, what's in it for them?"

"All good points," I said. "I just thought it would be worth exploring."

"I think we have a lot of obstacles to overcome, and honestly, what is the point? We should focus on finding the crystals and getting the California Witches back on board," he said.

"I don't know. I just feel like maybe we are missing something." I gnawed on my cheek. "I know it sounds crazy but maybe Mia is a Witch, and she is somehow connected to us finding Amelia and connecting with the others. It's just a weird hunch."

"I think you may be letting your disdain for her cloud your judgement. I don't see how she could be connected to the Alliance but if you can think of someone to send in as a spy, more power to you. We need to figure out our next step."

"Well thanks for your help," I sulked. "Let's set up a meeting with the others. And Amantes too. Right now though, I'm going to visit Steele; do you want to come?" I asked, hoping he'd say yes.

"I can't. We have a scrimmage today, remember?" he said referring to his position on the Valiant Lacrosse team. "I can drop you off on my way though and pick you up after if you're okay spending a few hours there."

"Yeah, sure that works. Thanks," I said.

"Great. I'll need to leave in about forty-five minutes." And with that he grabbed his sandwich and headed downstairs.

I went to my room to change and try to get some math homework done before leaving. Omega followed and hopped up onto my bed staring at me. I had all these feelings for Jules I couldn't seem to reconcile, and the feeling was clearly not mutual. Even after we literally stopped time and created our own multiverse, he was barely phased. He treated me like nothing more than a friend. I guess it didn't help that our private universe also resulted in me stealing his powers. I emptied my heart out to Omega, and like a good, trusted pal he just listened.

"Alright, buddy. See you when I get back from the hospital." I doubted Jules would be able to coerce the staff to let me bring Omega in again and I wasn't completely confident in my abilities yet.

When I got back downstairs, I stopped short and nearly gasped. Jules was dressed in his lacrosse practice gear, giving me a small glimpse of his flat stomach peeking out between his jersey and his pants. He grabbed his huge jug of water, and we headed out the door.

Brock was already at the hospital when I arrived. I listened at the door.

"Steele, I know this is difficult to grasp, but if you can find the silver lining here it will help you grow from this experience and get closer to your true essence," he said. "Deep inside you, your soul understands that everything that happens to us is an opportunity. The greatest light comes after the darkest hours. Learn from what happened here and take accountability for it. Do not let your grief and guilt consume you, but let it mold you, temper you, and give you strength to become better."

My brother sobbed.

"That's it, let it out. Let it all wash out and find your light."

I gave him a few minutes to compose himself and then I knocked on the door.

"Hey there, can I come in?" I asked peeking inside the room. Steele nodded.

Brock said his goodbyes and then I just hung out with my little brother for the next few hours, watched TV, and made small talk. I silently thanked the universe that he was okay.

"For a moment, everything seems right in the world," I said to him, something my Dad always used to say when our family was enjoying a particularly peaceful moment that we wanted to savor.

"Give it a minute," he said with a wink. That was something Mom would always follow up with, along with a lesson about life being a series of ups and downs. The key was pushing through hardships to get to the other side.

"I miss them, too," I told my brother. "A lot. And you know they would want us to be here for each other and to be happy."

"I know," Steele responded.

Jules texted to let me know he was waiting for me. I said my good-byes and made my way outside. Just as I was about to grab the car door handle, a stabbing pain engulfed my side. It took me completely by surprise and dropped me to my knees. Within seconds, Jules was by my side.

"What is it? Are you okay?" he asked.

I couldn't move and couldn't speak. I looked into Jules's eyes and tried to send him the message, but it still wasn't working. It took all of my strength to muster the words, "Home, now."

He scooped me up and gently placed me inside the car. He sped out of the parking lot. The next wave of pain came over me and I screamed.

"Sera, what is it? What is happening?" he yelled. "I am taking you back to the hospital."

"No!" I managed to get out. "It's Omega."

Jules picked up his speed sensing my despair. He knew, besides Steele, Omega was the last remaining part of my family still left on Earth. I doubled over in pain, knowing something had happened to him. We squealed into the driveway and Jules came over to get me. I told him to go check on Omega and I would get myself inside. He was gone in a flash. I mustered the strength to stand and the pain was gone. Instantly. But it was replaced with a knowing sense of dread. I ran inside and the look on Jules's face said it all. Omega lay limp on the kitchen floor.

"Can you do something?" I screamed. "Can I do something? Suck out his blood, replace it with venom, do what you did to me. Please Jules! Do something!" I pleaded with him and grabbed his shirt. "You can't let him die. We can't!"

Jules stood motionless, just staring at me and shaking his head. "Seraphina, I can't. He's gone. His soul has ascended. I can't get it back. Therions can't be changed anyway. I'm sorry."

I collapsed on top of my beloved friend. My protector. My Omega. I put my head down on his body and sobbed. I must have laid there with Omega for an hour before Jules dragged me upstairs to the bedroom and told me he'd deliver Omega to Brock and the others at camp for a proper burial.

Jules had inspected Omega's body but found no visible sign of injury but was sure that Brock would be able to figure out what happened. I immediately thought something was suspicious. There is no way he would have just passed out and died. I demanded that Jules inspect the camera system at the house. He complied. There was a power outage for about five minutes, which was common for the neighborhood, but the solar power kicked everything back on after thirty seconds. Besides that very small window, nothing out of the ordinary was captured on the cameras. Before the short blip, Omega could be seen patrolling the grounds as usual around the mansion or chilling out in front of the fireplace. I knew in my heart that something was amiss.

The next few days passed slowly and miserably, for all of us. Jules took Omega home to Brock and the other Therions, and I skipped school basking in my sorrow. I spent most of each day with Steele, who was as distraught as I was. His physical wounds were healing quickly, however, and the doctor said he could be released in time for Omega's consecration and memorial ceremony in a few days. We planned to regroup and figure out the next phase of the plan then.

29. WE ARE STARS
WRAPPED IN SKIN

IT WAS EXACTLY FOUR WEEKS FROM THE SNOW MOON. WE HAD
no new crystals and no new plan to get them. Today, after Omega's consecration, we would hopefully come up with a new plan. For everything we'd
been through, there had to be something we could do. This couldn't be how
it was meant to end.

I wasn't at all sure what to expect from the ceremony, but on the ride
out Thane assured me it would be beautiful and help us gain closure. Jules
agreed to attend with us, at Thane's request and prodding, and to be there
in person for our meeting afterward.

Brock had prepared Omega's body on a sacrimonial basket made
from vines and twigs surrounded by flowers, plants, and crystals. Ten
Therions carried the basket and laid it along a gravel path leading to a
pristine alpine lake about a half mile from the main camp. The pathway
and site were illuminated with hundreds of white candles of all shapes and
sizes. The entire village, plus me, Steele, Jules, and Thane gathered around
the shrine in a circle. Noah stood on one side of me, and Jules was on the

other. It was only awkward for me since Noah had no idea about my feelings for Jules and Jules had zero feelings for me at all.

After chanting in that strange language I did not understand, Brock led us through the most amazing and fitting goodbye ceremony for our dear friend, protector, and confidante. Then one by one those who wanted to issue their own private farewell took turns approaching his body, touching it and placing personal items, all from nature like rocks or crystals, into the basket. I had his collar firmly gripped in my hand as I slowly walked over to him. I knew he wasn't here; I could sense that his soul had left. Nevertheless, I placed my hand on his head and told him how much I loved him, thanked him for his unconditional friendship and protection, and promised that we would meet again one day. After me, Steele, walking on crutches, made his way over, and said his goodbyes as well. When everyone was done, the same ten creatures lifted the basket off its riser and carried it to the edge of the lake. Each Therion grabbed a candle and lit the plants and twigs on fire and sent our beloved Omega's body into the crystal clear water.

After the ceremony, Brock advised us to all chill out for a bit and regroup in his tent in a few hours. Thane and Jules went to track down Amantes and Steele wanted to get in a nap. After the others dispersed, Noah asked me if I wanted to go for a hike to blow off some energy. I agreed. We walked in silence for a while, and he could tell I was upset. Finally, he broke the silence.

"Seraphina, I am so sorry for your terrible loss, for everything you've lost." He stopped walking and turned to face me. "If there is anything I can do..." He put his hand on my shoulder.

I didn't let him finish. I was completely overwhelmed with emotion and began to cry. He wrapped his arms around me, and the crying turned to uncontrollable, ugly sobbing.

"It's okay, Seraphina. It's okay. I'm here," he consoled.

We stood like that for a while until I could regain my composure. It felt wonderful to be there with him in that way.

"Do you trust me?" he asked after I stopped crying.

"I don't really know you but for some reason, I do. Yes," I said.

"Okay then, follow me." He motioned for me to walk with him through a hidden pathway in the woods.

I would never have known there was a path hidden behind thick shrubs. He pushed aside trees and bushes, and we trampled through the unmarked, makeshift dirt trail for about a hundred yards until the trail turned to stone and ended at a rock ledge over a huge pond. Steam billowed from the water. There was an enormous tree that curved over the ledge, and had a thick rope hanging down from it. Noah took off his shoes, shirt, and pants, leaving him standing there in nothing but boxer shorts. Even though there was still snow on the ground and the temperature was brisk, neither of us seemed to notice. He had an insane six-pack and long lean muscles…well everywhere. I tried to look away but couldn't stop staring.

"Follow me!" He grabbed the rope, backed up to give himself a running start, and swung out over the ledge. He let go at the highest point of his swing and did a backflip before he dropped into the water.

"Show off!" I yelled. For about five seconds I hesitated, realizing this would be the first time a guy had ever seen me take my clothes off. But I felt confident about my soccer-toned abs and legs. I stripped to my bra and panties—thanking the universe that they matched—and followed him minus the backflip.

The warm water felt amazing, like a hidden oasis in the middle of snow and ice patches.

"What is this place?" I asked as I swam over to him.

"Natural hot springs, open to Therions only!"

"Well, technically, I'm not a Therion," I said coyly.

"It will be our little secret." He touched my waist tentatively, but when I didn't shy away, took it as an invitation. He dragged me closer, water rippling around us, until his bare stomach pressed against mine.

"I think," I said, gaze locked on his. "I would like sharing secrets with you."

He kissed me, gently at first, as if to make sure it was okay. I responded back and, in that moment, the ugliness of the world faded away.

30. UNDER YOUR SPELL

WHEN NOAH AND I GOT BACK FROM OUR HIKE THE OTHERS were all waiting for us inside Brock's tent—Brock, Jules, Thane, Steele and Amantes. Noah excused himself.

We decided that since the Witches were a dead end, for now, the biggest opportunity we had was to track down the three sacred Human gemstones. I relayed my suspicions about Mia and her possible involvement.

"We've known about her for a while, Sera, and if she's involved, I don't understand what her agenda would be," said Thane.

"And if she's evil, her umbra would have shifted," added Jules. "We've had her in our sights for two years, and she's been steady that whole time."

"Are you implying that my instincts aren't accurate?" I asked, annoyed.

"We're not implying anything," said Jules. "If she is *that* evil and if she is responsible for Omega's death, then we have a much bigger problem."

"Exactly what I was thinking," added Brock. "We'd be dealing with some seriously strong magic."

Amantes sat quietly, just listening.

"You're supposed to know everything about energy," Jules said to him. "Are we missing something?"

"My only guidance is that you should concern yourselves more with your own challenges," Amantes said. "You are asking the wrong questions."

"Oh, here we go again, with the useless information," muttered Jules.

"Julian," Amantes said. "You've seen a shift at the school. You've felt The Stirring, right?"

"Yes," Jules replied.

"Think about what you know of the Great Old Ones. Why the Alliance was formed," said Amantes. "Positive or negative actions impact the entire world on a quantum level. Positive actions create a ripple effect that helps others also choose positivity. On the flip side, negative actions tip the scale in a way that brings the energy of chaos and darkness upon the world. That is what the Old Ones want. That is why Arete 8 was formed. To counteract that negative force with united positive energy among all the earthly factions."

"You're right," Thane said. "Our number one priority has got to be finding the sacred gems. Forget Mia for now."

The group agreed. Jules recounted a story about these so-called sacred stones.

Back at the beginning of time, there were twelve sacred gemstones that came from the Mountain of God. It was the place where Moses received the ten commandments. The stones were entrusted to Moses, and he emblazoned them upon a holy breastplate to protect his brother, the high priest Aaron. Each stone represented one of the Israelite tribes. They are the Stones of Fire—Jasper, Sapphire, Chalcedony, Emerald, Sardonyx, Sardius, Chrysolite, Beryl, Topaz, Chrysoprasus, Jacinth and Amethyst. When assembled correctly, they held tremendous power. Ancient priests wore them as ornamental armor during the thirteenth century for protection and to speak with God. These stones, when together, had the power to summon angels and demons, and would allow us to open the correct door to locate Amelia's body and then reunite Arete 8.

"We only have six," said Thane.

"Right," said Jules, pulling out his laptop.

He opened up a document with pictures and details of each crystal group.

"Each faction was given three to guard. Therion gems are Jasper for healing, Sardonyx for protection, and Emerald for truth; Vampire gems are Sapphire for strength, Sardius for blood, and Chrysoprasus for release. The Witches should have Topaz for abundance, Chrysolite for durability, and Amethyst for connection to the divine. We need those gems plus the ones the Humans guard—Beryl for demon protection, Chalcedony for balance, and Jacinth for steadiness. We'll need a huge pulse of magical energy to find the Human stones without the help of our Witches."

"And then we still have the issue of their gems," I added.

"We should just go and steal them," Jules said.

"Let's concentrate on the Human stones," Brock added. "There are those who are born Witches and practice, and others who are born Human but have witchcraft in their ancestry, but the gene is dormant in this life. They are still drawn to it though. If we can find a way to tap into those Humans all at once…" his voice trailed off.

"I can do that with technology," said Jules. "We are all connected but we've lost our connection. Especially the Humans. If we can connect those Humans with witchcraft in their souls, at least on a small scale, we can harness that energy to reveal who's holding the Human crystals. We must get Humans to inadvertently perform a collective spell. I've helped manipulate, er, I've seen it done before," he said with a smirk as he jumped onto his computer and shared his screen with us.

"Here's an example of what I'm talking about. During an intense political climate back in 2017, a lot of these digital covens started popping up online, like this one," he said while navigating through social media pages. "It ignited matriarchal energy all over the country. Online covens formed mostly as a way to protest the so-called patriarchy but also to speak out against everything from war to injustice to politics. They would do live events to recruit members, light candles together, make music, honor the dead, things like that. I pretty much ignored it but studied it. It was fascinating. Sometimes they would even do collective spells."

"Seriously?" Steele asked.

"Dead ass. The line between collective actions and actual witchcraft can get a little fuzzy." He chuckled and zeroed in on one particular Facebook group. "Thanks to social media, self-proclaimed Witches don't have to gather in the woods or in front of the White House to perform collective spells anymore. A group of 'Witches' on this Facebook group actually tried to bind the President of the United States after he was elected. They informed their followers to gather certain ingredients and to all chant this one spell at the same time, every month—at midnight on every crescent moon. While there is power in collectively chanting a spell at a precise time to try and influence mass energy, it doesn't really work without certain elements and the right amount of people with witchcraft in their blood."

"Interesting," Brock replied. "I mean I can see how thoughts are powerful things and when those thoughts become words and words become actions, it can lead to physical manifestation. Like collective praying."

"Exactly. This Bind the President group has over five thousand members online," he laughed. "That group sparked others. Online covens hexed the guy being appointed to the Supreme Court, others formed so they could hex rapists and those who protect them, and on and on. The problem all these groups had—which we can avoid—is too many variables, not a specific enough goal, and too many mixed energies and intentions. It didn't work how they intended because they were novices. I, on the other hand, have been thinking about it for years. With my limited knowledge of witchcraft, plus a little help from a few friends, I think I can perfect it. We could smoke out the true Witch/Human energy and lead us right to crystals' exact location."

Just then my phone vibrated with a text.

It was Hannah.

Hannah! And just when we've thought the Witches were a dead end.

In the text she said she was going to try and send me a message via witchcraft and to watch for it. I texted back *"how?"*

But before she could even respond via text, a small piece of paper materialized in my hand. The others were staring at me. I unfolded the paper and read it aloud.

Dear Seraphina,

First, we have to apologize for our initial meeting. We were rude and you were nothing but sincere. To be fully transparent, Rachael has never known of our Wiccan background and my mother wanted to keep it that way for safety purposes. When the three of us (myself, Rachael, and our third sister—more about her later) have our powers activated, we are quite trackable. Our mother passed on yesterday and she left detailed instructions on what to do in the event of her death. First and foremost was to connect with you. I do not want to communicate digitally as that can be tracked as well. Rachael and I are on our way to Emberglow to meet with you and your brother immediately. Our flight lands at DIA tomorrow at 2 p.m. on Delta flight 516. If you could pick us up, that would be great.

Sincerely,

Hannah

I looked up at the others and all eyes were on me, hanging on every word.

"This is amazing!" I said.

"Interesting timing," said Jules, always the skeptic. "Coincidence?"

"There are no coincidences," said Amantes.

I think we all rolled our eyes at the exact same time.

"I can take you to the airport tomorrow," said Jules.

"That would be great," I said.

"I think I'd like to hang here tomorrow," said Steele, giving me a pleading glance. I knew he wanted to speed up his rehab and reconnect with Cayla, and whether it was the crystals, the positive energy or feeling the safety of the pack, his attitude had turned around.

"That works; I'll make sure to keep you posted," I told him. "The most important thing is that you're healing and regaining your strength, baby boy." It was a term of endearment I used to use sarcastically with him as kids, but in this case, I meant it more sincerely. Mostly. "You look tired. You should probably turn in for the night."

"Yeah, I am. And sounds good. Are you going to stay the night?"

"I think we should head back tonight," said Thane.

"Agreed," said Jules. "Brock, do you have a few more minutes? I had a few questions about Seraphina and her powers. I'm not sure you'll know the answers, but..."

"I can help explain," said Amantes.

I gave Steele a hug and he promised I would keep him posted about our quest. He left for his own tent.

That left me alone with Jules, Thane, Amantes and Brock. All eyes were on Jules.

"Sera's powers are growing and mine are fading," he began. "We are also sharing thoughts, but sporadically, and have stopped time between us for brief moments, creating this weird realm where only she and I exist."

I wouldn't call it weird; I'd call it amazing. I purposefully hid that thought from him. *How did I do that?*

"As your umbra gets darker, Seraphina, Julian's will get lighter," Amantes said. "That facilitates the power exchange. It would make perfect sense that you can share thoughts. Thoughts are just energy, out in the universe. When you are tuned in to one another's frequency, you can share that energy. I would imagine that has happened between you and Steele?"

"Yes, it has, but we've never created a separate space or stopped time," I said.

"That will become more frequent for you and Julian as your umbras reach equilibrium with each other," Amantes said.

"So how long before my powers are completely gone?" Jules asked.

"Only time will tell," said Amantes. "As long as it takes for your umbras to align."

"And then they'll be gone forever?" I asked.

"That depends, too," said Amantes.

"Great, thanks for all of these specific answers," said Jules.

"We'll figure it out," said Thane. "Hey, look on the bright side, Jules, you always wanted to be normal, right?"

Jules stood up. "Let's head back," he said. "Maybe one of our new Witch friends will be more helpful."

31. PROGRESS

THE GIRLS LOOKED DIFFERENT THAN WHEN I SAW THEM ON the field in California. Now, with their hair down and in normal clothes, they made quite a scene walking together through the airport. Boys and men alike did double takes as they drifted past. Women took notice of them too; these two were drop dead gorgeous and seemed to float rather than walk. They did have some some quirky and eccentric attributes, especially in the way they dressed. Rachael was more goth and wore black combat boots, black jeans, a black hard rock band t-shirt, and a black leather jacket. Hannah wore a long flowery pink and red dress but also paired it with black combat boots and a black leather jacket.

They saw us as we rounded the corner into the baggage claim area and made a beeline for us. Hannah came right up to me for a warm embrace and Rachael followed suit, albeit a little more awkwardly. I couldn't imagine how she must be feeling with the newfound knowledge of being a Witch coupled with her mom's death. I could relate and tried to send that feeling to her telepathically when we hugged. I guess that was becoming a habit, but with the girls, it didn't work. We made our basic introductions to Jules and Thane, explaining only that they were trusted friends, and headed to the car.

On the ride back they told us that their completely healthy fifty-five-year-old mom named Ruth, died in her sleep two nights ago.

"She was fine all night. She made her standard cup of turmeric and moringa tea, and went to bed around ten," said Rachael. "Then in the morning, she just wouldn't wake up."

She dropped her head into her hands and began to cry.

"We're going to have an autopsy done, but first her body has to be consecrated," added Hannah, her voice cracking.

"Mom left implicit instructions for us in the event of her death," Hannah continued. "Her friend, another Witch, gave us our family grimoire and inside the front cover was a note to find you. She said it was our number one top priority."

"What did you do with your mom's, um, body?" I asked.

"Our mom's friend is the town mortician. She has it and will keep it until we sort things out here," said Hannah.

Reading the grimoire brought them both enormous knowledge about their family tree. They uncovered many things that shocked them and others that they knew in their hearts since birth.

"Mom bound Rachael's powers when she was super young in order to protect the family from people who were hunting us," said Hannah.

"I have no memory of ever being a Witch," said Rachael.

Hannah on the other hand, knew witchcraft but said she never used it. Well, hardly ever, unless of course she was in a giant hurry and needed to quickly open a door or clean her room, but she was mostly a rookie and only knew enough to get her in trouble. Unfortunately, whenever she'd try to get better, her mom would always know when she was "using."

"I know first-hand how hurtful using magic can be," said Hannah. "But sometimes I would just dabble here or there."

She didn't elaborate further about magic being hurtful. I got the feeling it had something to do with their father, who they also didn't talk about except for saying that he too, died when the girls were young. Finding their mother's grimoire after she died opened their eyes to their lineage and ignited a strong passion for them to help reunite the Alliance, mostly because their mom had instructed them to.

"I'm sure our mom would have preferred to have told us these things in person," Hannah said. "But she had reasons for keeping us in the dark. Reasons that we now understand." She almost sounded like she was trying to convince Rachael of the facts.

"We understand that we have an obligation to help you reunite Arete 8. We will do whatever you need and whatever it takes," said Hannah.

"You mentioned something about a third sister in your note," I said.

"Yes," said Hannah, glancing at Rachael for a split second. She clasped her hands together before continuing. "We don't really like talking about it, but she died around the same time as our Dad. We were born Triad Witches and when we all cast magic at the same time, we were intensely powerful but also very easy to find."

I could tell that was all we were going to hear on that topic for the time being.

That night after our new allies settled into a guest room at Jules's place and freshened up, we all gathered in the basement to start planning. Jules and Thane gave them a basic intro course on Vampires and Therions, which they had grown up believing were fairytales and legends. They didn't seem too surprised to hear about their existence.

"I'm pretty sure our history teacher is a Vampire," Rachael said.

"If he lives out in the open, then a Therion would be a close ally," Thane said.

"I did see something about that in here," said Hannah, opening up their mother's grimoire.

It was the coolest book I had ever seen with thick brown leather binding and a giant seal stitched on the cover of three triangles intertwined. The sisters revealed that they did have the Witch faction crystals and would produce them when the time came but were currently somewhere safe. They also had a map, albeit encoded, that led to Amelia's location.

"The map is written in ancient Sazianu and encoded with a few cryptic proverbs. It looks like Amelia's body is inside an ancient Sazianu dwelling?" Hannah asked.

"Yes, the Sazianu moved her body here years after her death to keep it hidden just as we were getting close to finding her," said Jules. "After we wiped them out, history moved on and things were built on top of their underground cities, like Valiant High School."

"The only time the path to her can be found is on the upcoming Snow Moon. The Sazianu magic cannot hide the light of the Alliance from the Tetrad, whoever that is," said Hannah. "And it will illuminate only on the astral plane for the Tetrad."

"May I see that?" Jules asked.

She handed him the map and he studied it carefully.

"We've heard the same prophesy," I said. "The Tetrad and the illumination."

"The Sazianu were one of the first creatures to inhabit the land here in Colorado," said Jules. "Their name literally means, ancient old enemy. They were a vicious coven of hybrid Witch/demons connected to The Third Air. We thought we killed them all trying to find Amelia," he said, mostly to Thane. "We have never been able to crack their code or illuminate the path."

"They were always a sneaky, slithering bunch of heathens," Thane responded.

"Some would say you're talking about Vampires," Jules said.

"You said it, not me," Thane said, shooting him a grin and a wink.

Jules continued to study the map, holding it gently as if it would burn him.

While he did, Hannah asked us about the Human crystals.

"We know the Humans are on Maui and in the Turks and Caicos Islands," said Thane. "And we're hoping, with the help of your crystals, we'll see exactly where."

"And the twelve gems will unlock the door," I added. "But we'll need some ancient knife too, right?"

"Yes," said Thane. "We need both the Blade of Black Tourmaline and the Selenite Dagger to combine into The Blade of Cain. That will energize the set for protection and officially re-form the Alliance."

"Well, one of them is lodged into my sister's chest," said Jules. "And I have a good idea about how to find the other one."

32. I CRAVE MORE

It was all coming together. Sooner than later, I would see her again. They were so close that I could smell her. Seraphina, with traits now from all four factions, is the key to the illumination.

I knew reuniting the Alliance was the ultimate goal but being so close to finding Amelia made me almost rabid with anxiety. Ancient scripts, like most historical texts, get my story about fifty percent correct. The date is off by about seven hundred years but besides that small detail, the beginning is somewhat correct. Like most modern urban legends, it's a story based in truth but one that has been distorted by time and fear over the centuries.

Books that told of my story were banned by the Church or laced with arsenic, but remnants have leaked out in more modern times and especially with the invention of the internet. Born Amantes Burchard, I came to this Earth as a peasant and was orphaned five years later when disease struck our village, and the savage Vampires came.

I lived on my own traveling from camp to camp and family to family for about nine years. Living like a nomad taught me many things, mostly how to feed and protect myself. I was a master at weaponry. I'd spend hours alone in the woods making spears, swords, slingshots, and arrows.

I became known as Hunter—and I made a name for myself. I killed for food and started killing for money…until I met Amelia. She was the most beautiful creature I had ever seen. I remember watching her feed on the villagers from my hidden lair in the woods. They were the evil ones, the ones who sold women into slavery and were known for debauchery and rape. She and her brother ended them with ease and shared in the prize of engorging themselves with their evil life force. She felt me watching, her instincts were like those of a lioness, sharp and quick. In less than a second, she was in front me, inspecting me carefully like prey, but she must have sensed something less than evil because she spared me that day. She came back to check in on me from time to time and we formed a friendship, even though I was completely taken by her from the moment we met.

She followed me, trained me, and honed my murderous skills. Then she recruited me to be the paid assassin for Arete 8, a human weapon that was expendable yet purposeful. The ruling Alliance of the day lived in the shadows; their identities were a secret, but rumors spread of the magic among them.

The Alliance used me to do away with their earthly enemies. I never failed. I exterminated anyone, at any time, no matter how influential or protected the victims may have been.

Among my victims were kings, princes, duchesses, even illustrious churchmen. My blade of choice was a mystical dagger, imbued with magic and capable of either ending someone's life, or sending them to renew. It could also imprison a soul in its own personal Hell inside the dagger. Their fate was chosen by the Alliance.

For a time, life was grand. Amelia and I grew closer over the years and by the time I was sixteen our romance had blossomed. I had risen from an impoverished peasant to a successful nobleman.

I never questioned my orders until I met Mara. She tricked me. Hexed me and bewitched me, and ultimately recruited me for her own needs. But she also made me question my existence. She showed me the possibilities of the lives I cut short. She showed me the families they left behind, the sons and daughters, the sisters and brothers, and the mother and fathers who wept for their losses. The guilt weighed on my conscious, slowly at first, but then it began to suffocate me, crush me. I could barely function. I couldn't share my feelings with Amelia because she was on the council and she was, after all, a Vampire. It forced a wedge between us and drew Mara closer to me. Unbeknownst to me, the people the Alliance ordered me to execute were evil, so evil that their actions strengthened the Great Ones. But Mara twisted reality. She eventually made me believe that one of the kings I had murdered had been a decent man. His only crime was to have defended his people, so he didn't deserve to die.

From that moment on, I changed my mentality about murder. One by one, I started making amends with my victim's families. I worked as a double agent of sorts, serving the Alliance but also helping people escape death. Still in love with Amelia, I met with Mara in secret. She used her spells to help me hide the victims I was ordered to kill. She altered the Blade, so the souls taken would be resurrected a short time later to trick the Alliance.

She lied. The Blade absorbed their souls, but they were all evil. It powered the Blade with darkness. With every kill it became more power-ful. Her ultimate goal was to charge it enough to trap the Alliance members and removing them from this realm of existence forever.

Eventually her true agenda was revealed when she told me that my latest mark was her father. He was an old Monk lying somewhere in an underground dungeon. The Monk's gossip had created a dangerous atmosphere for the council, and I was ordered to execute him. But Mara convinced me to save him instead.

I had only little time to save the Monk, as he was about to be executed the very next day. I left the bed that Amelia and I shared with her thinking I was about to go to work. But she knew something was off. I went to the Monk and took the sick, old man out of the dungeon. I did not realize Amelia was following me, silently and swiftly, hoping to understand why I had become so distant. I carried the Monk out of the dungeon on my back and fought off several soldiers on the way out, sustaining serious injury. My wounds were not lethal at first, but I knew that losing so much blood may attract dangerous predators.

Weighing the odds, I decided to take the man to rest in a nearby forest until dawn. I'll never forget our odd conversation then. The old man said to me "God bless you child," but since I didn't believe in Heaven or in Hell at that time, I told him that I saved him according to my own decision, not to worship any deity. I had lost a lot of blood. I could sense the beasts nearby. If I had only known that my love was also watching so close by, things may have turned out differently.

I bid farewell to the Monk, asking him to let me die alone, in peace; and then I thrust my dagger into the ground. The Monk disappeared just before Mara appeared. She looked different. She touched my face and kissed me. She then grabbed the dagger out of the ground and lifted it toward the sky. I was so weak I couldn't speak and the whole time, Amelia was watching.

Mara's face was flush with anger, and it distorted the features so that I almost didn't recognize her. Relieved to see her nonetheless, I was completely taken by surprise when she lifted the glowing blade from the ground. The last thing I saw was my reflection in its shiny surface as she severed my head from my body in one fell swoop. Amelia emerged from the shadows a millisecond too late. Distraught by my adultery and conflicted by my murder she grabbed Mara by the hair and threw her like a ragdoll against a tree. Amelia grabbed Mara's injured body and literally squeezed her to death, draining every drop of blood. That was when the Blade glowed so intensely that it split in two in an enormous explosion, both halves falling to the ground.

By this time my soul had left my body and I floated above the scene, helplessly watching every heart wrenching moment. Completely manic at this point, Amelia grabbed the weapon closest to her and thrust it inside her heart. The Monk returned to see the bloody scene and lost his mind over the death of his daughter. He harnessed the power from the other half, the Selenite Dagger, to curse Amelia and all of the Alliance members, hiding them from each other in perpetuity to never be able to form against him again.

Meanwhile, in limbo, I noticed a hole opening in the ground and a demon emerged to claim my soul. The demon told me he was sent to take me to Hell with full honors, as a reward for the considerable number of murders I had perpetrated. I hesitated and did not want to go.

"No," I told it. "I do not belong there and if you insist, I will raise a palace from your bones and the bones of every last demon in Hell!"

That was when an angel of pure light appeared and spoke to the demon, "He isn't yours! This soul has chosen so much good that it exceeded the evil, and he will come along with us to heaven."

But the angel of darkness did not retreat, and both pulled out their swords.

Much to the angels' fright, exactly at that moment something else appeared, something the angels knew about, but had never seen before. It was iL Separatio, wearing a cloak with a hood, underneath which neither the face, nor the hands or feet could be seen. iL Separatio made a sign with his hand and at once the two angels trembled in fear.

It told them, "You are both wrong. This man has done as many good deeds as evil. So everything is balanced – you won't have him, neither of you. He belongs to me."

The absolute power of iL Separatio made the angels disappear. It then turned to me and said, "Get up, Amantes, as you have no more wounds now. You will live as long as you wish. If you will do evil deeds, it doesn't matter. The balance will compensate for it, as other people will be born to do good deeds. If you decide to do good deeds, it still won't matter, as other people will be born to do evil deeds. You no longer exist for this universe. You are Karma. Live on Earth as long as you want, until this species goes extinct. You can move everywhere you wish with the power of your mind; you may not directly interfere, but your essence will enact balance in the world, and you must use that to teach others."

iL Separatio vanished and from that point forward I have lived among men, and beasts, and supernaturals, and I've watched, assisted and helped maintain the balance of the world, always trying to understand further on what is good, what is bad, and why. I regretted those last few months of my time on Earth tremendously and especially regretted the wasted time I spent with Mara and being so easily manipulated by her. All I wanted was to have that time back. To have Amelia back and to spend the rest of my days making memories together. I took for granted the little things. The walks in the woods, the way she walked, her intensely beautiful smile, and the way she smelled. I missed the days we spent together laying in the forest doing nothing at all but being together. I was tired of balance. I needed love. Her love.

33. LIKE MAGIC

I TRIED TO PICTURE WHAT AMELIA LOOKED LIKE IN MY MIND. I had a blurry vision of her through my time inside Jules's mind and from my mother. I knew she had long dark hair and silver eyes with a blue ring around the iris. I wondered what she was like. How would she change the dynamic of my relationship with Jules? Would we get along? And how would she affect Jules? His voice broke my train of thought.

"We are closer than we have ever been to having all twelve stones and locating Amelia's body," said Jules.

"Careful buddy," interjected Thane. "If I didn't know better, I would think you sound a little optimistic."

That made me smile. Maybe his umbra was shifting more positive.

"No positive thinking here," he snapped back. "I am just stating the facts."

Or maybe not.

"The Sazianu didn't use a written language; they only used symbols and drawings. They were also known for their ridiculously complex network of underground tunnels and hidden rooms that led to the temples they called Vikus. Looking at the Sazianu symbols on this map, it seems like they form a path to where she is hidden, and if I had to guess it's inside a Viku pit."

Hannah opened the grimoire to a page she had dog eared.

"This whole section is devoted to the Sazianu and their symbols," she said, showing the pages to the group. "They worshipped the ground and the spirits within it," she read.

"More like they worshipped the Great Ones, and their evil essence that poisons the Earth," Jules added.

Hannah ignored him and continued.

"They believed the Earth gave their leaders supernatural powers, like super strength, and animalistic qualities similar to Therions—great climbing skills, speed, and telepathy. They built their cities on the sides of cliffs and extended underground. They weren't all evil creatures, but a specific cult emerged among them."

"Yeah, and it was hard to tell the difference," Thane chimed in. "They initiated their members into the cult when they turned ten."

"You're right," Hannah said. "The cult was into things like cannibalism and devil worship. They thought eating their members would give them powers."

"I hate relying on some ancient prophesy about seeing the illumination on the astral plane during the Snow Moon. If you give me and Thane some time, I think we'll be able to decipher the map. Once upon a time we got pretty good at speaking their language," Jules said, giving Thane a wink.

"Okay, well good luck with that," said Hannah.

"I think we should concentrate on finding the Human crystals," I said. "Jules, let's insert the Witch crystals into your simulation and see exactly where these Humans are."

After we linked the Witches' crystals with ours, we were able to pinpoint the exact location of the Humans who should hold the crystals. Like a beacon, their locations pulsed on the screen.

"My mother had been tracking the Humans over the years and I cannot believe how easy it was with our gems linked like this," Hannah said, amazed at the technologically savvy set up of our Vampire host.

"I actually don't find that hard to believe at all," said Thane. "Everything seems to be lining up at this exact moment in time for either us reuniting the Alliance or..." his voice trailed off.

"The world as we know it spiraling into chaos and exploding!" Jules chimed in happily.

"There's the Jules I know and love," said Thane.

"If your mom was tracking them, then wouldn't it stand to reason that other Witches—like bad ones—are doing the same thing?" I asked.

"Absolutely," said Hannah. "Why, what are you thinking?"

That's when we told the girls about Mia. We gave them the background information about the student club at school, my interactions with her, and the herbs she peddles at school. I unloaded my suspicions that she is somehow involved even though Jules and Thane doubted me. Hannah and Rachael agreed that if she were able to hide her true intentions from a Vampire, she must be into some seriously dark and powerful magic.

"If dark forces get control of the blades, even one of them, that will not be good," Hannah said. "It's an extremely powerful weapon. Whether this girl is involved or not, we need to make sure one of us gets to Amelia first."

"How would another Witch track the crystals if all of us just barely managed to do it?" asked Rachael.

"There is a huge amount of energy coming from Valiant High School, most likely due to its Sazianu connection and from Amelia and the Blade. Technically another Witch could use that energy to try and find the crystals," said Thane.

"I am telling you. Mia is bad news. Somehow, she is involved and so is the Students With Light group," I said.

Jules explained to the Witches about the group and how it had been gaining momentum not only online but also at the school. He took the girls deeper into his digital dungeon and showed them his massive social media enterprise and tracking devices. He ran through it quickly and efficiently without so much of a peep out of either sister, but I could tell their heads were spinning.

"This is incredible," Rachael said.

"Humans, and unawakened Witches, no offense, are dumb," said Jules. "They put their entire lives online. Whether it's a ten-year photo challenge that arms our facial recognition software or a silly survey that lets us know every hint we need to figure out their passwords, people have completely surrendered their lives to these computers and smart phones. I've never seen such ignorance in the thousands of years I have been on this planet, and trust me, I've seen a lot of ignorance. It's super helpful to a Vampire like me though, who needs to know where to feed, when to hide, or what groups to join."

"If mom would have had access to these types of resources," Hannah said. "Maybe we wouldn't have had to live on the run and things may have turned out differently for her."

"Which is why we are going to make a formidable team together," I said. "So back to the student group. I suggested this before, but we need to send in a spy. There are still about four weeks until the Snow Moon. We cannot take any chances that anyone will find Amelia and the blade before we do."

"I'll do it," Rachael said almost instantly.

"What are you talking about?" asked Hannah, sending Rachael a look that could kill.

I could tell there was a lot more meaning to that look than any of us knew.

"It's fiiine," Rachael insisted. "I feel...helpless. I'm this supposedly powerful Witch who has no powers and I want to do something helpful. Please, it's not a big deal. It's just going to high school, meeting new people, and joining a group."

"It's a good idea," Jules chimed in.

"Oh, *now* you think it's a good idea," I muttered under my breath, knowing he could hear me.

"If there is anything magical or supernatural about the group, they'd pick up on a practicing Witch in an instant," said Jules. "But since her powers are bound, she's our best bet."

Hannah shook her head. "No. Absolutely not. It's too dangerous."

"Hannah! I am literally going to school and talking to people! You are not my mother! I am doing it and I am not asking your permission!" replied Rachael.

"Fine, go get yourself killed," Hannah scolded.

"But before that, make sure to befriend Cole," Jules said. "He's Mia's best friend. Get in good with him, maybe flirt a little, and get him to trust you. Also, the best way to turn an enemy into a friend is to make a problem for them, and then help them solve it. I can take care of that."

Jules hopped onto his computer and hacked into their Facebook group. "A little computer problem should get their attention. Just show up and pretend to be a tech- head. I'll walk you through how to fix the bug I just planted."

"They also love newcomers," I added. "So most likely the vulture will pounce on you the instant she sees you," I told Rachael.

"While you all handle the teenager stuff, Thane and I can go spend a few days in the islands hunting Humans,"

"Human crystals, he means," Thane added.

We had a plan, and we all knew our parts. Tomorrow we would execute.

34. I LIKE THE WAY IT HURTS

He had the three deviants lined up in chairs against the wall of the dimly lit warehouse, with their hands zip-tied and mouths bound with duct tape. Their captor asked them, not expecting a response, how they would like to die.

"The drugs you were selling to those kids, those middle school minors, are not only toxic," he said. "But they also, in small doses, make people highly suggestible."

The vigilante took out a business card, cut the ties on one of his hostage's wrists, and handed him the card.

"In other words, just touching a piece of paper laced with it, can begin to have an effect," he said.

The hostage's eyes widened, and his pupils slowly began to dilate.

"That's it, already working," said the captor as he revealed a sharp-edged blade from his back pocket. "But you already know that, don't you? You've known all along about how many kids have died from your drugs. How many girls have been raped because of them, and the trail of destruction you have left behind, haven't you? Now why don't you take this blade from me. Turn to your friend over there and cut his throat. Go ahead, take it," he commanded.

The hostage, his will diminished from the drug, had no choice but to take the blade. He visibly struggled with the choice which made it even sweeter to watch. He held the blade to his friend's neck, stopping just short of cutting it.

"That's it," the captor urged. "Do it, now."

The hostage slit his friend's throat. The victim began to gurgle as blood spilled. Right before he lost consciousness and slipped into the after-life, the overseer knew that the dying delinquent would see his distorted reflection in the glowing blade that ended him, and the shimmering blue and silver eyes that bore into his soul as the beast muttered three words to him.

"*Nam-tar, Tesh, Kur.*"

The monster then leaped on top of him and finished him off, drain-ing every last bit of blood from his body as the remaining two hostages watched in horror. The demon came up for air with blood dripping from his mouth and asked, "Who's next?"

35. BIG WITCH ENERGY

THE NEXT DAY AT SCHOOL PLAYED OUT EXACTLY HOW I thought it would. Mia basically throttled Rachael and Hannah with her insincere, sickening, sugary sweet talk to welcome them to school and coerce—*I mean convince*—them to join the club. Trying to act uninterested in their conversation while I loaded books into my locker, I overheard Hannah say she'd be too busy with her STEM classes but as planned, Rachael acted excited and interested and agreed to attend today's meeting after school. *Not bad acting.* We all agreed that we shouldn't act too friendly toward each other at school so as not to arouse suspicion, so I closed my locker and walked right by the girls without giving them a second glance.

Morning announcements informed the student body about the upcoming girls basketball playoff game this evening, reminded everyone about this afternoon's SWL meeting in the chapel, and announced ticket sales for the upcoming Winter Dance. It was exactly three weeks before the Snow Moon. I could hear Amantes's words in my head about coincidences loud and clear. The theme for the Winter Dance was masquerade formal which made me daydream about dancing the night away in a beautiful gown. I pictured two scenarios—one with Noah and one with Jules. My heart beating faster at the thought of Jules in a tuxedo. I bet he'd look so damn good. My Bible teacher's voice broke my train of thought.

"Seraphina, that is your name correct?" he said staring at me.

"Oh sorry Mr. Engulu," I answered. "Yes, the Bible verse I chose for my project is Revelation 21:15-21." I chose the passage due to its connection to our quest and figured if I was researching the stones, I might as well get school credit for it.

"Interesting choice Ms. Grayson. I'm going to assign Josh as your work partner since your verses are complementary and I'll put you both down for an in-class presentation on Monday."

"Ugh, okay," I said awkwardly, looking over at Josh, an upperclassman who did not seem thrilled to be working with me at all. Rachael, on the other hand got paired up with Cole for the project and he looked rather pleased to be "stuck" with her. I wasn't sure it was exactly a coincidence but either way, it was fortuitous for us. The sooner she could figure out what that group was up to, the better.

Not surprisingly, after Hannah turned down Mia's request to join the club, she was suddenly the school pariah. Mia didn't hunt her down and harass her like she did with me, most likely due to our knock down drag out fight in the hallway. And despite Hannah being gorgeous, the boys avoided her, and the girls whispered behind her back. It was hard to imagine what they could be possibly whispering about since she literally just arrived here, and no one even knew anything about her but that was Mia for you. She was able to either anoint or dethrone someone depending on their feelings toward that stupid club. So, Hannah's best effort at meeting people was to get involved with student leadership and try to get onto the upcoming Winter Dance decoration committee. Apparently, event planning was kind of her thing back in California.

As for her sister, it took a matter of days for Rachael to get cozy with Cole. She was miraculously able to fix the club's Facebook glitch after attending the first meeting and overhearing Cole and Mia discussing the issue. After that, Cole took to her immediately. He even asked Rachael to the Winter Ball. If I didn't know better, I would have thought she may actually have feelings for him. She insisted otherwise.

While Hannah was having a much harder time making friends, Rachael was instantly popular. Most days Rachael and Cole would sit with Mia and her crowd during lunch and Hannah would hang with me, Avery, and a few other loners but today Hannah and I decided to go off campus for lunch and Rachael decided to join us, sensing something was wrong with Hannah.

She was certainly in a bad mood and had been grumpy all morning. The three of us texted our plan to meet in the back of the school and walk to the shopping center behind it. It was a beautiful sunny day and a great opportunity to get some fresh air. Jules mentioned that as a new Vampire, the sunlight would weaken me, but I didn't feel that effect yet and the bright UV rays shining on my face felt exhilarating. I felt the same way with the Full Moon. It energized me even though Brock gave me the same warning about its light, that most Therions were weakened by it. I hoped I would never have to hide from either. We walked across the street to our favorite Sushi restaurant to talk privately. We sat down and ordered a literal boatload of sushi. I was ravenous.

"Okay, spill it," Rachael said to Hannah. "You look miserable. What happened?"

"I'm just over this school already. It's a bunch of stuck up, privileged rich kids who are mean and I hate everyone," Hannah unloaded and began to tear up. "I have no friends, everyone is talking about me behind my back and bullying me. Then today I even got a snap from some jackass about resigning from student leadership, because no one wants me there."

"Are you kidding me?' I said. "That's bullshit. We need to have Jules track that snap down and then confront that asshole! But can't you do some spell from your grimoire to like…be popular or something?"

"I told you, Sera. Witchcraft can be dangerous. Especially when used for personal gain or petty things like that," Hannah said.

"Hannah," Rachael said, "the only reason people like me is because of Mia and her stupid club. As soon as I get the info we need from Cole, we can leave this dumb school and go wherever we want. For that matter we can take our GED, and just go travel the world. Screw high school!"

Hannah mustered a smile. "Thanks, Rach. That sounds like a good plan to me."

"On that note," I said. "Find anything good out yet from Cole?"

"Well," Rachael whispered and leaned in closer. "Something is definitely up. He keeps mentioning some big event that Mia has planned, and it has something to do with the tattoos, but I haven't been able to get close enough to him…I mean…get enough info out of him yet. I think I'll get him nice and talkative though the night of the dance. We're going to a pre-party, and he definitely gets chatty after a beer or two."

"The sooner the better," Hannah replied.

"I've been trying to watch for Mia's umbra to reveal itself, but I've had absolutely zero luck. I just don't understand how she'd be hiding it," I said almost to myself.

"Have you heard anything from Thane and Jules about the Human crystals?" Hannah asked.

"Last I heard was yesterday. They found the Humans on Maui, but they could not find the crystals. They struck out there and were headed to the Caribbean to try for the others."

"Couldn't his Vampire skills make them turn the gems over?" said Rachael.

"He said the Humans on Maui were clueless descendants and...he can't compel people anymore," I said.

They both looked at me perplexed and I explained the backstory of Jules turning me into a Vampire and me now being some sort of hybrid.

"Sera. This is huge," said Hannah.

"Yeah, I know," I said. "Jules is pretty damaged about the whole thing. He can still feed but his strength and speed and compulsion..."

"No, no, not that," said Hannah. "The prophecy. It talks about the Tetrad. We didn't know what that meant. The one with powers from all four factions. You are a Human with Therion DNA and you've been turned into a Vampire. Do you have Witchcraft in your line?"

"I don't think so, but I guess I'm not sure," I said. "I had no idea about being a Therion for sixteen years of my life, so... but what would that mean anyway?"

"On the night of the Snow Moon, the Tetrad will see the illumination," said Hannah.

I swallowed. I didn't know what to say. "How would we know if I had Witchcraft in my line?"

"I actually don't know," said Hannah. "I'll have to do some research."

"Have you ever practiced astral projection?" Rachael asked.

"I don't even know what that really means," I answered.

"Let's work on that later tonight," said Hannah. "You have three weeks to master it. I think it's you. I think you're the Tetrad."

"Focus on the goal Hannah," said Rachael, patting her sister's arm. Our job is to help reunite the Alliance. Nothing else matters. Don't let these petty idiots at school get to you. But I am curious, did you get the spot on the dance decoration committee?"

"Get the spot? That's a thing?" I asked. "Like can't you just volunteer?"

"It's a big thing, if you ask her," said Rachael. "Saving the world comes first, of course, but the dance committee is a close second."

We all collapsed into giggles.

"It's a popularity contest at this school, and you have to be chosen, voted for, to be on it,' said Hannah. We had the vote, and they are announcing the winners this afternoon at the student leadership meeting, but I seriously doubt anyone voted for me. Bunch of assclowns." Hannah shoved a huge piece of sushi in her mouth.

Who ever heard of an election to choose volunteers? What a joke.

We finished up lunch and headed back to school. I couldn't stop thinking about astral projection and wanted to get home to interrogate the girls further about it, but first I promised Hannah I would pop into the leadership meeting for moral support.

After school that day about fifty kids shuffled inside one of the larger Language Arts classrooms for the student leadership meeting. I found Hannah lingering at the doorway and we walked inside together and found a seat near the back of the room. It was mass chaos as everyone was buzzing about the school dance and excitedly waiting to hear if they had been voted onto the five-person decoration committee.

"Okay, quiet. Quiet everyone!" the President of the club yelled out to try and gain control of the room. Her name was Kelly, and she was a super annoying junior who had major control issues.

"The first name on the decoration committee is…" she announced, pausing for dramatic effect and the room fell into total silence. "Christy Edmonds!"

Hannah rolled her eyes and the rest of the room clapped.

"Okay, one down and four to go!" Kelly said like she was announcing the winner of the Nobel Peace Prize or something.

Just then the door opened and in walked Rachael. Every eye in the room turned onto her.

"Can I help you?" asked Kelly.

"Oh, yeah, I was just looking for… my sister," Rachael said, scanning the room. "There she is! Hey Hannah," she said as she walked toward us and sat in an empty chair next to Hannah amidst whispers and stares.

No one at school knew the two were related, and we had talked about not revealing that to anyone, but I guess now the cat was out of the bag. So much for the strategy of keeping our distance from each other.

"Oh boy," Hannah said under her breath and smirking.

Ignoring the interruption, Kelly continued with her announcements.

"The second person voted onto the committee is…Abigail Little!" exclaimed Kelly. Everyone clapped and cheered.

"Is this for real?" Rachael said to me and Hannah.

Just then the girl in front of us whispered to her friend, "Sisters from two different misters if you ask me."

The girl next to her let out a guffaw. But just as she did, a tiny piece of metal from her three-ring binder snapped off and hit her in the mouth.

"Ow!" she wailed.

Rachael smiled with an evil grin

Hannah elbowed her. "Don't do that."

"What? That wasn't me? That was Karma," Rachael whispered.

Hannah snorted.

"And the last three people to get a spot on the committee are Aubrey Burwood, Melanie Walker and finally..." she paused and flipped through her papers. "Um, finally, I am so happy to announce," she paused again, seeming flustered and flipped through more papers. "It's...um...it's," she faltered.

I looked at Rachael and she had her elbows on the desk, her chin gently resting on her hands, glaring right at Kelly but looking very pleased with herself.

"Well, who is it?" Rachael demanded.

"It's Hannah Adams."

Everyone in the room began whispering.

"Yes!" Rachael exclaimed, clapping loudly. "Go Hannah!" she said, still the only one in the room clapping, besides me of course.

She turned toward both us and whispered, "*Now that was me.*"

Hannah smiled. I guess someone *did* know how to do magic after all. So much for that speech at lunch. It made me like them both even more.

36. CRIPPLED ANGER

JULES AND THANE WERE SET TO RETURN HOME TONIGHT. THEY struck out in Maui and the Turks and Caicos Islands and had zero to show for their travels. I was anxious to hear what happened and to plan our next step. I scoured the internet about signs that might show that I was Witch. Am I drawn to nature, do I see repeating numbers, have I made a deal with the devil. Ugh. It was entirely unhelpful.

One thing was certain. While the boys had been away, my Vampire senses continued to improve daily. I wondered if that meant that Jules's skill had diminished even more. Amantes said eventually he would lose all supernatural powers except the ability to feed.

My hearing was so good now that I could make out every word Hannah and her new committee friend Aubrey were saying in the next room as clearly as if they were right in front of me. They were busy planning for the decorations at the dance. I tried to tune them out by turning on the TV and mindlessly flipping through the channels. I stopped on the local news when something caught my attention. It was a picture of a cop and the newscaster was saying he had been missing for three days. He looked super familiar and that's what held my gaze.

Normally, I never watched the news. I hated it. My mom was a TV news reporter when she was right out of college and because of that, she was a huge critic. She'd say the news was a bunch of garbage with the lines blurred between entertainment and true journalism. She taught us to never believe anything we saw on the news or in print without questioning the agendas that might be at play.

How did I know that police officer? I couldn't place it. He was last seen heading out on patrol three nights ago in downtown Denver and virtually disappeared. His GPS tracker on his patrol car had been turned off and the dash cam video had been erased. They suspected either foul play or possible suicide. That's when it came back to me. He was the officer that Jules had compelled the night that Steele was arrested. Dang, he was a super nice guy. I'd have to ask Jules about it later. I really hoped he would be found. I turned the channel to the food network to numb my mind. Brainless TV is what I was searching for and yet, I couldn't turn my mind off the dance.

The dance was coming up in two weeks and I still didn't have a date. Everyone I knew either had a date or was going with friends or was on a dance committee. Somewhere inside my irrational mind, I thought Jules might ask me, but he'd been extremely distant lately and hardly checked in at all while off in the islands. I had no idea what time they were getting back, and I could tell I needed to feed.

I knew it was time because at night when the moon was at its brightest, I felt shaky, and my eyes shimmered if I stared at myself in the mirror. I tried to put it off as long as I could, but it was approaching three weeks since I last fed. The darkness of others was calling to me, drawing me in. I just didn't feel comfortable doing it alone so that night when the urge was almost unbearable, I contemplated texting Scarlett to ask for help. She hadn't shown her face since the Steele incident, and I didn't want to reignite that argument so I decided against reaching out to her.

One level down, Jules's Vampire minions were monitoring away in their digital dungeon. I thought I'd head down there and maybe ask Devyn to help me. Just as I landed on the bottom step though I saw a dark shadow exit the sliding glass doors. It was Jules. Why didn't he tell me he was back? The lights were on in the back room, meaning the other vamps were working so I slowly and quietly slid out the doors behind him. I saw his smoke plume heading out across the backyard and toward the Denver city skyline. What a jerk.

I reached into my pocket and grabbed the crystal he gave me a couple of weeks back determined to follow him and demand an explanation and his help feeding tonight.

I took off my shoes and socks and stepped out onto the snow to ground myself and felt the cold encompass my feet and ankles. I was able to reach alpha level much quicker. Instead of focusing in on the blackness that called to me, I focused in on Jules. His scent and his aura. I locked on and instantly turned to smoke, following his trail. I materialized in front of a desolate warehouse somewhere downtown. There was a door slightly ajar with a faint light on inside. I heard voices. One of them was Jules's. I walked toward the door and tuned my hearing inside.

"What exactly was your thought process?" he asked,. "Did you actually think you would get away with kidnapping a cop? How did you see this playing out? Were you going to leave him here to starve and die or were you planning on killing him with a weapon of some sort, like this knife?"

I heard muffled groans coming from inside the room. I decided to peek in. What I saw terrified me. There was a man, in uniform, curled up on the floor, bleeding from the head and unconscious. It was the cop I recognized from the news. Was he alive? There were two other men sitting in chairs tied up with duct tape across their mouths. They were also bleeding, but from their necks. And there was Jules, hovering above them, mostly back in physical form but still smoking near his feet. His face was contorted, angry, demonic. I had never seen it like that before. He was seething. He was ugly. He ripped the tape off one of the men's mouths.

"You seem like the more rational one," Jules said to him. "And you have less blackness oozing from your skin."

"We weren't going to kill him, I swear," pleaded the man as he gasped for air. "At least I wasn't. I kept trying to convince Billy to let him go. And I brought him water every day. It just…it just got out of hand. We saw him at the gas station and Billy yelled at him, called him a pig, and threw a beer can at his head. He turned toward us and was about to shoot his taser thing at us and Billy just—he just grabbed his baseball bat from the car and hit him with it. He was bleeding, like everywhere and we panicked. We didn't want to go down as no cop killers, you know? But I swear I was bringing him water. Billy was the one who wanted to shoot him to erase all evidence, not me! Please dude, don't kill me."

"Shut up, you imbecile. Your umbra is literally hemorrhaging darkness," Jules sneered at him and lunged at the man's throat, biting it so hard he screamed out with the highest pitched moan I had ever heard. His partner squirmed in his restraints and tried to free himself, screaming himself underneath the duct tape.

"Jules," I said I as entered the room, making myself visible.

He stopped mid suck and lifted his face from the criminal's neck, who had now lost so much blood that he'd passed out. Jules almost looked embarrassed.

"What the hell are you doing here?" he said to me with the man's blood dripping from his mouth and chin. It made me salivate.

"You are killing him," I said.

"So what?" he retorted back. "You can see his umbra, right? He's a vile, evil creature. They both are. Creatures like this who exploit children, sell drugs, kill cops? They don't deserve to remain on this planet. And they don't deserve a refresh, a do over, or whatever happens when Humans die. Let the Devil deal with them for a few thousand years inside this Dagger," he said pulling a glowing dagger from his back pocket.

"You know you want to feed on them too. Their umbras call to you, just like they do for me."

"How many people have you done this to?" I asked, not really expecting an answer. I continued, "It is not our job to kill them. Feed on them, sure. Push them toward their dark impulses, okay. But killing them makes us just as bad!"

"They beat a police officer to within inches of his life. And this scumbag was about to shoot him. He has a family. He helps people. He may have made some mistakes and made some bad choices, but he does not deserve to die. I fed on him. We were connected. His umbra was leaning brighter and then this happens to him? I may not be able to use compulsion anymore but I can still avenge him."

"That is not for you to decide Jules. Is this what you do when you go off every night? Go on a killing spree? You have got to fight this urge. You need to let them go," I said as I walked toward the criminal with the tape on his mouth.

"Seraphina, DO NOT TOUCH HIM," he said, face turning ugly and contorted again.

I put my body between the criminal and Jules and just as I did the bad guy broke free from his restraints and grabbed a pocketknife out of his jeans. In a split-second Jules knocked me out of the way stepping right in front of the criminal's thrusting knife. Just before the weapon entered his stomach it happened again. We left the real world. We entered our private realm when everything else around us faded away and time seemed to stop. I knew as soon as it ended though, he was about to be stabbed. He threw himself in front of the knife for me.

"Jules, I..." I started to speak but then stopped. "Thank you for doing that."

He seemed taken aback.

"Whenever this private reality ends, I imagine you're about to be stabbed," I stated.

"I'll be fine. There's only one way to kill a Vampire, and that's not it," he replied.

I thought about that and definitely wanted to ask about it but there were more pressing matters at hand, and I had no idea how long this would last.

"This does not involve you, Sera. It's something I have to do. I have no other powers left. You took them."

"That's not fair," I said.

"*This* sustains me. It gives me pleasure and purpose," he said. "And if you join me, it will give you pleasure as well."

"I understand you want to kill bad people," I replied. "But we are only supposed to kill those who are already dying, at the point of no return. You killing bad people is the light inside of you battling the dark. You want to do good; you want to get rid of the bad, and stop them from hurting others, but this isn't the way. They have to make their own choices. If they choose to continue down a dark path, the universe balances it out. They eventually get what they deserve. In fact, they get it back times ten. We all do. I truly believe that."

"Whether that is true or not, this has become a habit I rather enjoy. I am not willing to fight this urge. Trust me, we are ridding the planet of evil, righting wrongs, punishing great evil. It is a feeling that is unmatched. It's the feeling you get when your fang first tastes the darkness of their blood. That first sip, but magnified times a hundred. Removing every last drop of their blood and eliminating them is, well, it's exhilarating. Try it with me."

Something about what he was saying resonated with me. It drew me in. Before I could respond, the realm dissolved, and Billy's knife plunged deep inside Jules's chest. Without uttering a sound, Jules slowly removed it, easing it out of his body, much to Billy's horror and within an instant Jules slashed the weasel's throat with his own blade, seeing the criminal's face distort in its reflection as his life force left his body. Jules then said three foreign words I didn't understand.

I watched without surprise, fully expecting he would finish the job he started. Now with both criminals laying on the ground bleeding and dying, we fed on them together until after their hearts stopped. Everything Jules said about the feel and taste of their intense umbras was right.

We closed up the bite marks and Jules picked up the police officer gently, told me he would take him to the hospital, and disappeared like a blur. I stood there over the dead bodies for a few minutes contemplating what had just happened.

It wasn't our job to kill bad people, was it? There was a fine line between feeding on evil, killing those who are already dying, and killing people who are bad. Isn't there? Their evil umbras did fulfill me intensely and entirely. I was totally conflicted.

One thing was for certain: ending them together with Jules was the most satisfying thing I had ever done in my life.

37. GRAVITY

I RETURNED HOME EMOTIONALLY DRAINED BUT PHYSICALLY fulfilled from the blood and darkness I had consumed. It made me feel powerful and intimately connected to my senses. I tried to remember the words Jules said. Nam-tar...something? I googled the fragment and found that it meant death or demon in ancient Sumerian.

The heat from my argument and relenting to the evil with Jules made me want him even more, despite the ugliness I had seen and felt tonight. I decided a cold shower would help me wash off those feelings. It did, slightly. I hopped into my coziest pajamas, a soft pair of Aviator Nation sweatpants and my new favorite Florida Gators t-shirt. Both purchases I'd made online through Jules's Amazon account. I had too many thoughts going through my head, so I decided to check in on Steele.

Nighttime was usually when we'd Facetime. He answered immediately.

"Hey Sera!" he said, sounding genuinely glad to see me.

We had a much better relationship on the phone than in person.

"Hey Steele. It's really good to see your face," I said, truly meaning it. He had a light surrounding him that made me happy.

"You look ugh, a little rough," he said back.

It was the first time I saw myself after getting back and he wasn't wrong. I looked horrid.

"Yeah. I can see that," I said examining my face on the phone screen. "Long story. I'll fill you in later. But how are things there at camp?"

It seemed like he was doing great, getting stronger, and training with Brock daily. He told me that Brock was giving him herbs to strengthen the Therion DNA to prepare him for an activation ceremony on the upcoming New Moon of Aries. They were also training daily to get his physical body ready. Even over FaceTime I could tell that he'd gained muscle mass. We'd perfected our telepathic bond and sometimes over Facetime we'd just look at each other and talk with our minds. It came in super handy if someone else came near my room.

It was how I told him about what happened this evening. Communicating this way was easier to convey emotions and felt less awkward when having to retell how killing someone evil and feeding on them made me feel good. He offered no judgement; he just listened all the way through to the end when he switched to verbal communication.

"Hey, I am the last one to lecture you about bad choices, Sera," he said. "But Brock warned us about Jules, you know." He hesitated and I could feel him trying to find the best way to say what was on his mind. "I think maybe you should separate yourself from him. Tune in to your Therion side. I know Brock thinks your gene was already triggered, but since you didn't turn during the last Full Moon, maybe you should fully activate your DNA after I do. If all goes well, that is."

I thought about what he said. I also told him about the prophecy of the Tetrad and the concept of me having to astral project to see the illumination.

"But you're not a Witch," he said.

"Well obviously," I responded.

"How's Cayla?" I asked, ready to change the subject.

He told me that him and Cayla were hanging out a lot, that he really liked her, and he was even planning to come back into Emberglow and take her to the dance next weekend. He told me I should ask Noah. Apparently, Noah talked about me all the time but didn't want to put any pressure on me or to force the relationship. In light of what happened earlier and completely writing off the possibility of going with Jules, I decided to text Noah as soon as I got off the phone with Steele. I told him I'd check in with him this weekend if I ever secured a date to the dance and hoped that maybe we could double date if so.

"Just make sure you clean yourself up before going out in public. And I think you still have blood on your face."

"Shut up," I said, knowing he was just giving me a hard time. "I already washed it off!"

"Love you! Bye!" he said, and he hung up.

I was really glad he was doing so well. Wish I could say the same for myself. It made me remember something Mom used to say to her friends. You are only ever as happy as your least happy kid. Meaning, when one of us was having a good day, the other one usually wasn't. It was a rare occasion in the Grayson home when Steele and I were both happy at the same time. I guess that still held true.

I laid on my bed for about another 2 minutes before deciding to text Noah.

Hi...

I knew he was typing back because I saw the ...

Hi Sera, how r u?

Good, how's camp?

It's good. Steele is doing great.

I've heard! That makes me happy.

FT?

Uh, sure. Let me finish up one last thing…10 min?

Sounds good

Ugh… now I had to go get ready. Guys are always ready to Facetime at a moment's notice. I was still fresh from the shower, with no makeup on and my hair was wet. I ran into the bathroom and brushed my hair and put on some mascara and ChapStick, and tried to look somewhat presentable before getting settled back onto the bed and calling him.

"Hi!" I said cheerily like it didn't just take a miracle to make the call.

"It's good to see you. I think this is so much better than texting, don't you?" he asked.

"Oh yeah, definitely," I lied.

We chatted for two hours and covered just about every topic: school, camp, Steele, and our quest to find the crystals and figure out what Mia and the others were up to. I filled him in on the Witches, the Sazianu, and soccer, like all topics were perfectly normal things to talk about in the same conversation. Conversation was easy, and he was fun to talk to. I could trust him completely. Just before we said our goodbyes, I got the nerve up and sprung it on him.

"So hey, uh, before you go, I wanted to ask you a question."

"Sure, what's up?" he said.

"Well," I started. "There's this Winter Dance next Saturday night at Valiant, and I know you have a lot going on and it's kind of silly, but Steele and Cayla are going and so are a bunch of my friends and I was, uh, just wondering if you'd want to go? With me?"

A huge grin formed on his face. "Sera, I'd love to go with you."

"Really? Awesome!" I said with relief. "Why don't you get here around six p.m. and we can take pictures, go out to dinner as a group, and then head to the dance. It's at the Emberglow Mansion," I told him.

"That sounds amazing. See you then," he said.

"Okay, bye, Noah." I ended the call.

I couldn't help feeling excited for my date.

38. I BET MY LIFE

NORMAL TEENAGE THINGS LIKE DRESS SHOPPING GOT MY MIND off being a mystical creature with the power of four ancient supernatural factions. After Rachael, Hannah and I all found the perfect outfits, we stopped to refuel at a fast-food Mexican place.

"I'll take a burrito please, with white rice, black beans, and peppers," I told the worker.

As he started to assemble my meal, I saw a guy in the back kitchen working on some fresh peppers that looked way better than the wilted ones I was about to get in my burrito. Dang, I thought. Just then the guy making my burrito caught the tongs on the edge of the pepper tray and accidentally flipped the entire container on the floor.

"Dammit!" he yelled. "I need new peppers!"

"Well, that was fortuitous," I said to the girls.

"Did you do that?" Rachael asked.

"No, I mean, I don't think so," I said.

As we sat down at a table outside, Rachael pressed me. "Sera, I think you do have witchcraft in your line. I'd bet my life on it."

"I'd chock it up more to Amantes," I said.

Both girls looked at me funny.

"Who?" Hannah said.

"Oh my gosh, we haven't told you about him yet," I said.

I explained who he was, how I met him, and how he was helping to guide our path to Amelia.

"Wow. I don't remember seeing anything about that in the grimoire," said Hannah.

"Yeah. Apparently, there are very few mentions of iL Separatio anywhere."

"Have you asked him about the Human crystals?" Hannah said.

"He's not really the most forthcoming with his information," I said. "He's more of like a North Star. Meeting him has definitely made me think about my choices more, that's for sure."

"Taking Karma into consideration, it makes even more sense that you are the Tetrad. Everything that has happened to all of us seems seren-dipitous," said Hannah.

"You are very smart," a voice behind me replied. "Just like your ancestors."

It was Amantes.

"You are not supposed to be here," I whispered.

"Humans are highly unobservant, Sera," he said, pulling up a chair. "Hello, Rachael. Hello, Hannah."

He shook each of their hands. "Don't mind me. I'm just here to listen."

"Can you tell us who killed our mother?" Rachael asked.

"All things in time," he said.

"Seriously?" Hannah said. "If you know, tell us!"

"Earth bound creatures have such an odd fascination with death," Amantes said. "As Witches, you should rise above that. You don't find it strange to feel tired at the end of every day, but when this happens at the end of a life, no one makes the obvious connection. Sure, some creatures die long before old age sets in but that was decided in the time before the renewal. It's the lack of memory that clouds your vision. Death is merely a longer slumber than an everyday night's sleep. Time has no place except for in this realm. You all mourn death so deeply, and yet you know deep inside, that you will see your loved ones again. That is if the Great Old Ones remain in slumber."

"Oh, wow," said Rachael, raising her eyebrows and widening her eyes. "Is this guy for real?"

"Yeah. He is full of responses like that," I said, chuckling.

"Much more importantly, you should focus on the upcoming day of power and the online covens," Amantes said. "The northern major lunar standstill."

Rachael typed it into her phone. "That's the same night as the Winter Dance. It only happens once every eighteen years."

I told the girls about Jules's idea to enlist the help of our digital Witches.

"That would definitely be a power boost," Hannah said.

"Indeed," agreed Amantes. "Also, this month, the duality of Pisces is present. It doubles the opportunity for light," Amantes said. "Pisces is a dual sign, with two fish swimming in opposite directions, just like the internal struggle Steele faces with the negative choices he has made pulling him in one direction but his ancestral Therion traits pulling him in the other."

We all sat awkwardly silent. The girls clearly didn't know what to make of our strange friend. Finally, Hannah broke the silence.

"We should try to harness its energy to find the Human crystals."

"How?" I asked.

"During the standstill, we can increase the power of the gems we do have. It might help with accuracy," Hannah said. "The waxing gibbous moon will rise between the windmill and the monument that sits behind Emberglow Mansion. Once it reaches the exact midpoint, we can put the crystals into the simulation again and see what happens."

"Excellent idea," Amantes said.

Rachael seemed disconnected to our conversation, off in her own world.

"You okay Rachael?" I asked.

She snapped out of it.

"Ya, I'm okay. I just really wish we were learning all of this from Mom. I can't believe she's gone."

"You will see her again," said Amantes. "Don't let your grief distract you."

Ignoring him, Hannah replied. "Rach—I miss her so much too. All of this talk about magic also scares me. I remember so clearly what happened before." Her voice trailed off.

"Sometimes you need to just put your baggage down. Push it aside," said Amantes. "It is not who you are, and you do not need to carry it. When you choose to put your baggage down, stop carrying it, the weight of which you have been carrying for most of your life, you will find that what you are left with is beautifully simple. Ladies, it was a pleasure meeting you in the flesh."

Amantes stood up and left as quickly as he had arrived.

39. INHALING
EVERY MOMENT

I TOOK MY TIME GETTING READY. MOSTLY BECAUSE IT WAS MY first chance to get dressed up in ages, and I wanted to look amazing for Noah. A tiny part of me wanted to look amazing for Jules. Okay, maybe it was fifty-fifty.

I wanted Jules to regret not asking me and feel a little jealous when he saw me and Noah together. I had the perfect little black dress. It was just slinky enough that Mom would have let me out of the house and Dad would have put up a tiny fight but would have been okay with it. Even though it was going to be cold out, I chose an off the shoulder tight dress that showed off a lot of leg and neck. My shoulders and neck were definitely my favorite body parts.

Hannah had to leave early to get the decorations finalized so Rachael and I did our hair together. Well, more like she did hers and mine. I was terrible at doing my own hair. I could barely even blow dry it. She blew mine out straight and put in some soft waves with the curling iron. I helped finish off her big curls on the back of her head.

"Are you excited for tonight?" I asked her as she finalized my perfect blond tresses.

"I guess," she said. "I am kind of sad to be manipulating Cole this way. I'm pretty sure I'll get the info we need from him tonight and then..."

"Do you like him?" I asked when her voice trailed off. "I mean like *really* like him?"

"No, I guess not. Not like that. He's a nice guy. He's cute. But he's really misguided. I mean he follows Mia around like a little puppy dog and I just can't relate to someone who has such blind faith in someone so . . . gross, you know?"

"Oh, I know," I said. "I can't stand that girl. How are you so sure you're going to get him to open up to you tonight?" I asked her.

"Let's just say I have a really good feeling about it," she said, implying something sinful.

I assumed she meant she'd be having sex with him. We both collapsed in giggles.

"What about you and Noah?" she asked, quickly changing the subject.

"I'm excited. I really like him," I said.

"More than you like Jules?" she said slyly.

"What do you mean?" I said, looking the other way so she didn't see if my face turned bright red.

"Oh, come on, Sera. It's so obvious you have a thing for him. I can see how you look at him and he makes you so nervous every time you're close to him. I can feel it. And so can everyone else."

"Hmm," I said. "There is something about him, I admit. But he's not good for me, you know? Noah is an all-around great guy. I like hanging out with him."

After we finished with hair and makeup, Rachael fluttered downstairs like a fairy to get a ride from Thane over to Cole's house. Since none of us had our own cars, we had to rely on the older members of the household for rides. I followed her downstairs and as I reached the main level, Thane and Jules were coming up from the basement. Jules and I almost collided at the landing.

"Oh, sorry," we both said in unison.

I hadn't seen him since that night and there was an unmistakable awkwardness between us. He did a double take when he saw me.

"Wow, Seraphina. You look stunning," he said in the sexiest voice ever.

He grabbed my arm and pulled me into him and pressed his nose against my neck.

"And you smell amazing," he said looking directly into my eyes.

So did he. But he always smelled amazing to me.

"Why, thank you," I responded.

The tension between us was pulled tight like a rope. Thane broke it.

"Alrighty, you ready for your big date, Rachael? And you look amazing too by the way," he said giving Jules a dirty look for ignoring her in his earlier remarks.

"Yep, I'm ready to go! Oh, wait. I forgot Cole's boutonniere. It's upstairs. Let me get it real quick," she said.

"I can go," I told her. "I've got to grab my bag anyway."

"No, no, it's fine. I'll go!" she said as she quickly turned to beat me up the stairs.

"Well, okedokey," I said to Thane and Jules.

And then the doorbell rang. It was Noah, Steele, and Cayla. Noah would be our designated driver tonight because after all he was like 150 years old, inside a teenager's body. I was excited for our double date with Steele and Cayla especially since I hadn't seen Steele face-to-face in forever.

He looked amazing. He was somehow tanned, taller and more muscular. He was absolutely dashing in his black suit with a dark blue button-down shirt and black and blue tie. It really made his eyes sparkle. Cayla looked beautiful in a teal green tank top dress and Noah…

Yum. His blond surfer hair was gelled to the side and he wore a navy-blue suit with a white shirt and brown belt and shoes. I was so excited to spend the night with him. It would be our last normal teenage night for a while. At least until midnight when we'd be trying to access the Human crystals during the northern lunar standstill. It was our last-ditch effort to find the remaining stones.

When they walked in, Jules gave Steele a fist bump and shook Noah's hand. He excused himself to ride with Thane and Rachael. I wasn't sure why she needed both of them to give her a ride. We all agreed to meet at eleven p.m. to activate the online coven during the lunar standstilll and re-link our crystals.

"Have fun tonight, kids. And don't miss curfew," Jules joked as he coolly strode toward the garage door. Thane and Rachael followed.

The rest of us headed for our dinner reservation at an Asian fusion restaurant in the Denver Tech Center. Noah drove a brand new gray Landrover Defender. The interior was spotless. It amazed me how there was no shortage of expensive cars in the Therion/Vampire world.

Clearly the place we chose was a student favorite. There was a frenzy of party buses and limousines dropping off groups of kids at our restaurant and others nearby. The plaza had about ten different spots to eat and lots of muraled walls for photo ops. It made me long to return to my normal life.

I looked at Noah and said, "Should we?"

"Should we what?" he asked.

"Get a photo! I mean we should commemorate the night, right?" I asked.

He and Cayla looked at each other nervously.

"I'm sorry, Sera. We really shouldn't. Let's just go get our table, okay?" he asked.

"Uh, sure," I said, giving Steele a weird look and asking him telepathically what the hell that was all about.

"No clue," he responded without uttering a sound.

The food was amazing and the conversation flowed easily. Cayla and Steele had obviously grown close as she was touching him every five seconds and giggling at literally everything he said. The feeling was clearly mutual. They were sickly cute together. Noah was acting like the perfect gentleman and opened all doors for me and even pulled out my chair.

"So, why so weird about the photo?"

"Oh that," replied Noah.

He leaned in. "So Therions exist at a higher frequency than others. Our cells are in a constant state of limbo depending on our will. We can exist in this Human form, or we can turn at will into our animal form. To the Human eye, they see no difference, and up until a few years ago, camera technology couldn't catch anything unusual either. But nowadays, technology has progressed so much that if we are photographed and it's an iPhone live photo, when you push the image down to see the live photo, you'll see us blur up, and in some cases, you'll see our face transition back and forth from Human to our animal form. It's uh, really difficult to explain away," he chuckled.

"Oh, that makes sense," I said.

"We can take pictures with older cameras," Cayla chimed in. "I'd imagine Thane and Jules spend a lot of time scrubbing photos off the internet when those who aren't as careful post pictures. It happens more than you'd think."

I made a mental note to buy a Polaroid camera.

After dinner we headed out to the dance at Emberglow Mansion. Located about a mile from Jules's neighborhood, the incredible historic home looked like a medieval castle sitting in the middle of a huge grassy lot with a long windy driveway, perfectly maintained shrubbery, and dramatic lighting leading the way. It sat among a working ranch, with a huge barn, bunkhouse, and an iconic windmill that we could see from Jules's house. Noah told us the mansion had belonged to some pretty famous families including cattle barons, oil tycoons, socialites, and a notorious Vampire at one time. Before I could ask more about that, we pulled up to the valet.

Inside the dance, the decorations were on point. Hannah stood just inside a giant black and gold balloon archway where she handed out ornate masquerade ball masks in all shapes and sizes.

"Wow, this looks amazing!" I told her.

"Thanks! It was so fun putting this together. Make sure to stop by the photo booth and check out the food table. The chocolate strawberries are to die for!"

It was good to see her so happy. Witchcraft or not, I was really glad Rachael got her on the committee.

I took a purple mask with black and gold feathers and strapped it around my head. We made our way into a complete winter wonderland.

They must not have spared any expense on the décor. The room was full of students. Some girls dressed like they were part of a fairytale. My senses were on full overload tonight, too. It was like I could hear every conversation, see into every interaction, and smell everyone's cologne and perfume like I was in one of those stores in the mall that only sell perfume.

I faltered to the side and Steele caught my elbow. I felt dizzy all of a sudden and half in the real world and half in another dimension, like the walls of reality were slipping away, confusing me.

"You okay?" Steele asked.

I grabbed his arm to steady myself. Noah and Cayla moved in closer, as if to get ready to catch me if I fainted.

"Yeah, all good. Just give me a minute," I said, holding Steele tighter and closing my eyes. I took a few deep breaths.

Just then one of my favorite slow songs came on. It brought me back to reality.

"I love this song," I said to no one in particular.

"May I have this dance?" Noah asked in a mock, formal tone.

"Absolutely," I replied, and he led me on to the dance floor.

He put his hands around my waist, and I put mine on his shoulders. He was way taller than me, probably about six-two to my five-four frame, but my three-inch heels made it a little more even. Dancing with him felt comfortable and familiar like we had done this before in another time and place. I put my head on his shoulder and just enjoyed the present moment with this amazing guy. I wasn't worried he would leave me to go on a killing spree or that he was longing to suck on everyone in the room.

I wondered if and when that would happen to me. Right now, I only started seeing umbras when I was hungry and needed to feed. Tonight, I was still full from our last feeding. I shook the thought from my mind and focused in on how right here and right now, everything felt right in the world.

That's when I felt a vibration. Noah got a text. He pulled his phone out of his back pocket and read it as a look of dread came over his face.

"Oh crap," he said.

"What's up?"

"I have to go."

"You're kidding, right?" I said, thinking there would be no way he was going to take off and leave me by myself at the dance.

"It's Brock. There's an emergency. He needs me, Steele, and Cayla back at camp right away. He would never ask if it wasn't important," he said.

I noticed Steele and Cayla must have received the same text because they were walking toward the door as well.

"But what about the spell and the crystals?" I asked, trying to make one last ditch effort to keep him there.

"They have you, Jules, Thane, and the Witches. Plus the online coven. That will be plenty of magic to channel," he said.

"I guess," I sulked.

He apologized profusely, kissed me on the side of my mouth, lingering just long enough to make me want more, and left me standing on the dance floor. I was kind of in shock. What could Brock possibly need that couldn't wait until the morning?

As I stood there, in the middle of the dance floor, awkwardly alone, I felt eyes on me, burning into the back of my head. I turned to find the source of the heat, and there in the far corner of the room, I saw him.

Jules's silvery eyes sparkled in the dark. He leaned against the wall, looking sexy in his black suit and white shirt with no tie, leaning against the wall with his hands in his pockets, just standing there, staring at me. Then came the butterflies. I crossed my arms and silently motioned with a tilt of my head for him to come over to me. He slowly made his way across the room.

"You look lonely," he said.

"Nope, all good. Just making sure everyone here on the dance floor is okay and accounted for," I said.

"Ah, okay. I'll just leave you to it, then," he replied but didn't move an inch.

"I mean, as long as you're here and all, you might as well ask me to dance."

"That makes sense." He offered me his hand. "Ms. Seraphina Paige, you look quite lovely this evening and it would be my absolute pleasure if I could have this dance."

"Since you asked so nicely. And also, I need a ride home."

He put one arm around my waist and pulled me in. Close. Our bodies fit together perfectly.

"Why are you here?" I asked.

"I'd never miss the Winter Dance," he replied. "I mean I have only been to ninety-nine of them and I wanted to hit a hundred," he smiled. "I think I win a set of steak knives or something."

"Ah. So it's just another year, another dance, another girl."

"Exactly," he said. "Although I must admit, I have never danced with a Human, who I turned into a Vampire, who has Therion DNA, and knows many of my secrets. This Winter Dance will definitely leave a lasting mark on my memory bank."

My senses were on fire. Everything about him was making me crazy. His shimmering eyes that saw into my soul, the smell and feel of his cool, perfect skin and the shock waves his touch sent through my body. It was as if we were dancing without anyone else around. As we swayed to the slow music, the world disappeared and for a few brief moments everything was perfect. The song ended and the DJ shifted to a faster beat.

"I don't do fast songs," I said, laughing nervously.

"Let's go get a drink," he said.

"Jules, why are you really here?"

"Something wasn't right about Rachael tonight," he answered. "I smelled something strange in the car so I thought I should stick around and make sure everything played out okay with her and Cole."

"What kind of smell?" I asked.

"I think it was the boutonniere," he replied.

Just then my ears tuned in to something odd. Jules heard it too. A gurgling sound coming from the back corner of the room. Our eyes peered in that direction. I saw Rachael with Cole in a shadowy corner of the room. She was trying to hold him up, but he was swaying from side to side, and then he gagged and almost threw up on her. Jules gave me a knowing look and we both made our way over to them and so did Hannah, who beat us over to their location.

"What did you give him, Rachael?" Hannah asked sternly.

"I think I gave him too much. I think I gave him too much," she said almost in tears at this point.

"It's nightshade. Are you crazy? I thought I smelled it in the car but then I thought there is no way she would be that stupid," Jules said.

"It worked so it wasn't that stupid," she barked. "I have to tell you guys what he told me. It's insane. They are poisoning the students. It's the tattoos."

At this point Cole's eyes were completely dilated and he could barely stand.

"Oh my God, is he going to die?" Rachael asked desperately.

His eyes were now rolling back into his head.

"Let's get him outside and get him some air," said Hannah. "Rachael, you come with me. Sera and Jules, can you grab some water and meet us outside?"

"Yes, we'll meet you guys out back," I said.

Hannah and Rachael walked Cole outside.

"What is nightshade?" I asked Jules as we hurried toward the drink station.

"It's an extremely powerful drug. All you have to do is touch something that has it on it and you get it in your system. Its nickname is Devil's Breath because you can actually blow it into someone's face for an immediate effect. It was very commonly used by Witches in the Middle Ages and is making a comeback now. It's kind of like a truth serum. It can be laced onto paper, like a business card, or made into a powder."

"That sounds like a made-up thing in the movies or something," I said.

"Oh, it's real. Just like Vampires, Therions and Witches," he said with a smirk. "It can turn someone into a zombie like state and at larger doses, it's lethal. It also doesn't show up in toxicology screens, leaving a lot of unexplained deaths because the bodies have no sign of..." his voice trailed off but I knew instantly what was he was about to say.

"Omega," I replied.

"Yes," he said.

"And you think Rachael has been using it on Cole?" I asked.

"She has some questions to answer, that is for sure," Jules said. "She clearly doesn't know what she's doing, and drugging someone isn't exactly Witchcraft."

We got five bottles of water and headed out back. Just as we exited the back door though we both heard an ear-piercing scream. It was coming from the bottom of the hill. Jules grabbed my arm, and he tried to transport us to the spot with Vampire speed. It didn't work. I tried and we were there in less than a second. But we were too late. Hannah collapsed on the ground, sobbing uncontrollably. Cole was passed out on the ground and Rachael was nowhere to be found.

"What happened? Where's Rachael?" I demanded.

"Mia took her," Hannah cried. "She was waiting for us, hiding in the woods and then she came out to us on the pathway. She walked right up to us, blew something into Rachael's face, and then they disappeared. I don't know what happened. It was all so fast."

"We need to get out of here," Jules said. "I'll grab Cole and we need to get to the car. Text Thane to meet us at the house. Now."

"But the spell!" I argued.

"Clearly that is not happening tonight," Jules said, realizing as I did, that we lost a serious opportunity.

Hannah was literally hyperventilating the entire ride back to the house and was inconsolable. Jules drove like a bat out of hell and looked sick to his stomach. He had worked on his virtual coven nearly every night for the past month getting them ready for a collective online spell to allow us to harness its energy, all for nothing it seemed. He was also fighting off the urge to finish Cole off since he was close to death. I sensed the feeling too, and while Cole's condition also distracted me, it was manageable. I wanted answers more than I wanted to taste his blood.

Thankfully the ride was short. Back at the house, Thane met us in the driveway, and he carried Cole inside and down to the basement to the cryo chamber prepped and ready. Jules had to excuse himself so he could control his urge to feed.

We met in the larger basement family room. Jules still looked ill, but Thane gave him some concoction and a blood bag that made his symptoms bearable.

Hannah was a hot mess, sitting on the couch alone, with her eyes closed, chanting and rocking back and forth.

"Hannah!" I screamed at her. "We need you here. You need to tell us what is going on."

She finished her chant and slowly opened her puffy, bloodshot eyes. She took a deep breath and slowly exhaled.

"I'm so sorry, you guys. We didn't tell you the truth earlier," she began. "Mia, is…she is, our sister. Rachael's twin and my younger sister."

We all sat stunned at her revelation and at the edge of our seats, staring at her, waiting for her to continue.

"We have different fathers but the same mother," she continued.

"How is it possible for twins to have the same mother but different fathers?" I asked.

"It's very rare," she answered. "It's a phenomenon called heteropaternal superfecundation, which is a really fancy term meaning my mom basically had sex with two different people on the same day," she said. "The woman's ovaries drop two eggs. One is fertilized by one man, and then if she has sex with someone else shortly afterward, his sperm fertilizes the second egg. It leads to two babies born as twins with two different dads."

"That is crazy," I responded.

"It happens," Jules said.

Of course, he'd heard of it. He was like a kazillion years old. Hannah continued.

"When I was two, our mom cheated on my dad with Mia's dad, Sam. When the girls were born, Sam somehow figured out Mia was his. He was a Witch too, but Dad was Human. Sam demanded she leave my dad and give him custody of Mia, but she wouldn't comply on either. She loved my dad, and Sam was just a fling. He wouldn't take no for an answer and tormented my parents for years. When I was seven and the girls were five, Sam killed my father. He made it out to look like an accident, but we knew. Our mom, Ruth, made a deal with Sam to never harm her other two daughters if she relinquished all parental rights to Mia and never contacted her again. She was crushed. We lost our sister and our father all at once. After that, Mom bound our powers because she didn't trust that Sam would keep his end of the bargain and she knew he couldn't find us if we weren't using magic. We changed our names, lived on the run, moving every few years, until we settled in Half Moon Bay.

"When you found us there, Sera, it made us very nervous, and we thought we'd have to move again. And you know the rest of the story," she finished with tears running down her face.

"It is unfathomable that you would think keeping something like that from us was a good idea," Jules retorted. "And then, sending in Rachael like a sitting duck. Are you kidding me?"

I ignored his rant and continued with my questions.

"So, does Mia know you are her sisters? She must have, right?" I asked.

"With our powers bound and it being ten years since we've seen her, we honestly didn't think she would," Hannah answered. "But since Mom died, the spell she did on us was broken and clearly Rachael has been dabbling in magic. That must have tipped Mia off. She is a very skilled Witch and with me and Rachael being such novices," her voice trailed off and she began sobbing again. "She must hate us, and I don't know what she'll do with Rachael," she said through her tears.

Cole walked into the room still groggy, but alive. "She needs her," he said.

He steadied himself by leaning on the couch.

"Glad to see you're feeling better," Jules said, meaning it more for himself than for Cole.

"What do you mean, Cole?" I asked.

"She needs her blood. She needs yours too, Hannah. The blood of the Triad will fuel a spell to activate the tattoos," he said. "I was so dumb. She had me under her power, convinced me it was the right thing to do. To start the world over again with a clean slate. But then Rachael came along and she, she changed me. She opened my eyes, before she tried to kill me, that is."

We ignored his self-loathing and pressed him more.

"What is in the tattoos?" I asked, remembering quite clearly that my brother had one that never washed off in the shower.

"It's a super small dose of nightshade. Just enough to get into their bloodstream so they can be controlled at will when needed but not enough to be noticed except for little headaches, maybe some nausea here and there. It's laced with a dormant mineral blend that can be activated with a spell using the blood of all three sisters. It only takes a few minutes to enter the bloodstream through someone's skin so even if you get it off, it doesn't matter."

"Activated for what?" I asked.

"To kill them. All of them. At the same time. She needs the dark energy to waken the Sazianu Royals and killing that positive energy from all the do-gooder students at one time will give her what she needs."

I was speechless. I was more than right about Mia. She was a psycho evil bitch. Hannah was stunned and buried her face in her hands. My phone buzzed signaling an incoming call from Noah.

"Answer it," Thane said, sensing my hesitation. "Put him on speaker."

I swiped to answer. "Hey Noah, you're on speaker with, well everyone, and Cole. You guys missed quite a night after you left."

"Hi Sera. Oh, good. I have Brock and Amantes here on speaker. The reason I left was because Brock needed me to verify something for him and timing was critical. The tattoo that Steele has, it's uh…"

"I know. It's poison," I said and filled him in on the events of the night leading up to his call.

"Oh wow," he responded.

Brock picked up where Noah left off.

"Hey, Sera and everyone. We have Steele in stasis, and he's fine. We want him out of the picture and safe from Mia if she decides to try anything to retaliate. We're not sure if she knows what you two are. But in stasis, she won't be able to sense him. We took many samples of his blood to test it and get it ready for DNA activation. The poison from the tattoo is the same poison that killed Omega."

My hatred for Mia simmered to the boiling point.

"Mia knows she is working against universal balance," said Amantes. "She is a very powerful Witch and knows that destroying all of that positive energy is the only way to awaken enough darkness to trigger the Great Ones and plunge this planet into absolute chaos."

"That's right," echoed Cole. "She's been planning it for years. Like lifetimes. Somehow, she can remember her past lives. Each time she reincarnates, when she turns twelve she has an 'awakening' as she calls it, and she gains knowledge from all of her previous lives. She's been not only planning this during this lifetime, but in many others before now. She has never succeeded before. This school will be the first test and if it works, she is going to broaden it to schools all across the country. She has three of the twelve sacred gemstones."

"The Human ones," Jules said.

"That explains a lot," said Thane. "But she still needs nine more."

"Make that six," said Hannah. "Rachael had our three with her tonight."

"Oh wow, the stupidity has no bounds," said Jules.

"We switched every day and thought it would be safer that way," Hannah said, looking down.

There was a heavy cloud of failure and desperation in the room as none of us knew what to do next.

"She is never getting my blood though, that's for sure," said Hannah. "Our only hope is that Sera is the Tetrad and we beat Mia to Amelia."

"What do you mean, that Sera is the Tetrad?" asked Jules.

Hannah told the others her theory. All eyes were planted firmly on me. I squirmed.

"We can't let her kill all those kids," I said, turning the focus to Mia.

"Now that we know we won't be finding the Human gemstones during the lunar standstill, I think we should focus on trying to save the students," said Jules.

He looked at his watch.

"It's 10:45," he said. "The online coven will be active in fifteen minutes. Why don't we switch gears and make it a protection spell? For the students?"

"It's worth a shot," Hannah said. "I have all the items needed in my bag and there is a protection spell in the grimoire. Sera, you and I can lead it together."

We raced outside into the backyard and formed a circle as Hannah set up the candles. Jules watched the app on his phone, setting a five-minute countdown and his phone on a tripod in front of me and Hannah, making the circle visible to the online participants. Thirty seconds before eleven, he hit the live button and Hannah and I broadcast our spell to the digital witches of the world.

40. DESPERATE TIMES

We hoped the spell worked but had no way of knowing unless Mia did get Hannah and Rachael's blood and all of the crystals. We were betting on us. Either way, we were worried.

"Even if we gather all of the gemstones first," Hannah said. "We'll only have a tiny window to get to Amelia first. We can't take any chances. Mia may have figured out her own way to see the illumination and we'll never beat her without a distraction," Hannah said, biting her lip while trying to think.

We all looked at each other, feeling the desperation of our situation and knowing we didn't have any time to waste.

"Hannah," Thane said. "I have an idea. But it would take a powerful spell."

"I'm up for anything at this point," she said.

"I've never actually seen it done but I've heard rumblings about a spell that thins the veil between the living and the dead, during a specific time of year. Back in ancient times, there were rumblings about Witches who meddled in necromancy."

"Like talking to the dead?" Hannah asked, while flipping quickly through the pages in her book.

"Well...and raising them," Thane replied slowly as if that would serve to not alarm any of us too much about the topic he was broaching. "I wonder if your mother would be a good distraction?"

"My mother?" she said aloud but then sat silently, thinking.

"Thousands of years ago when Witches were at their most power-ful, I heard of some who called upon the spirits to reveal secret hiding places of lost jewels or even the identity of who murdered their loved ones. I feel like in some cases they were able to raise the dead but only for a few moments, with some pretty intense magic. I don't know—obviously I know just enough to be dangerous and maybe it's impossible."

"No actually, I feel like I may have seen something about that in the book," Hannah said still skimming its pages. "I just don't know how I feel about it. I know how important this would have been to my mom, but I wouldn't want it to interfere in her reincarnation or trigger any severe con-sequences, you know? Black magic always has consequences. You never know how or where or when, but there is always a price to pay. Let me do some research, okay?"

The rest of us all needed some downtime, so we agreed to shower and change into some comfortable clothes and meet back in the kitchen in an hour. Jules said he'd order Chinese delivery.

When we met to eat, Hannah was armed with information. We called Brock so the others at camp could listen in.

"So here is what I found," Hannah began. "I think I can do it since she's been gone less than a year and her body hasn't been consecrated. There are specific elements we would need, and we'd also need my mom to be a willing participant once we reach her. The elements we need are scattered."

She pointed to a drawing in the grimoire.

"First, there is a flower that grows underwater at Hanging Lake."

"That's about four hours away," Brock said.

"Then there's a plant on the Devil's Pathway at Pike's Peak," Hannah said.

"That's two hours south in the other direction," Thane said.

"We need soil from the Garden of the Gods," Hannah continued.

"That's on the way to Pike's Peak," said Jules.

"And finally, we need serum from a specific beetle, and flower pollen from the mustard fields back in Half Moon Bay," said Hannah. "And of course, we need her body. The ceremony has to be done on sacred ground, so Valiant would probably work for that. Even if we did gather all of those elements and it all worked out, her spirit would only have access to her physical body for about eighteen minutes," she sighed and slumped back into her chair as if she just finished a race.

"Wow. And do we need to have a pepperoni and pineapple pizza waiting for her as well?" Jules asked sarcastically.

"Also, if everything worked out perfectly," Hannah said, ignoring him. "It's still kind of a crap shoot. But whatever. Let's give it a shot."

41. COME CLOSER

WE DECIDED TO SPLIT UP TO GET AS MUCH DONE AS FAST AS possible. We only had one week.

Hannah said she would head back to Half Moon Bay to get the wild mustard flower pollen and her mom's body. Noah agreed to go with her, and I had a small pang of jealousy. Jules offered the jet and volunteered to help me find the beetles. Interesting that he paired us up, but I tried not to read too much into it. Thane offered to head to Hanging Lake and then Pike's Peak with Brock and Cayla and a few others from the Therion camp who are good at climbing. He also offered to swing by the Garden of the Gods on their way back.

"So, tell me about this beetle we need to find," said Jules to Hannah.

"It's called a *cicindela theatina* aka a tiger beetle," Hannah said, "It's endemic to the Great Sand Dunes in the southern part of the state, meaning it's the only place on Earth where it lives."

"Yes, I am aware of the definition of the word endemic," Jules responded dryly.

She ignored him and continued. "There are a ton of them there, but they only exist on the remote backside of the dunes and are only visible when the Milky Way is at its brightest. They have a violin pattern on their backs and the stars illuminate their blue-green iridescent heads. You won't be able to miss them."

"Great. You up for a camping trip, Seraphina?" Jules asked. "They allow overnight camping in the Dunes but only by permit. Since the Milky Way will be at its brightest around two or three a.m., I guess we're in for an all-nighter. We can feed on the way down. Pagosa Springs is full of dark umbras and it's right on the way!" He sounded happier than I'd ever heard him.

"I won't be able to sleep anyway worrying about Rachael," I said trying not to sound too excited despite the quick hit of the stomach butterflies I got thinking about spending the whole night with Jules alone under the stars.

Jules convinced Brock to let us borrow his Wrangler—an uneven trade for the jet if you asked me—since he didn't want to get the Tesla or the Range Rover dirty. Such a snob when it came to his cars. We all went our separate ways with no time to waste.

Jules and I hit the small rural town of Pagosa Springs for a quick 'dinner' before making our way to the dunes park. I felt strong but anxious to spend the entire night alone with him. Or so I thought. Just as we were pulling out of Pagosa Springs and onto the highway, he got a call.

"Yello," he answered.

I homed in on the voice.

"Okay, yep. We're at mile marker 145 on state road 160. We'll wait here. See ya."

"Why?" I asked, dreading the response before even hearing it. No answer. "Uh hello, Jules. Why would you invite Scarlett?"

"Look. It won't hurt to have help finding and gathering the beetles, so this is really not up for discussion. I have no powers and you barely know how to control yours. She'll be here in twenty minutes."

My face flushed and I felt queasy. It was as if I could feel the anger's journey, slowly coursing from my fingertips through my arms, into my torso before attacking my heart and taking control of every cell in my body. I wanted to explode and rip his head off. But instead, I heard Brock's voice inside my head. *Don't let the anger consume you. Find a competing response. Don't let it out of its cage. I am in control, not the monster inside me. Put the energy into something else.*

I clenched my fists and squeezed my toes. Then relaxed them. How could he ever think I would be okay with this? *Don't let the thoughts take your inner peace. Remember the relaxation techniques.* Next, I squeezed my eyes shut tight. Then opened them slowly. *Breathe in for three seconds and breathe out for four.* It was working. After about three minutes of working to relax before responding, Jules finally broke the awkward silence.

"Look Seraphina," he started slowly. "We have to work together. This is too important. I have known Scarlett for hundreds of years and she is trustworthy. She wants to help us. She cannot help her nature. Like me, she is a demon. We feed on those who allow us in, and Steele was in a dark place. He invited her in. I understand why you would be angry about that, but it was his actions that invited her, and he is the one who should be held accountable for that, not her. Think about when we just fed. Did you care about whether that teenager passed out in his car from drinking too much had a sister who loves him? Did you consider that the sinful woman in the gray house with the white columns had an innocent five-year-old who was sleeping in the next room? No, you didn't wonder and you didn't care because you were fulfilling your vampire traits. Your job in nature to promote balance. It was their choices that invited you in, and just as easily as they invited you, they can turn the other way and make new choices that will shut you out."

I considered everything he was saying. I knew it made sense. I was just so angry that he wouldn't even ask me if it was okay for her to join us before telling her she was welcome. But to be honest it was so much more selfish than that. My dreams of being alone together all night under the skies in a remote park came crashing down. I had so been looking forward to this night. I carefully considered what I would say next. And despite my best efforts to sound normal I just blurted out, "It's fine. Whatever."

We sat in silence until a motorcycle pulled up alongside the Jeep.

"Who's up for an adventure?" she said with a wink.

I rolled my eyes. It was better than throttling her.

"You bring me an extra board?" she asked Jules.

"I am always prepared," he replied back. "Follow me if you can keep up."

And with that we squealed out.

"What board is she talking about?" I asked.

"Sandboards!" he replied. "We've got a few hours to kill before beetle hunting begins and you're in for a treat. It's way better than walking to the back side of the dunes, too."

I had no idea what he was talking about but still reeling from the news about adding a third wheel, all I could do was look away and stare out the window in silence.

I had never been to this part of Colorado before. It was desolate. We passed farmland and a few motels every few miles and even drove past a

UFO watch tower with a plastic alien sitting at the entrance. The mountains were all around us, covered in snow on their peaks but with the sun out most of the roads and farmland were already clear with only small patches of the white stuff scattered sporadically. I didn't see any sand dunes anywhere until about five minutes before entering the park. They were an anomaly in an otherwise mountainous and fertile area. Huge sandy dunes that filled up the bottom half of an enormous mountain. The dunes looked to get taller as we drove closer. Welcome to The Great Sand Dunes National Park and Preserve, the sign read. It is a national park that is more like a natural wonder of the world in my opinion. Located on the eastern edge of the San Luis Valley, a two-lane road approaches the park, which is flanked by the enormous Sangre de Cristo Mountain range.

"This is amazing," I said.

"It really is beautiful," said Jules. "I haven't been here in years."

We pulled into the visitor center parking lot with Scarlett close behind. Jules and Scarlett ran in to secure our camping pass for the night. We drove about a half mile farther and found a parking spot just before the entrance to the park. Jules and I grabbed our backpacks from the trunk, and he pulled out three brown boards that looked just like snow boards.

"These are sandboards," he said. "They look, feel and respond pretty much the same as a snowboard except for the backside has special rubber strips for gripping the sand. Also falling hurts more."

We hooked into the boards the same way you would a snowboard but using our own shoes. The next few hours were exhilarating. We hiked what felt like miles up and sand boarded down at breakneck speeds.

As dusk approached and we finished our last runs on the sand and snow, Jules suggested we hike the last bit to the backside of the dunes and set up camp. Brock equipped us with a pretty fantastic set up including a smaller version of the glamping tents. Scarlett opened up her backpack to reveal towels, four bottles of wine, paper cups and ingredients for smores.

"What?" she said when she saw me give her an incredulous look. "Vampires enjoy wine and chocolate as much as anyone else."

Okay, I had to admit she may be growing on me. She laid three blue and white striped beach towels on the sandy snow and handed me a cup. I hated wine but succumbed to the peer pressure of sipping from a plastic cup and laid back on the sand as Jules quickly started up a makeshift campfire.

"You're not really supposed to make fires on the dunes at night, but not sure anyone is going to stop us," he said. "Are you cold?"

"No, strangely, not at all. Should I be?"

"Well as a Vampire, we are cold blooded and our bodies don't conduct heat. We can regulate our internal temperature to match the environment. Therions run hotter always so the cold would be more comfortable. I'd imagine you're kind of a combination?"

I concentrated on my body temperature and was just comfortable, neutral; neither too hot or too cold.

Just then Jules's phone rang. It was Thane's signature ring tone. Jules answered it on speaker.

"Hey what's up?" he answered.

"So, we got the flower from Hanging Lake. I had to hold my breath for like ten minutes but I'm fine in case you were worried," Thane joked.

"I wasn't, but thanks for the extra info. Go on," Jules prodded.

"We've run into a little problem here at the Devil's Pathway. We found the trail leading to where the plant should be, but we can't access it."

"You have how many pounds of Therion muscle and can't dig up a little plant?" Jules ribbed him.

"It's covered in Death Camas," Thane replied.

"Oh, for the love of Lucifer," Jules yelled.

He looked at Scarlett who sighed before saying, "I'll handle it."

"Thanks, sweet Scar. You are just the absolute best," Thane remarked sarcastically. "And hurry the freak up," he added before ending the call abruptly.

She downed the rest of her wine and said, "Well, it's been real. See ya'll back in Emberglow tomorrow."

And with that she disappeared into a blur of black smoke and faded away toward the North.

"What was that all about?" I asked, now starting to sweat about being alone with him, despite my perfect body temperature.

"Death Camas is this beautiful white flowering plant that's all over Pike's Peak. It's highly poisonous to animals and Therions. It's pretty bad for Humans too. Won't kill them but will give them a nasty stomach bug. For us though, clearly the dominant species, no issues. Scarlett will handle it so it's all good and I'm sure we can get a few beetles on our own."

After Scarlett left, we still had a few hours to kill before the Milky Way would reveal itself and the beetles, so we kicked back on the towels and stared up at the sky. Jules knocked off a whole bottle of wine on his own while I took slow sips from my red solo cup. I'd had wine before but only out of Mom and Dad's glasses when they weren't looking. Jules's head was inches from mine, sending a burning sensation through my brain. The sky turned from day to dusk blessing us with a stunning cotton candy sunset that faded to a deep purple with pinprick stars.

"If I didn't know better, it sure seems like all of these hurdles and everything we've gone through is lining up for a purpose. Like it was intended to be a team effort," I said.

"Yes, it sure seems that way," Jules replied, seemingly lost in his own thoughts, and not really paying attention to what I was saying.

"I'm sure Amantes would have something to say about that," I continued, trying my best at making small talk.

My hormones were going crazy at this point. Laying so close to him was making me tipsier than the wine. I sat up to take a sip out of my cup and as I laid back down, I subliminally moved my body just a tad bit closer to his. Ever the predator, he immediately turned his head to mine, millimeters away from my face and said, "What are you doing?"

He was so close that I could feel and practically taste his cool, sweet, wine-tinged breath. It made me lose all self-control and I could barely speak.

"I-I'm not doing anything," I whispered huskily.

"Seraphina do not tempt me," he said to me. "I am a demon, a monster, a vessel of the devil, a creature that exists to corrupt others. I will corrupt you and I will be fine with it. I am trying to go against my nature, but I won't try hard. I am doing it for your parents, my friends. But even they would understand the limits of my abilities."

He moved his body even closer as if he were smelling me, scrutinizing my slightest movement, teasing me to make a move. He continued.

"When I look at people, I can see their umbra immediately. If they are evil, it's like I can see a mark on their forehead and that is an invitation to feed off that evil, harness it, grow it. I have learned to go against my nature and instead of perpetuating the greatest evil, I destroy it. I consume it inside of me and it makes me stronger."

"I understand that. It's a part of me too," I said. "But I also know that you can see if they are righteous too, in which case you have to stay away. But what you don't understand is that darkness cannot defeat darkness. Only the light can do that. I think—no I believe— that if you purposefully tried to tune in to the light inside of you, it would be difficult, almost impossible at first. Like any habit, it would get easier over time. Like blades of grass on a soccer field. Without anyone running on the grass they stand up straight. But when wind or players continually push the blades of grass down, over time, the grass stays flat. Yes, you are a creature of darkness; cold blooded. But deep inside you have a spark of warm light. I've seen it. I know it. Let me help you. Let me help strengthen your..."

That was the last word I could get out. He rolled on top of me, put his mouth on mine and the world disappeared. It was like last time, when we bloodshared, but this time it was kissing. It was way more intimate and way more intense. The world stood still, time stopped, and only he and I existed in our own private reality. We could see the stars above us and the sand beneath us, yet we were removed from it all, in our own alternate dimension.

"Stealing my power again, are you?" he asked me.

"Me? No, I am not..."I didn't finish my sentence before he kissed me again and we were lost in time once more.

42. DANCING IN THE STAR LIGHT

LIKE CLOCKWORK AT 2 A.M., THE MILKY WAY REVEALED ITSELF in all of its incredible glory. We had emerged from our private realm and were back on the planet and yet it was still utterly magical. Laying there together in the vast dune park under the blanket of stars that surrounded us made me feel as if anything was possible. Like the world was at our feet and that together we could conquer anything. His back on the ground, I laid next to him closely on my side, with one hand on his shoulder and my head resting on his chest.

"We are so small," Jules said out loud, giving me a glimpse into his thoughts. "We are bound to this tiny marble floating among the stars and dust. One of many small marbles that can at any moment in time, be completely obliterated and consumed by its monsters within."

"That's a kind of depressing thought," I replied.

"When you look up there, you are looking into the past. The light you see right now up there is 2.5 million years old," he said.

"I don't follow?" I asked.

"Look at that star right there," he said, pointing to Sirius, one of the brightest stars in the sky. "It is 8.6 light years away. That means that the light we see now was first emitted 8.6 years ago. When you look at that one," he said pointing to the Big Dipper, "the stars in that constellation began shining that specific light about seventy-five years ago. The light from the Milky Way we are seeing now is coming from a time before modern Humans were even on the planet. Seeing it so clearly now in the sky makes me long for those days. The days before technology, bombs, and so much chaos. When creatures could just exist. I sometimes question why we are so fixated on saving a planet that is already dying. There are so many galaxies in the universe, Seraphina. Don't you ever wonder why we are bound to this one?" he asked somewhat rhetorically. "Our quest to save this planet is really just a quest to save some time. Up there inside that highway of stars is the Andromeda nebula. One day, albeit in four to five billion years from now, if this planet is even still in existence, it will collide with our galaxy and bring our end regardless. In the meantime, we are merely a virus that exists on the Earth. Little ants who consume and destroy it, killing it slowly while we also kill each other."

I took in the magnitude and depth of what he was saying, and it gave me pause. I remained silent for a few moments before responding.

"I think all we have is the present moment. Sure, we might fail. Mia may beat us to Amelia, and the Great Ones may take over this planet. And sure, the planet is dying anyway, but right now, right here, we have this moment. And so do millions of others on this planet. Many waste it, many throw their lives away or give in to their dark impulses, but there is also so much love here. Creatures helping creatures, wonderful moments like watching the sun rise and set, swimming in the oceans, skiing or sandboarding down a mountain, or truly connecting with another soul on a deeper level," I said, turning to look into his deep silvery eyes. "We have those moments, and they fill our souls with light. And if enough people connect to that light, maybe we can not only save the planet now, but save our souls to live again somewhere else in five billion years, you know?"

He stared back at me, searching my eyes for something, but didn't say a word. As the cosmic highway reached its brightest peak, like a milky interstate beaming across the sky, we saw them.

"I wonder what the beetles think about time and space," he said.

It made me giggle.

Hundreds of tiny beetles emerged from the sand and scurried across the dunes. We saw the iridescent violin shape glowing on their backs and we collected about 100 of them into the special container that Hannah made for us that would keep them alive until right before she needed them. I was hoping that maybe Jules would want to stay the rest of the night contemplating life, and recreating what had happened earlier. No such luck. He immediately set to cleaning up our campsite and began walking back to the parking lot in silence.

43. DANCING IN
THE MOONLIGHT

JULIAN AND SERAPHINA REPRESENT THE EPITOME OF YIN AND Yang. Perfectly complementary. Yin is negative, dark and feminine, like Lilith. Yang is positive, bright and masculine like Adam. Their interaction is the true manifestation of harmony and balance in the universe. The mixing of two energies that make life possible. When they worked together for a shared common goal, they were intensely powerful, and could stop time. But even in Yin, there resides a small point of Yang, and vice versa. They were two halves of one whole. He was the moon, a dependable object that reflects the light of the sun and is a sensor for what is happening around it. If he allowed himself to be consumed by emotions, it jeopardized his existence. What he did not realize was that he did in fact have light of his own. If he could connect to it and go against his nature and seek others who needed his energy, he would not be governed by energy of limitation.

Sera was like the sun. The essence of sharing. The center of the universe. The light that shines on the moon. Just as easily as she could shine her light on Julian, he could distort hers, altering it on a lower level and forcing her to succumb to darkness.

44. EVERY LITTLE THING
SHE DOES IS MAGIC

EXCEPT FOR HANNAH AND NOAH WHO WERE STILL IN California, we all regrouped back in Emberglow the next day. We gathered in the basement and called the others on Facetime, projecting their faces on the huge movie screen monitor. Scarlett had successfully retrieved the plant from the Death Camas. We had all the items needed now for the spell to distract Mia.

The Snow Moon was in three days. It just happened to coincide with Valiant's Practicum week so there were no classes in schedule, meaning we would have zero contact with Mia.

"My mom's friend has been helping me learn new spell work," said Hannah. "We've been trying to use a scrying spell to find Rachael's location every night, but nothing is working."

"Mia will keep Rachael alive," I said, trying to convince myself as much as the others. "At least until the Snow Moon. She needs her blood, right?"

"Yes, thank goodness we at least have a few more days," said Hannah. "Triad blood will be needed to 'activate' her followers all at once to create an energy portal of darkness and awaken the Great Ones."

"If only the Tetrad can see the path, how do you think Mia plans to find Amelia?" I asked.

"That's a good question, Sera," said Brock. "We have to assume she is one step ahead of us, and that she will be there when we are, during the first few minutes of totality."

Everything hinged on a few key miracles. Me being able to see the illuminated Sazianu symbols showing the pathway, beating Mia there, distracting her with Ruth, and stealing the Witch and Human crystals from her during the distraction window to open the door to Amelia. Oh, and also saving Rachael's life.

Mia also needed Hannah's blood, something we would have to guard closely.

While we knew the symbols were supposed to light up leading the way to Amelia during that time, we couldn't be sure that I'd be able to see them. Brock and I planned to research everything we could about astral projection and Hannah was convinced she could teach it to me after interrogating her mom's friend in California.

"Sera, why don't you come out to camp and meet with Hannah and Noah when they get back. I have some herbal teas that should aide your ascension into the astral plane. It's very similar to achieving Alpha Level and with the right mindset, I know you'll be able to do it," said Brock.

"We should be back late, the night before the Snow Moon," said Noah.

"I can give you a ride out there," said Thane.

"Thanks," I said. "Sounds good."

Noah and Hannah would bring Ruth's body back on the jet and Jules would hang back at Emberglow to reinforce and reengage our specific online groups for a strengthened protection spell from Hannah's new skills.

"How's Steele?" I asked Brock.

"He's fine. He's still in stasis. I am going to begin triggering his Therion DNA so that he'll be strong enough to wake up in time for the Snow Moon. It will be important for him to be with us," said Brock.

We ended the call, all knowing our separate missions. We had a lot to do. First on my mind was astral projection.

When Thane and I arrived back to camp it was late, after most of the others had already gone to sleep except the nocturnals who were pacing around or playing in the woods. Steele looked to be in a peaceful sleep when I entered our tent. I walked over and kissed him on the head, thankful that we had each other and this special place full of what felt like family.

As soon as Hannah and Noah got back to camp, I cornered her, eager to learn.

"Let's find a quiet spot," she said.

We headed into the woods and sat down on the ground.

"So it should be pretty simple for you," Hannah began.

"If I am the Tetrad," I said.

"You are. You must be. Why else would all of this have happened?" she asked.

I inhaled deeply, then exhaled slowly and tried to clear my mind.

"Okay, let's do this," I said.

"You have within you great spiritual power. So first, concentrate on a destination, or a person, you want to visit," Hannah said.

Of course, my mind went to Jules. Would it be weird to spy on him in this way? Oh well.

"Okay, I have it. I have my, um, person," I said.

"Now concentrate only on that person and cast your soul into space," Hannah said. "Lift away from your body. Disconnect from the physical and send yourself into the astral plane."

She made it sound so easy. I wondered where these instructions were coming from. I tried with all of my will power to exit my body. Leap into the astral plane. For a second, I thought I did it. But then I realized I was just thinking about Jules; I wasn't with him.

"It's not working," I said.

"Don't think with words," Hannah said.

"What does that mean?"

"It means just think. Don't use words. Words tie you to the planet. Just think," Hannah insisted.

"I cannot think without words," I said.

"Sera, stop talking. Just feel," Hannah said.

We sat there in silence for thirty more minutes without success.

"I think we should go find Brock," I said finally. "Either I am just really bad at this, or I am not the Tetrad."

Hannah sighed loudly, exasperated.

Back at camp, we found Brock and Noah. They were with Amantes. We told them what happened.

"Steele is ready," Amantes said to Brock. "His umbra is bright. His energy will help her."

That made my heart so happy. I couldn't wait to see him awake.

"Will he be a Therion?" I asked.

"No, not yet," Brock said. "But the poison will be gone from his bloodstream, and he will be in transition, and strong."

And he was. He looked better than I'd ever seen him. Muscular and toned, strong and powerful and above all else, happy. Brock suggested we all gather in circle.

He mixed up a potion of herbs and leaves into some sort of aromatic tea and began to fill several small clay cups to be passed around. As everyone received their cup, they began to sip from it. After everyone had gotten a cup and taken a sip, Brock instructed us all to hold hands and began with a short sermon.

"We gather in circle for a momentous event. One we haven't experienced in any of our lifetimes. The royal family joins us tonight for an opportunity to reveal great light."

All eyes were squarely on Brock, hanging to his every word.

"During every Full Moon phase, the sun and the moon face each other, creating what is known in astrology as an opposition. The sun throws all its light out into the solar system and the moon reflects it. The opposition of the two great luminaries, similar to Therions and Vampires, suggests a balance, a search for a middle point between two extremes. It is up to us, the Earth dwellers, all species, to find the middle ground and balance. It grounds this world into existence."

"When the balance is off," added Amantes. "Great calamities plague the planet and evil energy gains space. This week's Snow Moon Eclipse is a unique opportunity to hone that balance and tap into the great power available to us because of it."

"The energy of a Full Moon represents completeness," Brock continued. "Where the moon reaches the highest point in relation to the sun.

This position denotes energy of culmination. It is a moment of splendor and brilliance. The Snow Moon is the second Full Moon of the year. For early cultures and our ancient ancestors February was a month of coldness, darkness, scarcity, and short days. It was a time when people were most in need of connection, light, positivity and oneness with each other and the planet. In our modern lives, we often forget the importance of this time of year and our connection with nature. This Snow Moon, as the two of you, Seraphina and Steele, have been awakened and great power seems to hang in the balance, will be an optimal time to gain knowledge from the universe."

He paused and intense silence fell upon the circle.

"When the Sun and Moon oppose each other," Amantes said. "A greater amplification of vision shines through."

"That is what we all manifest for you tonight, Seraphina. Use the energy all around you, the energy from tomorrow's Snow Moon, and access your alpha level, the state between wakefulness and sleep," said Brock.

"Imagine a rope hanging from the heavens down to where you sit," said Amantes. "The rope has five knots on it. Use your soul, your essence, and grab on to the closest knot."

I did. I felt it working.

"Grab on to the second knot," Amantes coaxed.

I heard his voice, but I didn't need to. I was rising. I felt my energy lift and saw myself from above. As my mind left my body and eased into space, my presence shifted. I was aware, in a subtle way, of everything around me. All emotional anguish vanished, and a profound sense of peace flowed through my body. Bliss enveloped me. Like when Jules first blood shared with me. Jules, that's who I wanted to go see. Something stopped me. Another energy blocked my path.

It was my mom.

She took my hand, and we flew through the cosmos together. Under space and over time, I felt her essence flow through me, and she shared sacred knowledge with me about my lineage. Our maternal line, while Therion based, had been infused with witchcraft along the centuries by infidelity and intermarriage. She showed me that I was something unique, not known in the world before, born a Human, with dormant Therion DNA, infused with witchcraft, and poisoned by a Vampire. The Tetrad. It was this unique combination of all four earthly breeds that would allow me to rule them, she said. I had to embrace my unique hybrid self and share my gifts with others to help reunite the Alliance. Then she vanished.

Next up was Dad. Oh, my father! What a joy it was to see him, smell him, and feel his protection. I had missed them both so dearly. He showed me a place we had visited when I was younger that held fond memories for me, a fishing pier in Key West. He told me how proud he was of me and implored me to keep the strong connection I had with Steele. To never let anyone come between us. We held hands and strolled the most magnificent stretch of beach with sparkling turquoise water.

"When we come into this world Seraphina Paige, we are given the exact amount of time necessary to complete our spiritual work."

He grabbed my hand.

"Most of us depart each life without completing the task we came here to do, and we may have even moved in the opposite direction. What is true for a single soul is also true for all souls. As long as any one spirit falls short of transformation, we will continue to anticipate in the cycle of birth, death, and rebirth until the critical mass of truly enlightened people comes into being to eradicate pain and death forever. The Great Ones would like that to never happen. They thrive on pain and wish to transform the world into a deep and dark chaos."

We rose above the ocean and flew across the waves. I dipped my hand into the sea and felt its warmth and smelled its salty breath.

"Your mother and I left this world so that you and Steele could be born. Truly born. You must reclaim our family's destiny. Remember though, when it comes to your Vampire traits, they are a part of you now, but you can control them. Think of them as habits you can override but know that you will be tested."

Just as I was about to ask about that, mostly for Jules's sake, Dad directed my attention down the beach where I saw something running like a lightning bolt at breakneck speed toward me. Oh my gosh! It was Omega!

The sense of happiness that overcame my senses was palpable. We ran toward each other and as we met, he tackled me. We rolled around in the warm sand and at the edge of the sweet briny ocean water for what felt like hours before he shared his own important message for me.

He assured me that he was okay, that we would meet again on the earthly plain and that it was his Karma to sacrifice himself for me because I had saved his life in several lifetimes before. He existed somehow in this realm in both his wolf and Human forms simultaneously, in pure harmony. He told me that he fulfilled an important duty by dying for me. He chose that. He was poisoned but it was meant for me.

"Never forget, Seraphina, light doesn't come through light. Light comes through darkness," Omega said. "It is revealed through difficulty, through pain. It is how you react to those circumstances that allow light to be revealed."

And then they both disappeared.

I could still see the others in circle below and I focused on my initial goal.

Jules. I wanted to see Jules.

In less than an instant I arrived. At his home in Emberglow. I was in the cryo chamber room with him. He couldn't see me. He was fumbling for something in the closet in the back of the room. It was the dagger. The one he used to kill the criminals that night at the warehouse. That's when I smelled her before I saw her. That unmistakable scent of lavender and vanilla. I had to warn him! Without his powers, she could hurt him.

"Jules!" I screamed but he couldn't hear me.

"Hey," he said to her.

"Hey, yourself," she said to him.

"I told you I had it," he held up the ancient relic.

It was bronze and serrated with a silver and gold handle, laced with leather bindings. It had ancient symbols emblazoned on the blade and dried blood on its edges.

"The Selenite Dagger," Mia said. "Looks like you've been busy," she said, noticing the blood.

"Let me hold it," she said.

Her eyes were glistening, and she looked like she was salivating. What was he doing with her? This must not be real.

He handed her the Dagger.

She touched its tip with her pointer finger and it sparked. "Definitely authentic," she said.

"Now do what you said. Channel its power to me. Give me back my strength," he said.

"Tired of using my drugs to compel people? As long as you keep up your end of the bargain, I will help you." Mia said.

"I'll keep my word. I just want to revive Amelia and get my powers back. After that, you can have the damn dagger."

What was he saying? That traitor! That asshole! And with the emotional anguish that returned, my connection to the astral plane was gone, and I opened my eyes. I landed back into my body, in the circle. "We need to get back to Emberglow," I said. "Now."

45. YOUR HEART
TAKES THE FALL

AFTER I FILLED IN THE OTHERS ABOUT WHAT I SAW, STEELE, Brock, and Amantes stayed at camp and Thane drove me and Hannah to Emberglow to confront Jules. I had an hour to decide what I would say. As we approached the house, I felt a pressure building in my chest and a knot in my stomach. I wished I could be happy about my ability for astral projection but that was all tarnished now. My heart hurt and I felt numb.

Everyone warned me. Even he warned me. I wouldn't see it.

"Why would he do that?" I said to Thane. "He betrayed all of us!"

"Do I need to point out that he's a Vampire?" said Hannah. "No offense, Sera."

"Let's just give it a beat. Maybe there's more to the story." Thane said. "My grandfather always said there are three sides to every story. His, hers, and the truth."

I was fuming.

"I know what I saw!"

After that outburst, I sat in silence for the rest of the ride.

When we arrived, I stormed into the house.

"Jules! Jules!" I yelled. "Jules Blakewell!"

He sauntered up the stairs from the basement. Thane and Hannah came in the front door and closed it behind them.

"What is the emergency?" Jules asked.

"Are you working with Mia?" I said, point blank.

He stared at me.

"I said, are you working with Mia? You know, the Witch who killed Omega and plans to kill thousands of students and unleash havoc onto the world?"

"She's helping me get back what you took," he said.

"At what cost?" I screamed.

"All I care about is finding my sister and getting my powers back. I have never cared about reuniting the Alliance and I have never made that a secret," he said.

"You have got to be kidding me? You would give her the dagger? How could you?"

"I have also never tried to hide who I am from you. I am a Vampire. Stop trying to make me out to be something more than a demon."

"What dagger?" Hannah asked.

I realized I had never told anyone that Jules had it.

"The Selenite Dagger?" she pressed. "How could you have had a weapon like that at your disposal and not told us about it?"

"Are you seriously lecturing me about holding back information?" Jules replied dryly.

"That weapon is insanely powerful. It is imbued with the power of Gods. When combined with the other half, it can open portals to other worlds, trap evil, kill... anything," Hannah said, raising her voice. "It should be in hiding, protected."

"This is a house full of Vampires and Therions. I'd say it's well protected. And its other half has been buried in a secret hiding place for fifteen hundred years, so there has never been any reason for concern for quite some time now."

"Until now, when you plan to give it to Mia!"

"I was never really planning on giving it to her," Jules said.

"That is a dangerous game you're playing Jules," said Thane.

"We do not have time for this," said Hannah. "My sister's life hangs in the balance. The fate of the world is at stake. Jules, I'm sorry, but I don't think you can be involved any further."

"You must be joking. My sister's life hangs in the balance too," he said.

"I think I speak for everyone when I say, no one wants you there tonight," Hannah said.

"Agreed," I said. "You are not welcome at the school or at the ceremony."

We turned around and left. Back in the car I buried my head in my hands, bit my lip, and choked back sobs. I was devastated. Heartbroken. I had to get it together. We didn't need him. I couldn't let this be a distraction. We had to turn our intentions to raising the dead.

46. ALL THE PRETTY LIGHTS

DUSK TURNED TO NIGHT. THE FULL MOON ROSE, LIGHTING UP the sky, almost as much as the sun. The eclipse would begin at 10:45 p.m. and the expected time of totality, when the Blood Snow Moon would emerge, was at 11:11pm. It would last for 7 minutes and 30 seconds. Since we'd have 18 minutes with Ruth after awakening her, we planned to do that first. We wanted to be as close to Valiant as possible to save time, so Noah hauled a trailer with Ruth's coffin hidden inside, to a secured a clearing in the woods behind the school for the spell. I found a comfortable spot for my ascent into the astral plane and Steele planted right beside me, to guard my body.

Noah and Cayla volunteered to keep watch for Mia and Rachael at the spot where the woods opened to the school's campus.

At the clearing, the rest of us, minus Jules, gathered at the site. Thane, me and Steele, and Hannah—a partially united Alliance fighting for our friends and for all of the souls on Earth.

Ruth's coffin lay in the middle of the circle. All of our hopes relied on Hannah being able to raise her dead mother, that being enough to distract Mia, and the Blood Moon activating the illumination of the symbols to light the way to Amelia's location. I would have to see the path and send it telepathically to Steele, who would relay it to the others to get a head start. Everything would have to play out exactly in our favor, and hopefully Rachael was still alive. I felt like Hannah would get a feeling if she wasn't, but she had been completely engrossed in preparing for the spell over the past few days and was checked out emotionally. She'd mixed the herbs and items we had gathered from our scavenger hunt inside a cauldron, and then began to pour them out carefully in a circle in front of us.

"Stand outside the circle please," she instructed.

She moved slowly over to the coffin, placed her hand on top of it and mumbled a spell quietly, almost inaudible to all of us. The latch came undone, and the lid popped opened ever so slowly. We collectively held our breath. She motioned to Thane and Steele to come over toward the coffin. She raised the lid and inside lay her mother. Only dead for about two months and carefully embalmed, she looked peaceful. It pained me to be part of disturbing her and I couldn't imagine how Hannah must feel.

Without any emotion, Hannah asked the boys to remove her body from the coffin and place it with her head toward the east and her arms out to the side, forming a T. Chains with eighteen links were bound around her wrists to bind the spell. It would also ensure the maximum length of her soul occupying her body for 18 magical minutes.

She set down a small bowl filled with liquid next to Ruth's right hand. Hannah walked toward the herb circle and lit it on fire, igniting the shape into a fiery blaze. She dipped her hand inside the liquid and touched it to her mother's head. She then set the liquid inside the bowl on fire as well. Once both blazes were fully burning, Hannah motioned to Steele and Thane to join us outside of the circle and for us all to take hands.

We looked toward the sky and saw the shadow begin to touch the moon. First contact. It was time. Hannah closed her eyes and began to chant. As she did, I began my ritual as well.

I reached Alpha Level quickly and left my physical body with ease, one rope knot at a time. My spirit became one with the sky and the stars. As I rose above the circle and the fires, I saw my brother and my friends anxiously watching me for some sign of success. Higher and higher I floated until the heavens and the stars enveloped me, shining brightly against the night sky. I turned among them, feeling powerful and at peace. I faced the Earth and saw the high school below. I stretched out my energy as if to spread my arms out wide and looked up to the moon. Its reflection illuminated my essence and filled me with joy. As I looked back down to the school, I saw it. From this high vantage point I could see that there was an outline on top and over the entire school, as if someone had traced a person's body over the entire campus. It was a giant drawing of a woman.

Amelia.

I couldn't make out her specific features, but I knew it was her. Pulsing lights were coming from her eyes, her heart, her hands, and her feet. The lights pointed toward an entrance. It was in the school library. I sent the celestial message to my brother below with my mind, who waited for it below. As he relayed the message to the others, they began to head inside the school. I went there too, in this elevated form and found the hidden entrance inside the library. Behind the wall was a glowing symbol, an alien looking hieroglyphic symbol. There were thousands of them inside the tunnels, but only certain ones lit up for me now, showing us the way. Telepathically I sent the mystical map to Steele and he led the others through the maze. As they winded through the dark tunnels, lit only by symbols on the walls and the flashlights the crew carried, someone else followed them close behind. I had to warn them.

47. CUT

Steele turned over body protection duty to Thane so I could telepathically show him the way to go. Thanks to my head start, Steele, Hannah, Noah, and Cayla made it underneath the school with Ruth in time to beat Mia, but she was close behind them. When I opened my eyes, the Earth had moved between the moon and the sun. The Blood Moon had emerged. As I acclimated quickly to being back in my body, Thane helped me up and we quickly headed inside the school. We entered through the door, hidden in plain sight for Humans, inside the library that I'd uncovered in my vision. Just like I saw, there was a symbol and a latch behind the Paradise Lost book in the Biblical literature section. It opened the entire bookshelf and led to a secret hallway that wound downward, bypassing the basement where the classrooms and the Bistro were and ended in a room shaped like a Pentagon. From there, pathways veered off in several different directions.

Like we had hoped, just as totality began, the symbols forged into the stone so many years ago lit the pathway to take. Without their light it would have been impossible to know which way to go. It was an intricate maze under the school with a large labyrinth of underground pathways used in the 1920's during prohibition but before that by Vampires and Therions to travel undetected and before that, by the Sazianu. Amelia had been right near the Vampires and the Therions for so long, but too far from their detection with dark magic.

Without the glowing symbols, we would have been utterly lost.

As Thane and I quietly approached, we heard a commotion. It was Mia.

She had cut the group off at the dead end of the magical pathway, which ended at a huge archway. Behind that was a smaller foyer looking room with a giant door. On it, was an imprint of what looked like a tree on its surface with twelve points. It looked just like Jules's simulation grid. Noah was with Ruth, hiding behind a pair of enormous stone pillars, just out of Mia's sight.

We inched close so that they all came into view. Mia's jeans pocket was glowing. The crystals must be inside. She was gripping Rachael's hand so tightly that it was white. Rachael was moaning in pain. We held close to our hiding spots.

"Well, it looks like a party down here," Mia said. "Except, I think you forgot to invite me. So I just invited myself."

"Let go of me!" Rachael yelled, trying to break free from Mia's grip.

Mia was too strong for Rachael and tersely replied, "The Sazianu sacrificed their unfaithful members to the Gods right here in this very spot and then ate their remains. I thought it fitting to be your place of death."

As they fought, I motioned silently to Thane that I was going to insert the crystals that we had into the grid. He nodded in agreement. I dissolved into smoke and made my way, undetected to the door with the seal. I knew behind this door was Amelia. We were so close.

"Mia, please. Let her go," Hannah said.

Mia threw Rachael down to the ground.

"Well, hello big sister," Mia replied. "I haven't listened to your demands for years. Not since we were toddlers. Did you really think I was that stupid that I wouldn't recognize the two of you? You played right into my hands. Dumb, dumb girls."

"I actually feel sorry for you," Rachael cried out. "You are so broken and so scared. The love and light in your soul died long, long ago. I used to think it was my fault but now I know you were broken way before me."

Mia scoffed. "Oh, you stupid girl. Darkness isn't born. It's created. It's a choice made from hatred. From the light being taken away time and time again. Lifetime after lifetime. I remember it all. Every death, every birth, every single time I was thrown aside. You think you did that to me? You think you mean so much to me? How vain! We may have been in mother's womb together, but you never meant anything to me. And now, whenever I look at you, I see mother. The one who threw me away, and who turned my heart to darkness long ago. With that darkness I will crush you, your sister, and every one of her allies from Arete 8."

That was my cue. I would not let her hurt them. I materialized into physical form and slipped out of the shadows, and Thane and I walked over to join the others. Mia looked our way.

"Oh fabulous, more party people," she said, glaring at me.

"I warned you once before Mia. We are not sheep," I said. "Let Rachael go."

She laughed.

"Or what? You'll turn into a wolf and eat me?" she asked.

Maybe she didn't know I was a Vampire.

"Tell you what," Mia said. "You have six crystals and I have six crystals. How about an even trade?"

Hannah seemed to be considering it.

"No way," said a voice from the shadows. It was Jules. But how? He walked closer, out of the dark, twirling a glowing Dagger in his hand.

Mia noticed the Dagger, and an evil grimace creeped across her face. She picked Rachael up from the ground and used her as a shield.

If Jules threw the weapon, he had no shot of hitting Mia without hitting Rachael as well. He needed to get them apart.

"Let my sister go, you evil bitch!" Hannah demanded.

"Now, now. Let's not be so nasty, sis," Mia said. "I would expect that from a Vampire but not from my own flesh and blood. Where are your manners? I am in control here. And this is such a pleasant surprise. You brought the Dagger *and* you have saved me the time of doing a spell to secure Hannah's blood. So, if you don't mind, sweetie, make it easy for me and give me just a tiny little drop, would you?"

"Enough Mia!" I yelled and lunged toward her with all of the powers I could muster – my Therion strength and my Vampire speed. In a blur, I circled her, grabbed the stones from her pocket, placed them into the seal on the door, and ended up right back in Mia's face. This time, I would not be backing down from the fight.

The gems glowed bright in their intended spaces and began to melt into the seal, dripping liquid along their journey of unlocking the door. Mia faltered backward a step, her eyebrows raised and her mouth fell open.

"Well look at that. It takes a lot to surprise me, but you've gone and done it," she said to me.

Before I could reply, Mia used her mind control to whip the Selenite Dagger from Jules's hand and threw it toward Hannah's hand. It cut her and wet the dagger with just a small drop of her blood before flying right back into Mia's hand, all within about two seconds. She then took the blade to Rachael's palm, made a small cut there and then to her own hand to do the same. The blade began to glow a more fiercely shade of bright crimson.

Jules exploded. "I will rip both of your arms off to get that Dagger back."

Oh, now now, Julian, I don't think you can do that anymore, sweetie," Mia taunted.

"Now whose manners are in question?" a voice spoke from just beyond the room.

Just then Noah walked in revealing Ruth, magically secured in the chains that bound her hands. It took Mia completely by surprise and her grip on Rachael's hand slackened.

Rachael gasped. "Mother?!"

Ruth looked at Mia and Rachael with deep sorrow on her face. Mia was visibly taken back, and the mother daughter duo stared at each other for what seemed like an eternity but was actually only a few seconds. Enough to turn her attention to what we needed to do. She let out a loud cackle.

"My mother, in chains? Is that your parting gift to me?" Mia said with evil laughter. "Because this is my gift to all of you."

She magically floated the glowing Dagger toward the sky.

"The blood of the Triad now imbues this Blade with the power to end you all."

Ruth screamed, "Mara, no!"

Did she just mess up her own daughter's name? I thought to myself. Why would she call her Mara? No one else seemed to notice.

I glanced down at my wrist and noticed we only had six minutes left with Ruth.

"Well," said Steele. "That may be a twist, but you only have one dagger and there are six of us. Even if you don't hesitate for a second, the ones who are left over will rip you apart," growled Steele as his eyes glowed gold.

"Someone has some new strength and a missing tattoo I see," Mia mocked. "But as usual, that's very small thinking on your part, Steele."

And with that Mia levitated the Dagger into the space above her head, said a quick chant and flicked the air. I glanced behind her at the door and the crystals had melted completely into the lock and it was unlatched. The Dagger burst into a million tiny pieces, and she threw them all toward us at once. They hit like shotgun pellets in a thousand places on our bodies all at the same time. Other remnants of the Blade fell on top of us like snowflakes, getting inside of our mouths, eyes, ears and hair. My entire body was on fire. I began to sputter and cough, and tears fell down my cheeks. The others screamed in agony.

Ruth watched with horror on her face. "Mara Isobella Adams, you're killing them!" she yelled.

"It's Mia!" she yelled back. "Mara died a long time ago!"

"Mara?" Jules said surprised, while coughing and gasping for air. "How is that possible?"

"How serendipitous for you to all be able to be here for this," said Mia. "Especially you, Mother. Now you can have a front row seat as we watch together as I kill your daughters and their friends from the inside out," Mia snarled. "And then you can watch as I open the crypt and kill that annoying bloodsucker Amelia once and for all, something I should have done right the first time."

That's when Jules, writhing in pain, realized that Mia was a reincarnation of Mara, who hexed Amantes, and murdered him all those years ago. Ruth clearly gained that knowledge as well after her death.

"You," he managed to get out. "You are the bitch who killed Amantes."

"Well, aren't you just the sharpest tool in the shed," she said to Jules.

Ruth approached Mara slowly and she began to cry.

"Oh, my sweet, sweet girl," she said as she walked closer. "You still carry around so much anger for me? After all these years? Lifetime after lifetime you choose darkness, and lifetime after lifetime I hope for better. I truly thought you would be cared for by your father. At that time, I had no idea how evil he was. I was blinded by the veils of the past, but I will not make that mistake again."

Mara gazed at Ruth intensely, with an unblinking stare. Her jawline tensed. "You. Gave. Me. Away. You took everything from me. My sisters, a mother's love. You have done it over and over and over again. You never thought of me for the Alliance. Lifetime after lifetime. You ended my family. You cursed me forever. You turned me over to the darkness. You never came for me!"

"You're right. I should have fought harder for you," Ruth said quietly. "That is on me, not them." Ruth moved closer to Mara, now standing just inches from her face.

As I felt the life force leaving my body and the fire inside my veins grew hotter and hotter, I struggled to remove the pieces of the poisonous weapon that pierced my skin. I couldn't manage to get enough of them out. There were too many. Three minutes left.

"Now, dear Mother," Mara said. "What's that thing they say…oh yes, a day late and a dollar short. It's way past time for apologies. Any last words or final thoughts for your daughters and their friends?"

We writhed in pain, and it emboldened her. With a magical flick of her wrist, Mara sped up the Dagger remnants piercing into our flesh, making the burning even more intense.

Just then out of the corner of my eye I saw a figure slip inside the crypt room. Could it be?

"Mara, please stop. You've won. You can have everything you ever wanted. A place on the council. Make amends with your sisters. It's my fault, not theirs." Ruth pleaded.

"I will never belong here with them! The Sazianu always welcomed me. The Old Ones will have me as a member of their family. I am their sister. Their family. A part of the Third Air. A place to finally be accepted and rule this world in the glorious chaos and darkness that calls to me!" Mara screamed.

"Daughter, please. I am so, so sorry. I made bad choices. I should have never let you go. I should have stayed by your side. Seeing all three of you together now makes me realize how selfish I was and makes me long for what could have been. If I get the chance again, I will do better. I will evolve. I promise. The power of the three of you together could have been such a strong force for good. Please forgive me."

Mara's face changed slightly. A bit of her darkness dissipated. Ruth seized the opportunity.

"The light and peace that I have found in death has been profound… and you can find it too. Heaven or Hell will renew your soul. *Nam-tar, Tesh, Kur*."

And with that Ruth wrapped the magical, poisonous chains from her wrists around Mara's neck and squeezed. The Blade pellets retreated from my body as Mara faltered. Ruth called out to the hidden figure that was in the back of the room behind the wall.

"Amelia, now."

Amelia, quite alive and stunningly beautiful with long dark hair and deep brown eyes was visibly paler than she should be. The silver-purple

Vampire shimmer was absent from her eyes, but she held the Blade of Black Tourmaline. As its other half began to slowly reform, their tips started to glow. Someone was watching it, directing it almost, from the shadows. Amelia flew toward Ruth and Mara with intense speed and purpose, and as she did, Jules did too, but with human speed. Using every last ounce of his strength, he grabbed me and threw me out of the way. As he did, Amelia used her Blade to sever both Mara and Ruth's heads off in one swipe.

"Now that was worth waking up for," she said with an air of confidence. Rachael regained her composure and joined Hannah in chanting a spell to suck the poisonous dust out of our lungs and the pellets completely out of our bodies. I gasped for air. It felt cold. I gasped again. The others were slowly recovering. I looked for Jules. He was motionless on the ground.

Out of the dark corner of the room, a shadowy figure lurked, and slowly walked out into the light.

He walked forward slowly; his eyes locked with Amelia's, and as she walked his way, she said to him, "You've either majorly screwed something up or you are about to," she paused, ignoring the rest of us, and staring deeply into his eyes. "Which is it?" she inquired.

Amantes swallowed hard. "Both."

EPILOGUE – SET ME FREE

I GRABBED MY FLANNEL SHIRT AND POLISHED OFF THE LAST OF the twelve crystals on the beautiful blade. After the Stones of Fire completed their mission of unlocking the door, and both halves of the powerful ancient weapon rejoined, it summoned the gems to attach to its handle. I handed it to Amantes and he gently cradled The Blade of Cain inside an intricate, framed box. It was whole again. For that, I envied it.

The Blade of Cain would protect Arete 8 once more. This time we would be more careful. We would only trust each other, and we would rule united, with the knowledge of what could happen if we allowed anyone to separate the factions again.

We transformed Amelia's crypt into the new headquarters for our semi formed Alliance, knowing that no one else would ever be able to find a way in. I looked around the room at the eight chairs that were pulled up to the octagonal table. Rachael and Hannah would take the Witch seats and Steele would occupy a Human seat for now. He decided to wait to unlock his Therion DNA until we found the right Human to take his seat. He also wanted to finish high school without the burden of becoming an animal every thirty days or so. Amelia reclaimed her Vampire seat. As a Tetrad, my leadership on the council would fulfill the second Vampire seat, the second Human seat, and a Therion seat, all at once. So for now, Arete 8, was comprised of only five. But it would do.

Turned out I didn't need Noah and I didn't need Jules after all. I had the power inside myself all along. Need and want are two entirely different things. I wanted so badly to see Jules again, to smell and taste him, to thank him for his sacrifice, and to be with him one more time.

His body lay right here in the crypt in the same coffin his sister laid in for fifteen hundred years. His soul, however, was trapped inside the blade. When Jules threw me out of the way, the Blade cut him and the gash took his energy and locked it inside.

"His sacrifice will shorten his stay," Amantes said.

"So you say," I replied.

"You are a Vampire, Seraphina. You can afford to be patient. You will see him again," Amantes said. "I waited what felt like a lifetime to see Amelia again and now that I have her back, the time we were apart has faded away. She recognized my soul inside this body and understood that I had been tricked."

I nodded and felt a knot form in my throat. To distract myself I took out my phone to text Steele.

Hey we're done down here, all clear up there in the library to come out?

Yes ma'am—come on up.

That was when I noticed the red number on my photo app, informing me that someone had invited me to a shared photo album. I opened it up and saw hundreds of photos suddenly populating into my phone.

My eyes welled with tears, and I smiled, then laughed. Tears streamed down my face.

It was my old photos. The ones I lost on my phone in the avalanche. I looked at the Blade on the wall and could have sworn I saw his shimmering purplish blue eyes with strands of silver staring at me from inside the Vampire crystals. The vision faded. But that's when I knew. I didn't care how long it took. I would be patient.

I would wait for him.